A
CARNIVÀLE
OF HORROR

A Carnivàle of Horror

Dark Tales from the Fairground

Edited by

Marie O'Regan & Paul Kane

2012

Contents

Contents cont...

Acknowledgements

Special thanks to Peter and Nicky Crowther, Mike Smith, Michelle Humphrey, Alicia Christensen, Tina Wexler and Christine Cohen, Paul Stark, and all the contributors.

ACKNOWLEDGEMENTS

TWITTERING FROM THE CIRCUS OF THE DEAD copyright © Joe Hill 2010—Originally published in *The New Dead: A Zombie Anthology*, 2010, St. Martins Press. Reprinted by permission of the author and his agent.

THE PILO FAMILY CIRCUS copyright © Will Elliott 2006— Originally published by ABC Books (Australian Broadcasting Corporation), 2006. Reprinted by permission of the author.

FACE OF THE CIRCUS copyright © Lou Morgan 2012

ESCARDY GAP copyright © Peter Crowther & James Lovegrove 1996—Originally published by Tor, 1996. Reprinted by permission of the authors.

THE CIRCUS OF DR LAO Reprinted by permission of International Creative Management, Inc. Copyright © 1935 by Charles Finney. First published by The Viking Press, July 1935. Reissued in 2002 by the University of Nebraska Press.

IN THE FOREST OF THE NIGHT copyright © Paul Finch 2012

ALL THE CLOWNS IN CLOWNTOWN copyright © Andrew McKiernan 2010—Originally published in *Macabre: A Journey Through Australia's Darkest Fears*. Reprinted with permission of the author.

NINE LETTERS ABOUT SPIT copyright © Robert Shearman 2011—Originally published online at justsospecial.com. Reprinted by permission of the author.

TO RUN AWAY AND JOIN THE CIRCUS copyright © Alison Littlewood 2012

Introduction: *Horror of the Carnivàle*

The circus.

A place of wonder and excitement, of laughter and fun. Right? Wrong... There's always been another side to carnivals and the circus, something not quite right about them—as if they're hiding a more sinister aspect beneath all that colour and showmanship. It's led to some of the most intriguing fiction, television and films of all time. Who could forget the movie *Freaks* (we've included the story that inspired it, "Spurs", right here in this anthology), the 1960 British horror film *Circus of Horrors*, directed by Sidney Hayers, or Ray Bradbury's *Something Wicked this Way Comes* (an extract from which is also included within these pages).

Then there's the stand-out episode of *The X-Files*, "Humbug", which sees Mulder and Scully investigating the death of Jerald Glazebrook, otherwise known as "The Alligator Man". And the superb HBO series *Carnivàle*, from *Battlestar Galactica*'s Ronald D. Moore, which injected a sense of the supernatural into a dustbowl sideshow from the 1930s (originally conceived as a trilogy of books). Before bringing things right up to date with the *Cirque du Freak* movies, based on the books by Darren Shan and introducing vampires into the mix. All this even before you get to the figure of the evil clown—fuelled by the very real affliction of Coulrophobia—which has inspired such disparate characters as Batman's nemesis, The Joker, and Stephen King's Pennywise from *IT* (so memorably portrayed by Tim Curry in the mini-series), right up to Papa Lazarou from *The League of Gentlemen*, and Violator from the *Spawn* comics. Not to mention the real life terrifying deeds of "Killer Clown" John Wayne Gacy, Jr.

In *A Carnivàle of Horror*, we're aiming to keep this tradition alive, whilst at the same time presenting you with some of the best historical genre fiction using the circus as its jumping off point. Our stories and extracts take in not just the concept of scary clowns (in stories like "Some Children Wander By Mistake" from John Connolly), but also the dangerous animals that inhabit the circus (for example "Tiger, Tiger" by Rio Youers), plus opening up the scope to include more traditional horror fare (such as zombies in Joe Hill's "Twittering from the Circus of the Dead"—soon to be a major movie—and fortune telling in Charles G. Finney's "The Circus of Dr Lao"). But they also do something else: they show the impact of those things on ordinary people and their lives, as all good tales should.

So, roll up, roll up—come one, come all. See the greatest show on earth . . .

If you dare, that is!

Marie O'Regan & Paul Kane
Derbyshire, May 2012

A
CARNIVÀLE
OF HORROR

Something Wicked This Way Comes

RAY BRADBURY

Midnight then and the town clocks chiming on toward one and two and then three in the deep morning and the peals of the great clocks shaking dust off old toys in high attics and shedding silver off old mirrors in yet higher attics and stirring up dreams about clocks in all the beds where children slept.

Will heard it.

Muffled away in the prairie lands, the chuffing of an engine, the slow-following dragon-glide of a train.

Will sat up in bed.

Across the way, like a mirror image, Jim sat up, too.

A calliope began to play oh so softly, grieving to itself, a million miles away.

In one single motion, Will leaned from his window, as did Jim. Without a word they gazed over the trembling surf of trees.

Their rooms were high, as boys' rooms should be. From these gaunt windows they could rifle-fire their gaze artillery distances past library, city hall, depot, cow barns, farmlands to empty prairie!

There, on the world's rim, the lovely snail-gleam of the railway tracks ran, flinging wild gesticulations of lemon or cherry-colored semaphore to the stars.

There, on the precipice of earth, a small steam feather uprose like the first of a storm cloud yet to come.

The train itself appeared, link by link, engine, coal-car, and numerous and numbered all-asleep-and-slumbering-dreamfilled cars that followed the firefly-sparked churn, chant, drowsy autumn hearth-fire roar. Hellfires flushed the stunned hills. Even at this remote view, one imagined men with buffalo-haunched arms shoveling black meteor falls of coal into the open boilers of the engine.

The engine!

Both boys vanished, came back to lift binoculars.

'The engine!"

"Civil War! No other stack like that since 1900!"

"The rest of the train, *all* of it's old!"

"The flags! The cages! It's the carnival!"

They listened. At first Will thought he heard the air whistling fast in his nostrils. But no—it was the train, and the calliope sighing, weeping, on that train.

"Sounds like church music!"

"Hell. Why would a carnival play church music?"

"Don't say hell," hissed Will.

"Hell." Jim ferociously leaned out. "I've saved up all day. Every-one's asleep so—hell!"

The music drifted by their windows. Goose pimples rose big as boils on Will's arms.

"That *is* church music. Changed."

"For cri-yi, I'm froze, let's go watch them set up!"

"At three a.m.?"

"At three a.m.!"

Jim vanished.

For a moment, Will watched Jim dance around over there, shirt uplifted, pants going on, while off in night country, panting, churning was this funeral train all black plumed cars, licorice-colored cages, and a sooty calliope clamoring, banging three different hymns mixed and lost, maybe not there at all.

"Here goes nothing!"

Jim slid down the drainpipe on his house, toward the sleeping lawns.

"Jim! Wait!"

Will thrashed into his clothes.

"Jim, don't go *alone*!"

And followed after.

৵৽

Sometimes you see a kite so high, so wise it almost knows the wind. It travels, then chooses to land in one spot and no other and no matter how you yank, run this way or that, it will simply break its cord, seek its resting place and bring you, blood-mouthed, running.

"Jim! Wait for me!"

So now Jim was the kite, the wild twine cut, and whatever wisdom was his taking him away from Will who could only run, earthbound, after one so high and dark silent and suddenly strange.

"Jim, here I come!"

And running, Will thought, Boy, it's the same old thing. I talk. Jim runs. I tilt stones, Jim grabs the cold junk under the stones and— lickety-split! I climb hills. Jim yells off church steeples. I got a bank account. Jim's got the hair on his head, the yell in his mouth, the shirt on his back and the tennis shoes on his feet. How come I think *he's* richer? Because, Will thought, I sit on a rock in the sun and old Jim, he prickles his arm-hairs by moonlight and dances with hoptoads. I tend cows. Jim tames Gila monsters. Fool! I yell at Jim. Coward! he yells back. And here we —*go!*

And they ran from town, across fields and both froze under a rail bridge with the moon ready beyond the hills and the meadows trembling with a fur of dew.

WHAM!

The carnival train thundered the bridge. The calliope wailed.

"There's no one playing it!" Jim stared up.

"Jim, no jokes!"

"Mother's honor, look!"

Going away, away, the calliope pipes shimmered with star explosions, but no one sat at the high keyboard. The wind, sluicing

5

ice-water air in the pipes, made the music.

The boys ran. The train curved away, gonging its undersea funeral bell, sunk, rusted, green-mossed, tolling, tolling. Then the engine whistle blew a great steam whiff and Will broke out in pearls of ice.

Way late at night Will had heard—how often?—train whistles jetting steam along the rim of sleep, forlorn, alone and far, no matter how near they came. Sometimes he woke to find tears on his cheek, asked why, lay back, listened and thought, Yes! *they* make me cry, going east, going west, the trams so far gone in country deeps they drown in tides of sleep that escape the towns.

Those trains and their grieving sounds were lost forever between stations, not remembering where they had been, not guessing where they might go, exhaling their last pale breaths over the horizon, gone. So it was with all trains, ever.

Yet *this* train's whistle!

The wails of a lifetime were gathered in it from other nights in other slumbering years; the howl of moon-dreamed dogs, the seep of river-cold winds through January porch screens which stopped the blood, a thousand fire sirens weeping, or worse! the outgone shreds of breath, the protests of a billion people dead or dying, not wanting to be dead, their groans, their sighs, burst over the earth!

Tears jumped to Will's eyes. He lurched. He knelt. He pretended to lace one shoe.

But then he saw Jim's hands clap *his* ears, his eyes wet, too. The whistle screamed. Jim screamed against the scream. The whistle shrieked. Will shrieked against the shriek.

Then the billion voices ceased, instantly, as if the train had plunged in a fire storm off the earth.

The train skimmed on softly, slithering, black pennants fluttering, black confetti lost on its own sick-sweet candy wind, down the hill, with the boys pursuing, the air so cold they ate ice cream with each breath.

They climbed a last rise to look down.

"Boy," whispered Jim.

The train had pulled off into Rolfe's moon meadow, so-called because town couples came out to see the moon rise here over a land so wide, so long, it was like an inland sea, filled with grass in spring, or hay in late summer or snow in winter, it was fine walking here along its crisp shore with the moon coming up to tremble in its tides.

Well, the carnival train was crouched there now in the autumn grass on the old rail spur near the woods, and the boys crept and lay down under a bush, waiting.

"It's so quiet," whispered Will.

The tram just stood in the middle of the dry autumn field, no one in the locomotive, no one in the tender, no one in any of the cars behind, all black under the moon, and just the small sounds of its metal cooling, ticking on the rails.

"Ssst," said Jim. "I *feel* them *moving* in there."

Will felt the cat fuzz on his body bramble up by the thousands.

"You think they *mind* us watching?"

"Maybe," said Jim, happily.

"Then why the noisy calliope?"

"When I figure that," Jim smiled, "I'll tell you. Look!"

Whisper.

As if exhaling itself straight down from the sky, a vast moss-green balloon touched at the moon.

It hovered two hundred yards above and away, quietly riding the wind.

"The basket under the balloon, someone *in* it!"

But then a tall man stepped down from the train caboose platform like a captain assaying the tidal weathers of this inland sea. All dark suit, shadow-faced, he waded to the center of the meadow, his shirt as black as the gloved hands he now stretched to the sky.

He gestured, once.

And the train came to life.

At first a head lifted in one window, then an arm, then another head like a puppet in a marionette theater. Suddenly two men in black were carrying a dark tent pole out across the hissing grass.

7

It was the silence that made Will pull back, even as Jim leaned forward, eyes moon-bright.

A carnival should be all growls, roars like timberlands stacked, bundled, rolled and crashed, great explosions of lion dust, men ablaze with working anger, pop bottles jangling, horse buckles shivering, engines and elephants in full stampede through rains of sweat while zebras neighed and trembled like cage trapped in cage.

But this was like old movies, the silent theater haunted with black-and-white ghosts, silvery mouths opening to let moonlight smoke out, gestures made in silence so hushed you could hear the wind fizz the hair on your cheeks.

More shadows rustled from the tram, passing the animal cages where darkness prowled with unlit eyes and the calliope stood mute save for the faintest idiot tune the breeze piped wandering up the flues.

The ringmaster stood in the middle of the land. The balloon like a vast moldy green cheese stood fixed to the sky. Then—darkness came.

The last thing Will saw was the balloon swooping down, as clouds covered the moon.

In the night he felt the men rush to unseen tasks. He sensed the balloon, like a great fat spider, fiddling with the lines and poles, rearing a tapestry in the sky.

The clouds arose. The balloon sifted up.

In the meadow stood the skeleton main poles and wires of the main tent, waiting for its canvas skin.

More clouds poured over the white moon. Shadowed, Will shivered. He heard Jim crawling forward, seized his ankle, felt him stiffen.

"Wait!" said Will. "They're bringing out the canvas!"

"No," said Jim. "Oh, no . . . "

For somehow instead, they both knew, the wires high-flung on the poles were catching swift clouds, ripping them free from the wind in streamers which, stitched and sewn by some great monster shadow, made canvas and more canvas as the tent took shape. At last there was the clear-water sound of vast flags blowing.

The motion stopped. The darkness within darkness was still.

Will lay, eyes shut, hearing the beat of great oil-black wings as if a huge, ancient bird had drummed down to live, to breathe, to survive in the night meadow.

The clouds blew away.

The balloon was gone.

The men were gone.

The tents rippled like black rain on their poles.

Suddenly it seemed a long way to town.

Instinctively, Will glanced behind himself.

Nothing but grass and whispers.

Slowly he looked back at the silent, dark, seemingly empty tents.

"I don't like it," he said.

Jim could not tear his eyes away.

"Yeah," he whispered. "Yeah."

Will stood up. Jim lay on the earth.

"Jim!" said Will.

Jim jerked his head as if slapped. He was on his knees, he swayed up. His body turned, but his eyes were fastened to those black flags, the great side-show signs swarming with unguessed wings, horns, and demon smiles.

A bird screamed.

Jim jumped. Jim gasped.

Cloud shadows panicked them over the hills to the edge of town.

From there, the two boys ran alone.

A Flat Patch of Grass

MURIEL GRAY

I'm looking at them all, one by one, but they're not looking at me. Except for the big men detectives. They haven't stopped staring since they came in and sat down. The lady lawyer is looking through some papers and the nice lady from the social work department is looking at her phone. The very fat lady from somewhere called The Children's Unit is looking at the big men detectives waiting for them to say something. At last one of them sits forward. He asks if I'd like a drink

I shake my head. The lady lawyer clears her throat.

She says I can have a drink any time I like. I just have to ask.

I shake my head again. The detective puts his hands together. He smells of cigarettes and aftershave. It's nice, after the smell of disinfectant in the room they kept me in.

He asks if I know why I'm here.

I say yes.

He says, can you tell me what happened?

I say, when?

He says, last night.

I say, which bit?

He looks at me to see if I'm being funny, but his eyes tell me he doesn't think so. The other one speaks. He's just as big, but he has close shaved ginger hair and his suit looks too small for him.

He says, any bit. I can start where I like.

I say I don't want to.

He says, why not?

I say she's gone now. I don't want to think about her any more.

He asks who's gone. I think for a minute if I should say. But then I think, why not? It's over now. She's not coming back.

I tell them. I say, Razbunare.

Everybody writes something down. I wish I was at home.

৵৽৵

That was a bad one. You see some weird shit in this game, but that was up there with the worst. I mean, what was stopping the old guy coming out? Nothing. We were shouting, yelling at him, but he just stood there in the doorway, metres away from safety, screaming. No. That's not right. Howling. That's what it sounded like. Like an animal in pain. And that kid. Just standing, watching, like he was in a trance. That's not normal. We get all kinds, you know? Kids that dance around excited like they're at a bonfire night party. Kids that cry, horrified and afraid. And kids on the estates that chuck stones while we get the hose up and running. They're the little bastards that half of you hopes will fall asleep with the chip pan on one day, and just when their faces are melting they suddenly remember throwing rocks at the guys who could have saved them. But this kid, he just stood, staring at the door. Frank scooped him up and hauled him away, and then the guys fought their way through to the old nutjob in the doorway. But he was burning properly by then. Really, really burning. They got bits of him back. Still alive. Still screaming. Trevor's taken the offer of counselling. That never happens. Six foot four of black love machine, pecs like Usain Bolt and he's going to spend an hour every Tuesday afternoon telling that skinny bird with the specs what he "feels" about what happened. Funny thing is, no one's taking the piss.

৵৽৵

These are not abusive parents. Twenty three years in this job, and believe you me, I can tell. They can be upper class, middle class, junkies, doctors, unemployed astronauts, you name it. Abusers come from every walk of life and you can smell it the moment you walk in. It's not just about eye contact or body language. Call it primeval instinct. You can feel a danger about them, a wrongness. Neville Benson's parents love him. Mary Benson looks as if her world has caved in. Her husband Adam is trying to be strong, but his eyes are hollow with pain. The little girl, Emma, is watchful, but not in the way that abused children are careful. She looks protective, angry even, but not furtive. Mary wants to talk. She's distraught, wringing a paper handkerchief and trembling. She's gabbling, telling me how clever her son is, how popular at school and how well behaved he is. Apart from being bloody cheeky, adds her husband as light relief. She laughs but it turns to crying again. I ask to see Neville's room.

They show me it like I'm a prospective house buyer. I search for the routine things they usually overlook; the discarded toy with its eyes poked out, the brutal scouring of deep pen marks on walls, the duvet tucked in too tight for protection. None of that. This is the room of a normal ten year old boy. There's some tadpoles wriggling in a tank in the corner. The water's clean. A poster on the wall lists all the fresh water fish of the UK, two thirds of them with big red ticks and a smiley face drawn beside them in red marker pen. The fishing rod propped beside it is gleaming and maintained. The Bensons stand silently by the door. I move to the window and look out. Beyond the large field on the other side of the tidy fence you can just see the charred remains of the farmhouse. Then I notice marks on the glass. Tape marks. All round the edges. I touch the curtains. They're thin, diaphanous, printed in a cheerful fish pattern. Something's been taped to the glass and now it's been taken down.

Was something over the window? I ask.

Mr Benson smiles a crooked grin, all agony and remembrance.

Neville's blackout screen, he says. Mrs Benson sniffs again. It keeps out the light, she says. He wakes easily she adds. Bad dreams. She points at the bed. I look across. Poking from beneath is the corner of a ragged piece of cardboard, painted black, the duct tape still sticking to the edges.

Mrs Benson buries her nose in her hanky.

He made it himself, she sobs. It helps him sleep.

The cops aren't saying anything. That means it's a juvenile. Always is when they clam up like that. So I sent Nancy in to talk to the neighbours. She's got a way with her. Doesn't sound or look like a reporter. Got that mumsy look that means none of the news boys want to shag her, they just tell her their problems. She hates that. Started wearing high heels and a low cut top for a while to try and change it, but they didn't notice. I watched her go back to wearing sandals and that frumpy cardigan. But I didn't say anything. Didn't make fun of her. Wouldn't want to lose an asset like that.

You see, people trust her. She did the business and it looks like we've got plenty without plod's help. It was an old guy. A farmer called Jack Rowntree. Few acres, bunch of miserable, tick infested sheep and a ramshackle old house. Never married, lived alone his whole life with his invalided mother until she died ten years ago. Are you getting the picture? If we'd hired a pantomime paedo from central casting they couldn't have got it more spot on. And surprise, surprise, blow me down with a fucking feather, it's the kid from over Rowntree's fence the rozzers are holding. Nancy's sure of that. So have I got a scoop? Have I fuck. In newspapers this is what you call a sinker. The old pervert is dead, burnt to a crisp, so we're never going to know what the cunt did. And if the kid started the fire then he's going to be kept away somewhere nice and private and safe, not named, cloak of anonymity and all that, meaning no chance to tell the poor little bastard's tale. All we can do with this one is hint, wink, make allusions. And when it's a juvenile the lawyers will be all over our arse like a case of the Bombay runs.

It's a dead end story. Shit. Sometimes I hate this fucking job.

Neville's a little old for standard play therapy. We normally use dolls with children up to the age of ten, but I've seen how a wily ten year old will read the subtext and respond accordingly. The abuser is a careful animal. They coach their prey. That's why I prefer more personalised methods. But Neville is proving a tough one. The damage must be deep, given how artfully concealed is it. The idea that this freckle faced, healthy and sociable little boy carefully assembled a dozen Molotov cocktails, crept to an old age pensioner's house in the middle of the night, threw them through the windows and watched the old man burn alive, is surreal. You never stop being surprised in this job. I'm looking at him now. He's a bright and friendly child. Lots of hobbies. He fly fishes. He makes things. And refreshingly, I admit as an old fogey, he seems more interested in animals and birds and fish than playing on a computer. So I'm trying books. Looking together at pictures of things that interest him, in the hope that casual conversation provides a clue. There's something about two people looking away from each other, flicking through a magazine, or forward out a car windscreen that makes them talk more easily. Connection without eye contact. Old as the hills. I've brought along a book called *Incredible But True*. It's like the Guinness Book of records, full of people eating aeroplanes, holy men with three feet long toenails and cats that can walk on their hind legs.

Neville is loving it. We browse through it together, laughing at the photographs of the world's ugliest dogs. I tell him about mine. He grins, delighted. Asks questions. We laugh. He stops at a page about an Amazonian fish that squirts water at insects to knock them out of trees into the water, and tells me more about it. He's very knowledgeable. I ask him if he ever fished on Mr Rowntree's farm. In the little river. Without flinching he says yes, he did, and he caught a beautiful brown trout on a special fly he tied himself. I ask him if Mr Rowntree was happy about him fishing there. He says, again without any change in emotion, that he doesn't know. He never met him. I glance at him to see if he's lying. If he is, it's incredible. His eyes are still bright, enjoying the book.

15

We turn a page to be confronted with the world's most tattooed man and I sense a tiny change in him. Almost imperceptible. I ask him if he knows anyone with tattoos. This time he just says no, and turns the page again. I make a mental note to check with the police to see if they knew if Rowntree had any tattoos. Neville cheers a little as we read about the world's biggest sand sculpture and tells me about a holiday they had in Spain where they saw a walrus made of sand, but smaller. Did you enjoy being on holiday with your family? I ask. He tells me he loved it. He got sunburned ears. We laugh again, though I can still feel that tiny shard of ice in his voice.

Then it happens.

We flick to a double spread of colourful photos. It's a circus performer, a woman, standing astride two feather-trimmed, galloping ponies. Dressed in a short basque with a sequined tutu, her hands are held high, her legs strong and wide as she grins from a thickly made up face running with sweat. She's a Russian acrobat who currently holds the record for the longest unbroken twin pony ride around a ring.

Neville pushes back as though he's been stung. His face is white and his eyes are wide in horror. He stabs at the book trying to get it away from him. I quickly close it and push it under the chair, but Neville is already back against the wall, knees up to his chest. I move quickly to him and lift a hand to comfort him, but he shrinks from me and buries his face in his arms.

I step back but ask him calmly, softly if he's ok.

She can't come back, can she? he whimpers.

I despise lying to children, but he needs to be reassured.

No. I say.

She can't.

∾∿

I'm looking hard. As hard as I can. But I still can't see it. But then he always sees things I miss. It's always been that way. From the very

16

beginning. He knows when it's about to rain, where the hotel is, even if we've never been there. He knows there's deer in the trees or where the big trout are lying near the bank. Once he ran in from the garden, put his head on my arm and told me not to be too sad. He hugged and kissed me and went back to his game. As he left, the hospital rang about Mum. I don't know what that means. Nothing, probably. It's just Nev.

Mary's downstairs making Emma's tea and then we'll drive to the unit to see him. But right now I'm at his window holding the cuddly toy trout we bought him in Hampshire, its beady glass eyes starting to come away from the silky fabric. He called it Robson after some fishing hero on a telly programme he loves. I hold it close to my face, breathing in the smell of my son, and stare harder. Rowntree's field looks the same as it always does. The scrubby, unkempt grass land is pock marked with tufts of inedible marsh grass, and his handful of remaining sheep move slowly across it, nuzzling to find enough to eat. It's just a field. Have I disappointed him because I can't see what he sees?

We've been here less than a year. Moved last summer when head office pushed me up the greasy pole. The kids loved it. A world away from the cramped suburban estate they grew up on. And all this space and freedom and beauty, only three miles from a quaint market town, made Mary happier than I've ever seen her.

When did he first say it? I can't remember. I know it was hot. I was in his room, looking for my socks that Mary always packs into Nev's drawer, as if she can't tell the difference between size four and size ten. He was standing at the window, just where I am now, and he said, look Dad. He pointed at the sheep. Look, he said. They won't go onto it. They just eat round it.

On to what? I said.

The patch, he said.

I looked then as I'm looking now.

What patch? I asked.

He hesitated, frowning, as if trying to find the words. Then he pointed down at the garden below.

17

Like Emma's paddling pool, he said.

I followed his finger to the empty lawn. A few scattered toys, but no paddling pool. But then, I admit to my mild irritation, I saw the round, yellowed mark on my pristine green grass that Neville was indicating. I like a nice lawn. I keep it well. The mark was where the paddling pool had been a few days ago. Nothing but a patch of flat, yellowed grass.

He looked up at me with those searching brown eyes.

It's the same, Dad. Do you see?

I looked back at the field. It was uniform in colour. No yellow bits. No dark bits. Just sheep.

No, I said, shaking my head. I don't see it.

I remember he looked sad, not angry or frustrated. He just put a hand up to the glass, looked back out of the window again and I left the room.

I put my own hand on the glass now, wishing it was touching Nev's. What if I could go back? What if I could say that yes, I did see a round patch of yellowed grass in the field? A mark where something had been, and now was gone. Would that have helped? Would he have believed me? Should we have called the doctor when his night terrors started? Should we have taken him to see someone? Was it really Rowntree to blame? He was so old and housebound. Felled by a stroke, reliant on meals on wheels. Never if rarely seen. Neville never went near the farm. It doesn't seem possible he was an abuser. Maybe it was us. Something we did. Something we didn't do.

Oh dear God, how have we failed our son?

☞❦

We get another chance to interview him today. We'll have to go slow until the psychiatric reports come in, but of course the game changed when he mentioned there was someone else involved. A woman. This Razbunare. If there's more to this than a good kid losing the plot with some paedo cunt we need to know, and know fast. Dennis says the name sounds Eastern European so we're checking the fruit pickers working on the two farms bordering Rowntree's.

I've done the digging on Rowntree's background. Not much there. Lonely old git, letting his farm fall about his ears for years. No accusations, rumours even, of molestation, flashing, any of the charming routine hobbies of the kiddie fiddler. Quiet and mundane life by all accounts, and almost totally housebound. Yeah, I know that doesn't mean much. I still remember that little sweetheart mucked around by her chair-bound morbidly obese uncle. He'd trained her to come to him. Fucking animal. But Rowntree. I mean, what went on? There's something not right about this. Nothing left of the farmhouse so we can't check for porn, but seems he wasn't even connected to the internet. Meals on wheels woman said he just had a phone when his mother was alive then even took that out when she died. Doesn't really add up. Did the kid wander in there, maybe? Find something weird? Maybe there was some Polak bird up to no good, working with Rowntree, bringing him kids for money. Who knows? We need that kid to talk.

I'll let Dennis do the farm hands and I'll talk to the gaffers. If there's a Miss fucking Razbunare hiding out there she's about to get her arse hauled in.

కొ౼

Emma's brought me my black-out shield. Even if she's a pain sometimes, like when she wants to come fishing and I take her and then she makes too much noise, talking all the time and scaring the fish, she's still a pretty sound sister. Lynn, the lady who looks after me, says I can put it up if I want, but I don't really need to. Nothing bad's coming here. Not outside this place. Or any place again, I hope. Not now that I set them all free. I just like that Emma brought it and I hugged her, although it was a bit icky and embarrassing. It made Mum cry again. I really want to go home now. Especially as it's safe again. But they won't let me until I tell them about everything. Dad says I should try and be brave and talk about it all to Vivien, the lady doctor, because that'll make me feel better about what happened. I asked him if that would mean I could come home again. The brown trout season's about to start and I don't want to miss the first days. They're ravenous after the winter. They'll take just about anything. It's awesome.

Dad looked very serious and said it would certainly help. Mum just cried again, in that way she's trying to hide that she's doing it with a weird, shaky smile. I think that's worse.

I don't really want to talk to the big, giant detective men, because of the way they look at me, but I think I would actually like to talk to Vivien. She's kind and funny, and she showed me some photos of her dog that she thinks would win the ugliest pet competition, even though she loves him very much. It's a bit scruffy, but not really that horrible. I've seen much uglier things. Much, much uglier.

$\approx\ll$

I'm sitting in my car outside the unit and I'm trying to control myself. I spend every working day helping people to understand what's wrong with their brains, to explore their emotions, to control their fears. And here I am shaking like a kitten.

He's not ill. That's the good news. It's also the very bad news. I've never encountered this before. It's impossible for a ten year old to have constructed such a conceit. I've listened to enough of them. There are always flaws, implausibility and errors. The damaged brain creates its own logic, but the illogic is plain to any psychiatrist even when consistent. But Neville's constructed horror is water tight.

This confident, well-loved little boy quite genuinely believes, without a shadow of a doubt, that he has saved, set free, dozens of men, women and mostly children. Animals, too. Horses, he insists. By the act of burning down Jack Rowntree's house, which he claims he was instructed to do, he feels somehow that he has performed a great duty. A duty that he freely admits caused him profound distress, but a duty nevertheless.

We'd started as normal. We talked about the weather, how the fishing might be, what he had for lunch. Then before I began the day's programme he asked me a question.

Had I ever been to a circus? I answered yes, I had. He asked me to describe it. I scrambled amongst my memories for long forgotten details of some visiting, amateurish, county circus of my childhood, and watched his eyes grow round as I described what I could recall.

He nodded. Went quiet.

I asked him if he'd ever been to one. He shook his head.

Razbunare worked in a circus, he said.

Did she, I asked. What did she do?

He thought about it.

She swung on a trapeze and stood on ponies, he said. But I never saw her do it. She just told me.

I thought of the book, the picture of the acrobat that upset him. Neville using it to invent this imaginary person was extremely intriguing. I knew I had to go carefully. I wanted to see how else he would employ it.

Where did you meet her? I asked.

Neville clenched and unclenched his little fists, then sat on his hands as though they were betraying him.

After I noticed the patch, he said.

I just nodded and it seemed to comfort him. He sat forward and started to speak.

I saw her standing in the middle of it, he said. It was a circle, like a giant paddling pool had been on the grass. But it was a tent that was there. She told me it had been her tent. She said there's not many people notice it and I was one of the few.

What was she like? I asked.

He shrugged. I thought she was nice at first, he said. She laughed a lot, and she's . . . He hesitated.

I waited.

She was pretty, he said. He looked embarrassed.

That's always nice, I said.

21

He looked up at me and his eyes were round and moist. His voice had lowered almost to a whisper.

But then she got . . . scary, he breathed.

I asked how.

She got angry all the time, he said.

He sat forward, conspiratorial, and continued.

When you ignore her she screams, and her whole mouth opens up like a great, gaping, black hole, bigger than anyone's mouth could ever be, and you think you'll be swallowed up in it.

That must be very frightening, I said.

It's worse when they all do it, he said.

Who, Neville? I asked.

The people from the tent. Children. Lots of children.

I asked him when he sees these people. He told me they come at night. They make lots of light and noise so it wakes him up, and they wait until he looks out the window, and then they scream. And the horses. Galloping and galloping, their backs and their manes on fire, screaming just like people.

I swallowed hard at the image but stayed calm. He'd clearly joined his fear of the woman in the picture book to the real event of the fire. Unusual, but the brain is a mysterious organ. I nodded sympathetically. He continued.

I made a blind, he said. A piece of board that would stop the light getting in. But she got really angry. That's when she started to come into my room.

So I had to make it stop.

He lowered his eyes.

Did she tell you how to make it stop Neville? I asked.

He nodded.

She said they didn't have much time. She said if Mr Rowntree died before they could say hello to him properly then they would all be there forever. I didn't want them to be there forever because I like it there. There's a river, and a big garden and everything. And Mum loves the market and the shops and I don't want to leave. But if they all start to come into the house like Razbunare did then Mum and Dad will want us to go. I know they will.

I nodded again.

She said if I could just make Mr Rowntree come out of his house and say hello to them everything would be alright. I said I would go and ask him and she said that wouldn't work and I had to do it her way.

With fire, I said.

He nodded and looked at me steadily.

Did Razbunare show you how to make the fire? I asked.

He said yes. I got the petrol from the can Dad uses for the mower and filled some empty squash bottles with it. Just like she said.

We sat quietly then for several minutes. He began to cry. The first time since the incident. I thought, here's the breakthrough. I moved to hold his hand. He offered no resistance.

Will Mr Rowntree forgive me? he asked.

I don't know Neville, I replied. Are you sorry?

He nodded.

He wiped his nose on his sleeve and said, I thought he would be pleased to see them. She said he would be. They were all standing there, waiting for him, right there at the front door. But when he saw them he wouldn't come out. I didn't know he wouldn't come out.

He pressed my hand hard.

I didn't know that.

My neck prickled and my mouth dried as I spoke next.

Do you know why didn't he come out?

Neville's grip on my hand tightened.

Because they weren't pleased to see him at all, he said.

How do you know? I said.

He kept his eyes on the floor.

They were screaming at him, he whispered, and their mouths were bigger than their heads.

I'm here now, sitting in the car, his file on my knee, and I'm lost. What report will I file? My decision is going to affect the rest of this little boy and his family's lives. I don't think he's psychotic. I don't think he's disturbed. I don't know what the hell I think. All I know is I need to go home and have a very big drink.

You see I Googled the woman's name. Razbunare. It's not a name. It's a Romanian word. It means revenge.

❧❦

Jesus fucking wept, Nancy must be well pissed off with this fire-bombing kid thing, because she won't let it fucking drop. I guess she's just so hungry for that by-line she'll turn naked cartwheels 'til she gets it. So when she bursts into my office I give her five minutes of my precious time to listen to what she's got. And what is it? It's a pile of horse shit that's no use to man nor beast, and certainly not to a fucking busy editor of a newspaper that needs to get some meat in it fast, to stop shedding readers faster than a leper loses toes.

Seems she went back and poked around the village, got talking to some old bastards in the pub and an old folks' home, you know, to get the low down on Rowntree. As if it bloody matters now.

She finds out some big disaster happened in his field, over fifty years ago, long before any of us on this paper were even pissing in nappies. Some Gypo circus that used to pitch up every year on the Rowntree's farm burnt to the ground killing 68 poor sods inside, mostly local children.

Tragic, sure, and would have been a hell of a story in its day. A corker. But right here and now, what's that got to do with the price of milk? Might as well report the sinking of the Titanic.

But then Nancy gets all excited and said that a couple of the old sods insisted that they still think Rowntree had done it. Fell for some sexy young acrobat apparently, had a fling then very publicly asked her to stay and marry him. They remember her laughing at him, mocking him in front of his friends. So one of the old geezers insists that Rowntree waited until the gypsy bird was giving it her all in the big top, then sealed up the exits and torched the fucking thing. Old guy blurting out this stuff lost his little sister in the blaze. Bound to be hacked off.

Turns out, of course, it was just village gossip. Plod was all over it and the mother swore Rowntree hadn't left her side all night. They formally declared it an accident. Sounds to me like the lonely old gits were treading on sour grapes to entertain Nancy.

So I'm listening to this stuff, and she's insisting it needs looking into, and I'm thinking, what does she think I look like? A fucking health and safety officer? What the fuck has all that ancient history got to do with a crazy kid who gets his own back on a paedo? This is a proper newspaper, not the *National Enquirer*.

I'm not being sexist or anything, but honestly. Women. Sometimes they just can't see the real story.

Some Children Wander By Mistake

JOHN CONNOLLY

The circus seldom came to the towns in the north. They were too scattered, their populations too poor, to justify the expense of transporting animals, sideshows and people down neglected roads in order to play to sparsely filled seats for a week. The bright colours of the circus vehicles looked out of place when reflected in the rain-filled potholes of such places, and the big top itself seemed to lose some of its power and vibrancy when set against gray storm clouds and relentless drizzle.

Occasionally some forgotten television star would pass through for a week of pantomime season, or a one-hit-wonder from the seventies might attempt to rustle up a weekend crowd in one of the grim, boxlike clubs that squatted in the larger suburbs, but the circus was a rare visitor. William could not recall a circus ever coming to his town, not in the whole ten years of his life, although his parents sometimes spoke of one that had played early in the year of his birth. In fact, his mother said that she had felt William kick in her womb as soon as the lights went down and the first of the clowns appeared, as though he were somehow aware of the events taking place outside his red world. Since then, no great tent had occupied the big field out by the forest. No lions had passed through here, and no elephants had trumpeted. There had been no trapeze artists, no ringmasters.

No clowns.

William had few friends. There was something about him that alienated his peers: an eagerness to please, perhaps, that was the flipside of something darker and more troubling. He spent much of his spare time alone, while school was a tightrope walk between a desire to be noticed and a profound wish to avoid the bullying that came with such attention. Small and weak, William was no match for his tormentors, and had developed strategies to keep them at bay. Mostly, he tried to make them laugh.

Mostly, he failed.

There were few bright spots to life in that place, and so it was with surprise and delight that William watched the first of the posters appear in shop windows and upon lampposts, adding a splash of colour to the dull streets. They were orange and yellow and green and blue, and at the centre of each poster was the figure of a ringmaster, dressed in red with a great top hat upon his head and moustaches that curled up at the ends like snail shells. Surrounding him were animals—lions and tigers and bears, oh my—and stilt walkers, and women in spangled costumes soaring gracefully through the air. Clowns occupied the corners, with big round noses and painted-on smiles. Sideshows and rides were promised, and feats never before witnessed in a big top. "From Europe," announced the posters, "For One Night Only: Circus Caliban!" The performance would take place on, of all dates, 9 December, the date of William's tenth birthday.

It took William only minutes to track down the circus folk responsible for distributing the posters. He found them on a sidestreet, using a stepladder to put up the advertisements for their great show. A cold north wind threatened to make off with a dwarf in a yellow suit who teetered at the top of the ladder as he tried to staple a pair of posters together around a lamppost, while a strongman in a vinyl cape and a thin man in a red coat held the ladder steady. William sat on his bicycle, watching them silently, until the man in the red coat turned to look at him and William saw those great curly moustaches above a pair of bright pink lips.

The ringmaster smiled. "You like the circus?" he said. His accent was funny. "Like" became "lak", and "circus" became "sow-coos". His voice was very deep.

William nodded, awestruck.

"You don't speak?" said the ringmaster.

William found his voice.

"I like the circus. At least, I think I do. I've never been."

The ringmaster staggered back in mock surprise, releasing his hold upon the ladder. The dwarf at the top stumbled a little, and only the actions of the bald strongman prevented the ladder from coming down, dwarf and all.

"You have never been to the circus?" said the ringmaster. "Well, you must come. You simply must come."

And from the pocket of his bright red coat he produced a trio of tickets and handed them to William.

"For you," he said. "For you, and your mother, and your father. One night only. Circus Caliban."

William took the tickets and held them tightly in his fist, unsure of the safest place in which to put them.

"Thank you," he said.

"You're welcome," said the ringmaster.

"Will there be clowns?" asked William. "There are clowns on the posters, but I just wanted to be sure."

The strongman stared at him silently, and the dwarf on the ladder grinned. The ringmaster leaned forward and gripped William's shoulder. For a moment, William felt stabs of pain that extended hotly through his upper body, as though the ringmaster's sharp nails were needles piercing his skin, injecting him with unknown toxins.

"There are always clowns," said the ringmaster, and William thought that his breath smelled very sweet, like bullseyes and gum drops and jelly babies all mixed together. "It would not be a circus without clowns."

Then he released William as the dwarf descended from the ladder and the three men moved on to another lamppost and another street. After all, they were here for "One Night Only", and there was much work to be done if that night was to be as special as it could possibly be.

❧

Over the course of the next week, more and more circus folk began to arrive in the town. Rides were assembled, and sideshow booths appeared. There was the stink of animals, and many children gathered at the edge of the field to watch the circus take shape, although the circus folk kept them back behind the wall by warning them that the animals were dangerous, or by telling them that they did not want the surprise to be spoiled. William tried to spot the clowns, but they were nowhere to be seen. He supposed that they looked like ordinary people most of the time, until they put on their makeup, and their big shoes, and their funny wigs. Until they did that, there was no way of telling if they were clowns or not. Until they dressed up and made you laugh they were just men, not clowns.

❧

On the night of the performance, while his tummy was still full of birthday cake and fizzy drinks, William and his mother and father drove into town and parked their car at the edge of the great field. People had come from all around to see the circus, and a "House Full" sign stood beside the ticket caravan. William could see the grown ups clutching yellow admission tickets. William's tickets—the special free tickets given to him by the ringmaster—were blue. He did not see anyone else holding blue tickets. He suspected that the ringmaster couldn't afford to give out too many tickets without charge if the circus was only in town for one night.

The big top itself stood at the centre of the field. It was black, with red trim, and a single red flag flew from the topmost support. Behind it were the performers' caravans, the animal cages, and the vehicles used to transport everything from town to town. Most of them looked very old, as though the circus had somehow transported itself from the middle of one century to the beginning of the next, travelling through time and space, its animals ageing but unchanging, its trapeze artists now very old but blessed with the bodies of younger people. William could see rust on the bars of the empty lions' cage, and the interior of one of the caravans, glimpsed through an open door, was all red velvet and rich, dark wood. A woman looked out at William, then pulled the door closed to prevent him from seeing anything more, but William briefly caught a glimpse of others within: a sullen fat man whose naked body was reflected in a mirror as a young girl bathed him by candlelight, her own figure barely concealed by the thinnest of slips. For an instant, William locked eyes with the girl as her hands moved upon the older man, and then she was gone and he was left with an unfamiliar feeling of disgust, as though he were somehow complicit in the commission of a bad deed.

He followed his parents through the sideshows and rides. There were shooting ranges and hoop toss, games of skill and games of chance. Men and women called out from behind the stalls promising wonderful prizes, but William saw nobody carrying the big stuffed elephants and teddy bears that stood arrayed on the topmost shelves of the game booths, their glass eyes gleaming emptily. In fact, William saw nobody win anything at all. Shots were missed by those who regarded themselves as fairground marksmen. Darts bounced from playing cards, and hoops failed to land around goldfish bowls. All was disappointment and broken promises. William could almost see the smiles beginning to fade, and the cries of unhappy children carried on the breeze. The hucksters exchanged glances and sly grins with one another from their booths as they called to the new arrivals, the ones who still had hopes, and expectations of success.

William was not aware of drifting away from his parents. One minute they were beside him, and the next it was as if the whole circus had shifted slightly, moving silently in a great circle so that William no longer stood among the rides and games but at the very periphery of the performers' caravans. He could see the lights of the sideshows and could hear the sound of the children on the merry-go-round, but they were hidden from him by vehicles and tents. These looked more dirty and worn than those close to the big top, the fabric of the tents shabbily mended where it had torn, the panels of the caravans slowly decaying into rust. There were puddles of waste on the ground, and a stale smell of cheap, cooked meat hung on the air.

Uncertain, and a little afraid, William began to pick his way carefully back to his parents, stepping over guy ropes and avoiding the tow bars of the caravans, until at last he came to a single yellow tent which stood apart from the others. Outside stood a red jalopy decorated with balloons, its wheels misshapen and its seats balanced on huge springs. William could hear voices speaking inside the tent, and knew that he had found the clowns. He crept closer and lay down on his belly so that he could peer beneath the bottom of the tent, for if he was seen at the entrance then they would surely send him away and he would learn nothing more about them.

William saw battered dressing tables with brightly-lit mirrors above them, the bulbs powered by a humming, unseen generator. Four men sat at the tables, dressed in suits of purple and green, yellow and orange. They had oversized shoes on their feet. Their heads were bald, but they wore no makeup. William was faintly disappointed. They were just men. They were not yet clowns. Then, while William watched, one of the men took a cloth and doused it in liquid from a black bottle. He looked at himself grimly in the mirror, then drew the cloth across his face. Instantly, a line of white appeared, and the rim of a big red mouth. The man wiped himself again, harder now, and circular red cheeks appeared. Finally, he hid his face in the cloth, rubbing furiously, and when the cloth came away it was covered in flesh-coloured makeup and a clown stared back from the mirror. The other men were engaged in similar activities, rubbing away the cosmetics that concealed the clown faces beneath.

But those faces were not in the least bit funny or engaging. True, the men *looked* like clowns. They had big smiling mouths, and oval shapes around their eyes, and fake redness painted onto their cheeks, but their eyeballs were yellow and their skin looked puckered and diseased. Their bare hands were very white, reminding William of cheap sausages, or lengths of uncooked dough. The clowns moved listlessly, and they spoke in a language William had never heard before, more to themselves than to one another. The tongue sounded very old, and very foreign, and William felt himself grow increasingly afraid. A voice in his head seemed to echo their words, as though someone close by were translating for his benefit.

Children, the voice said. *We hate 'em. Foul things. They laugh at what they doesn't understand. They laugh at things they should be afeared of. Oh, but we know. We know what the circus hides. We know what all circuses hide. Foul children. We make them laugh, but when we can . . .*

We take 'em!

And then the nearest clown turned and stared down at William, and the boy felt moist hands gripping his own as he was dragged beneath the canvas and into the tent. Two clowns, unseen until now, knelt by him, holding him down. William tried to cry out for help, but one of the clowns placed a hand over William's lips, stilling any sound within.

"Quiet, child," he said, and although he still spoke in that strange language William understood each word. The clown's painted mouth smiled, but his other mouth, his *real* mouth, remained grim. The other clowns crowded around, some with a little of their old make-up still in place, so that they seemed half-human and half-other. Their eyes were tinged with yellow, and their eye sockets were rimmed with bright red flesh. One of them, now with an orange wig upon his head, placed his face very close to William's and sniffed at the boy's skin. Then he opened his mouth, revealing very white, very thin, and very sharp teeth. They curved inward at the bottom, like hooks, and William could see great spaces of red gum between them. A tongue emerged, long and purple and covered with tiny barbs. It unfolded like a fly's, or the end of a paper whistle, slowly uncurling from deep in the clown's mouth. The tongue licked at William, tasting his tears, and it felt to William like having a thistle or a cactus rubbed against his face. The clown stepped back, preparing his tongue to lick again, but another clown with blue hair, bigger and taller than his fellows, grabbed it between his thumb and forefinger and squeezed it so hard that his stubby nails punctured the flesh and yellow liquid dripped from the wound.

"Look!" said the clown.

The others drew closer, and William could see a streak of something pink upon the orange clown's tongue before it was released to slide back into its owner's mouth with a slapping sound. The blue clown raised his finger so William could see what was upon it.

It looked like pink make-up.

Instantly, William was dragged to his feet and brought to one of the dressing tables. He was forced into a chair, and an old cloth handkerchief was stuffed into his mouth. William struggled and tried to cry out, but the cloth smothered the sounds and the clowns held him in place. There were hands on his shoulders, on his legs, on the top of his skull and beneath his jaw, keeping his mouth closed on the gag.

And then the clowns descended upon him, their long tongues unfolding from their mouths, their breaths stale with the lingering taste of tobacco and alcohol. He felt their tongues upon him, licking his face, scouring his eyelids and his cheeks with their tiny barbs, exploring his ears and his lips and his nostrils as they covered him with their saliva. William closed his eyes tightly as his skin began to burn, the pain like the stinging of nettles. Just as he felt sure that he could take no more, the clowns stopped. They stared down upon him, and now there were real smiles beneath the painted ones as their tongues withdrew into the cages of their mouths. They backed away, revealing William's reflection to him.

Another William stared back at him from the mirror, this one palefaced and yellow-eyed, with a fixed smile and rosy-red cheeks. The blue clown rubbed William's head gently, and a handful of William's dark hair came away in his hand. The other clowns joined in, rubbing their sharp nails through William's hair until there was nothing of it left but a few stray strands. William's face crumpled, the tears flowing freely now, but the clown smile never left his face, so that he seemed to be laughing even as he cried, crying harder than he had ever cried before, crying for all that he had now lost and that would never be his again.

"I want my mum," whimpered William. "I want my dad."

"No need," said the blue clown. His accent was thick and foreign, like the ringmaster's. He looked very old. "No need for family. New family now."

"Why are you doing this to me?" said William. "Why have you done this to my face?"

"Done?" asked the blue clown, and there was real surprise in his voice. "What done? Done nothing. Clown not learned. Clown chosen in the mudderwomb. Clown does not become: Clown *is*. Clown is not made: Clown is *born*."

❧

And the show went on that night, while William's parents searched and searched for him, and the police came, and laughter rose from the circus tent as the clowns drove on in their happy jalopy and gave balloons to the children, the hated children, and when they left there were smiles on the faces of nearly all of those in the audience, except for the very clever children who sensed that there was more to clowns than bright suits and funny cars and oversized feet, and that if you were wise you didn't laugh at them, and you stayed out of their way, and you never pried into their business, for clowns are lonely and angry and want company in their misery. They are always seeking, always searching, always looking for new clowns to join them.

The Circus Caliban was gone the next day, and there was no sign that it had ever visited the town. The police looked, but William was never seen again, and a new clown was added to the act of the Circus Caliban when next it appeared at the edge of a forest in a country far, far from this one. He was smaller than the rest, and seemed always to be looking into the laughing audience, searching for the parents that he still hoped would find him, but they never came.

And his teeth fell out and were replaced by sharp, white hooks that were kept hidden behind shields of plastic; and his nails decayed to hard yellow stumps at the end of soft, pale fingers. He grew tall and strong, until at last he forgot his name and became only "Clown", and a great clown he was. His tongue grew like a snake's, and he tasted children with it as they laughed, for clowns are hungry and sad and envious of humanity. They travel from town to town looking for those that they can steal away, always marking the child that kicks in the womb, and always finding him upon their return. For clowns are not made. Clowns are *born*.

Spurs
(AKA Freaks)

TOD ROBBINS

I

Jacques Courbé was a romanticist. He measured only twenty-eight inches from the soles of his diminutive feet to the crown of his head; but there were times, as he rode into the arena on his gallant charger, St. Eustache, when he felt himself a doughty knight of old about to do battle for his lady.

What matter that St. Eustache was not a gallant charger except in his master's imagination—not even a pony, indeed, but a large dog of a nondescript breed, with the long snout and upstanding ears of a wolf? What matter that M. Courbé's entrance was invariably greeted with shouts of derisive laughter and bombardments of banana skins and orange peel? What matter that he had no lady, and that his daring deeds were severely curtailed to a mimicry of the bareback riders who preceded him? What mattered all these things to the tiny man who lived in dreams, and who resolutely closed his shoe-button eyes to the drab realities of life?

The dwarf had no friends among the other freaks in Copo's Circus. They considered him ill-tempered and egotistical, and he loathed them for their acceptance of things as they were. Imagination was the armour that protected him from the curious glances of a cruel, gaping world, from the stinging lash of ridicule, from the bombardments of banana skins and orange peel. Without it, he must have shrivelled up and died. But these others? Ah, they had no armour except their own thick hides! The door that opened on the kingdom of imagination was closed and locked to them; and although they did not wish to open this door, although they did not miss what lay beyond it, they resented and mistrusted anyone who possessed the key.

Now it came about, after many humiliating performances in the arena, made palatable only by dreams, that love entered the circus tent and beckoned commandingly to M. Jacques Courbé. In an instant the dwarf was engulfed in a sea of wild, tumultuous passion.

Mlle. Jeanne Marie was a daring bareback rider. It made M. Jacques Courbé's tiny heart stand still to see her that first night of her appearance in the arena, performing brilliantly on the broad back of her aged mare, Sappho. A tall, blonde woman of the amazon type, she had round eyes of baby blue which held no spark of her avaricious peasant's soul, carmine lips and cheeks, large white teeth which flashed continually in a smile, and hands which, when doubled up, were nearly the size of the dwarf's head.

Her partner in the act was Simon Lafleur, the Romeo of the circus tent — a swarthy, Herculean young man with bold black eyes and hair that glistened with grease like the back of Solon, the trained seal.

From the first performance, M. Jacques Courbé loved Mlle. Jeanne Marie. All his tiny body was shaken with longing for her. Her buxom charms, so generously revealed in tights and spangles, made him flush and cast down his eyes. The familiarities allowed to Simon Lafleur, the bodily acrobatic contacts of the two performers, made the dwarf's blood boil. Mounted on St. Eustache, awaiting his turn at the entrance, he would grind his teeth in impotent rage to see Simon circling round and round the ring, standing proudly on the back of Sappho and holding Mlle. Jeanne Marie in an ecstatic embrace, while she kicked one shapely bespangled leg skyward.

"Ah, the dog!" M. Jacques Courbé would mutter. "Some day I shall teach this hulking stable-boy his place! *Ma foi*, I will clip his ears for him!"

St. Eustache did not share his master's admiration for Mlle. Jeanne Marie. From the first he evinced his hearty detestation for her by low

growls and a ferocious display of long, sharp fangs. It was little conso-
lation for the dwarf to know that St. Eustache showed still more
marked signs of rage when Simon Lafleur approached him. It pained
M. Jacques Courbé to think that his gallant charger, his sole
companion, his bedfellow, should not also love and admire the
splendid giantess who each night risked life and limb before the awed
populace. Often, when they were alone together, he would chide St.
Eustache on his churlishness.

"Ah, you devil of a dog!" the dwarf would cry. "Why must you
always growl and show your ugly teeth when the lovely Jeanne Marie
condescends to notice you? Have you no feelings under your tough
hide? Cur, she is an angel and you snarl at her! Do you not remember
how I found you, a starving puppy in a Paris gutter? And now you
must threaten the hand of my princess! So this is your gratitude, great
hairy pig!"

M. Jacques Courbé had one living relative—not a dwarf, like
himself, but a fine figure of a man, a prosperous farmer living just
outside the town of Roubaix. The elder Courbé had never married
and so one day, when he was found dead from heart failure, his tiny
nephew—for whom, it must be confessed, the farmer had always felt
an instinctive aversion—fell heir to a comfortable property. When the
tidings were brought to him, the dwarf threw both arms about the
shaggy neck of St. Eustache and cried out:

"Ah, now we can retire, marry and settle down, old friend! I am
worth many times my weight in gold!"

That evening as Mlle. Jeanne Marie was changing her gaudy
costume after the performance, a light tap sounded on the door.

"Enter!" she called, believing it to be Simon Lafleur, who had promised to take her that evening to the Sign of the Wild Boar for a glass of
wine to wash the sawdust out of her throat. *"Enter, mon chéri!"*

The door swung slowly open and in stepped M. Jacques Courbé,
very proud and upright, in the silks and laces of a courtier, with a tiny
gold-hilted sword swinging at his hip. Up he came, his shoe-button
eyes all a-glitter to see the more than partially revealed charms of his

robust lady. Up he came to within a yard of where she sat, and down on one knee he went and pressed his lips to her red-slippered foot.

"Oh, most beautiful and daring lady," he cried, in a voice as shrill as a pin scratching on a window pane, "Will you not take mercy on the unfortunate Jacques Courbé? He is hungry for your smiles, he is starving for your lips! All night long he tosses on his couch and dreams of Jeanne Marie!"

"What play acting is this, my brave little fellow?" she asked, bending down with the smile of an ogress. "Has Simon Lafleur sent you to tease me?"

"May the black plague have Simon!" the dwarf cried, his eyes seeming to flash blue sparks. "I am not play-acting. It is only too true that I love you, mademoiselle, that I wish to make you my lady. And now that I have a fortune, now that—" He broke off suddenly and his face resembled a withered apple. "What is this, mademoiselle?" he said, in the low, droning tone of a hornet about to sting. "Do you laugh at my love? I warn you, mademoiselle—do not laugh at Jacques Courbé!"

Mlle. Jeanne Marie's large, florid face had turned purple from suppressed merriment. Her lips twitched at the corners. It was all she could do not to burst out into a roar of laughter.

Why, this ridiculous little manikin was serious in his love-making! This pocket-sized edition of a courtier was proposing marriage to her! He, this splinter of a fellow, wished to make her his wife! Why, she could carry him about on her shoulder like a trained marmoset!

What a joke this was—what a colossal, corset-creaking joke! Wait till she told Simon Lafleur! She could fairly see him throw back his sleek head, open his mouth to its widest dimensions and shake with silent laughter. But *she* must not laugh—not now. First she must listen to everything the dwarf had to say, draw all the sweetness of this bonbon of humour before she crushed it under the heel of ridicule.

"I am not laughing," she managed to say. "You have taken me by surprise. I never thought, I never even guessed—"

"That is well, mademoiselle," the dwarf broke in. "I do not tolerate

40

laughter. In the arena I am paid to make laughter, but these others pay to laugh at *me*. I always make people pay to laugh at me!"

"But do I understand you aright, M. Courbé? Are you proposing an honourable marriage?"

The dwarf rested his hand on his heart and bowed. "Yes, mademoiselle, an honourable marriage, and the wherewithal to keep the wolf from the door. A week ago my uncle died and left me a large estate. We shall have a servant to wait on our wants, a horse and carriage, food and wine of the best, and leisure to amuse ourselves. And you? Why, you will be a fine lady! I will clothe that beautiful big body of yours with silks and laces! You will be as happy, mademoiselle, as a cherry tree in June!"

The dark blood slowly receded from Mlle. Jeanne Marie's full cheeks, her lips no longer twitched at the corners, her eyes had narrowed slightly. She had been a bareback rider for years and she was weary of it. The life of the circus tent had lost its tinsel. She loved the dashing Simon Lafleur, but she knew well enough that this Romeo in tights would never espouse a dowerless girl.

The dwarf's words had woven themselves into a rich mental tapestry. She saw herself a proud lady, ruling over a country estate, and later welcoming Simon Lafleur with all the luxuries that were so near his heart. Simon would be overjoyed to marry into a country estate. These pygmies were a puny lot. They died young! She would do nothing to hasten the end of Jacques Courbé. No, she would be kindness itself to the poor little fellow; but, on the other hand, she would not lose her beauty mourning for him.

"Nothing that you wish shall be withheld from you as long as you love me, mademoiselle," the dwarf continued. "Your answer?"

Mlle. Jeanne Marie bent forward and, with a single movement of her powerful arms, raised M. Jacques Courbé and placed him on her knee. For an ecstatic instant she held him thus, as if he were a large French doll, with his tiny sword cocked coquettishly out behind. Then she planted on his cheek a huge kiss that covered his entire face from chin to brow.

41

"I am yours!" she murmured, pressing him to her ample bosom. "From the first I loved you, M. Jacques Courbé!"

II

The wedding of Mlle. Jeanne Marie was celebrated in the town of Roubaix, where Copo's Circus had taken up its temporary quarters. Following the ceremony, a feast was served in one of the tents, which was attended by a whole galaxy of celebrities.

The bridegroom, his dark little face flushed with happiness and wine, sat at the head of the board. His chin was just above the tablecloth, so that his head looked like a large orange that had rolled off the fruit dish. Immediately beneath his dangling feet, St. Eustache, who had more than once evinced by deep growls his disapproval of the proceedings, now worried a bone with quick, sly glances from time to time at the plump legs of his new mistress. Papa Copo was on the dwarf's right, his large round face as red and benevolent as a harvest moon. Next to him sat Griffo, the giraffe boy, who was covered with spots, and whose neck was so long that he looked down on all the rest, including M. Hercule Hippo, the giant. The rest of the company included Mlle. Lupa, who had sharp white teeth of an incredible length, and who growled when she tried to talk; the tiresome M. Jegongle, who insisted on juggling fruit, plates and knives, although the whole company was heartily sick of his tricks; Mme. Samson, with her trained baby boa constrictors coiled about her neck and peeping out timidly, one above each ear; Simon Lafleur and a score of others.

The bareback rider had laughed silently and almost continually ever since Jeanne Marie had told him of her engagement. Now he sat next to her in his crimson tights. His black hair was brushed back from his forehead and so glistened with grease that it reflected the lights overhead, like a burnished helmet. From time to time, he tossed off a brimming goblet of burgundy, nudged the bride in the ribs with his elbow and threw back his sleek head in another silent outburst of laughter.

"And you are sure that you will not forget me, Simon?" she whispered. "It may be some time before I can get the little ape's money."

"Forget you, Jeanne?" he muttered. "By all the dancing devils in champagne, never! I will wait as patiently as Job till you have fed that mouse some poisoned cheese. But what will you do with him in the meantime, Jeanne? You must allow him no liberties. I grind my teeth to think of you in his arms!"

The bride smiled and regarded her diminutive husband with an appraising glance. What an atom of a man! And yet life might linger in his bones for a long time to come. M. Jacques Courbé had allowed himself only one glass of wine and yet he was far gone in intoxication. His tiny face was suffused with blood and he stared at Simon Lafleur belligerently. Did he suspect the truth?

"Your husband is flushed with wine!" the bareback rider whispered. "*Ma foi, madame*, later he may knock you about! Possibly he is a dangerous fellow in his cups. Should he maltreat you, Jeanne, do no forget that you have a protector in Simon Lafleur."

"You clown!" Jeanne Marie rolled her large eyes roguishly and laid her hand for an instant on the bareback rider's knee. "Simon, I could crack his skull between my finger and thumb, like this hickory nut!" She paused to illustrate her example, and then added reflectively: "And, perhaps, I shall do that very thing, if he attempts any familiarities. Ugh! The little ape turns my stomach!"

By now the wedding guests were beginning to show the effects of their potations. This was especially marked in the case of M. Jacques Courbé's associates in the side-show.

Griffo, the giraffe boy, had closed his large brown eyes and was swaying his small head languidly above the assembly, while a slightly supercilious expression drew his lips down at the corners. M. Hercule Hippo, swollen out by his libations to even more colossal proportions, was repeating over and over: "I tell you I am not like other men. When I walk, the earth trembles!" Mlle. Lupa, her hairy upper lip lifted

43

above her long white teeth, was gnawing at a bone, growling unintelligible phrases to herself and shooting savage, suspicious glances at her companions. M. Jejongle's hands had grown unsteady and, as he insisted on juggling the knives and plates of each new course, broken bits of crockery littered the floor. Mme. Samson, uncoiling her necklace of baby boa constrictors, was feeding them lumps of sugar soaked in rum. M. Jacques Courbé had finished his second glass of wine and was surveying the whispering Simon Lafleur through narrowed eyes.

There can be no genial companionship among great egotists who have drunk too much. Each one of these human oddities thought that he or she alone was responsible for the crowds that daily gathered at Copo's Circus; so now, heated with the good Burgundy, they were not slow in asserting themselves. Their separate egos rattled angrily together, like so many pebbles in a bag. Here was gunpowder which needed only a spark.

"I am a big—a very big man!" M. Hercule Hippo said sleepily. "Women love me. The pretty little creatures leave their pygmy husbands, so that they may come and stare at Hercule Hippo of Copo's Circus. Ha, and when they return home, they laugh at other men always! 'You may kiss me again when you grow up,' they tell their sweethearts."

"Fat bullock, here is one woman who has no love for you!" cried Mlle. Lupa, glaring sidewise at the giant over her bone. "That great carcass of yours is only so much food gone to waste. You have cheated the butcher, my friend. Fool, women do not come to see *you*! As well might they stare at the cattle being let through the street. Ah, no, they come from far and near to see one of their own sex who is not a cat!"

"Quite right," cried Papa Copo in a conciliatory tone, smiling and rubbing his hands together. "Not a cat, mademoiselle, but a wolf. Ah, you have a sense of humour! How droll!"

"I *have* a sense of humour," Mlle. Lupa agreed, returning to her bone, "and also sharp teeth. Let the erring hand not stray too near!"

"You, M. Hippo and Mlle. Lupa, are both wrong," said a voice which seemed to come from the roof. "Surely it is none other than me whom the people come to stare at!"

44

All raised their eyes to the supercilious face of Griffo, the giraffe boy, which swayed slowly from side to side on its long, pipe-stem neck. It was he who had spoken, although his eyes were still closed.

"Of all the colossal impudence!" cried the matronly Mme. Samson. "As if my little dears had nothing to say on the subject!" She picked up the two baby boa constrictors, which lay in drunken slumber on her lap, and shook them like whips at the wedding guests. "Papa Copo knows only too well that it is on account of these little charmers, Mark Antony and Cleopatra, that the side-show is so well-attended!"

The circus owner, thus directly appealed to, frowned in perplexity. He felt himself in a quandary. These freaks of his were difficult to handle. Why had he been fool enough to come to M. Jacques Courbé's wedding feast? Whatever he said would be used against him.

As Papa Copo hesitated, his round, red face wreathed in ingratiating smiles, the long deferred spark suddenly alighted in the powder. It all came about on account of the carelessness of M. Jejongle, who had become engrossed in the conversation and wished to put in a word for himself. Absent-mindedly juggling two heavy plates and a spoon, he said in a petulant tone: "You all appear to forget me!"

Scarcely were the words out of his mouth when one of the heavy plates descended with a crash on the thick skull of M. Hippo, and M. Jejongle was instantly remembered. Indeed he was more than remembered, for the giant, already irritated to the boiling point by Mlle. Lupa's insults, at the new affront struck out savagely past her and knocked the juggler head-over-heels under the table.

Mlle. Lupa, always quick-tempered and especially so when her attention was focused on a juicy chicken bone, evidently considered her dinner companion's conduct far from decorous and promptly inserted her sharp teeth in the offending hand that had administered the blow. M. Hippo, squealing from rage and pain like a wounded elephant, bounded to his feet, overturning the table.

Pandemonium followed. Every freak's hands, teeth, feet, were turned against the others. Above the shouts, screams, growls, and hisses of the combat, Papa Copo's voice could be heard bellowing for peace:

"Ah, my children, my children! This is no way to behave! Calm yourselves, I pray you! Mlle. Lupa, remember that you are a lady as well as a wolf!"

There is no doubt that M. Jacques Courbé would have suffered most in this undignified fracas had it not been for St. Eustache, who had stationed himself over his tiny master and who now drove off all would-be assailants. As it was, Griffo, the unfortunate giraffe boy, was the most defenceless and therefore became the victim. His small, round head swayed back and forth to blows like a punching bag. He was bitten by Mlle. Lupa, buffeted by M. Hippo, kicked by M. Jejongle, clawed by Mme. Samson, and nearly strangled by both of the baby boa constrictors, which had wound themselves about his neck like hangmen's nooses. Undoubtedly he would have fallen a victim to circumstances had it not been for Simon Lafleur, the bride and half a dozen of her acrobatic friends, whom Papa Copo had implored to restore peace. Roaring with laughter, they sprang forward and tore the combatants apart.

M. Jacques Courbé was found sitting grimly under a fold of table-cloth. He held a broken bottle of wine in one hand. The dwarf was very drunk and in a towering rage. As Simon Lafleur approached with one of his silent laughs, M. Jacques Courbé hurled the bottle at his head.

"Ah, the little wasp!" the bareback rider cried, picking up the dwarf by his waistband. "Here is your fine husband, Jeanne! Take him away before he does me some mischief. *Parbleu*, he is a bloodthirsty fellow in his cups!"

The bride approached, her blonde face crimson from wine and laughter. Now that she was safely married to a country estate she took no more pains to conceal her true feelings.

"Oh, *la, la*!" she cried, seizing the struggling dwarf and holding him forcibly on her shoulder. "What a temper the little ape has! Well, we shall spank it out of him before long!"

"Let me down!" M. Jacques Courbé screamed in a paroxysm of fury. "You will regret this, madame! Let me down, I say!"

But the stalwart bride shook her head. "No, no, my little one!" she laughed. "You cannot escape your wife so easily! What, you would fly from my arms before the honeymoon!"

"Let me down!" he cried again. "Can't you see that they are laughing at me!"

"And why should they not laugh, my little ape? Let them laugh, if they will, but I will not put you down. No, I will carry you thus, perched on my shoulder, to the farm. It will set a precedent which brides of the future may find a certain difficulty in following!"

"But the farm is quite a distance from here, my Jeanne," said Simon Lafleur. "You are strong as an ox and he is only a marmoset, still, I will wager a bottle of Burgundy that you set him down by the roadside."

"Done, Simon!" the bride cried, which a flash of her strong white teeth. "You shall lose your wager, for I swear that I could carry my little ape from one end of France to the other!"

M. Jacques Courbé no longer struggled. He now sat bolt upright on his bride's broad shoulder. From the flaming peaks of blind passion, he had fallen into an abyss of cold fury. His love was dead, but some quite alien emotion was rearing an evil head from its ashes.

"So, madame, you could carry me from one end of France to the other!" he droned in a monotonous undertone. "From one end of France to the other! I will remember that always, madame!"

"Come!" cried the bride suddenly. "I am off. Do you and the others, Simon, follow to see me win my wager."

They all trooped out of the tent. A full moon rode the heavens and showed the road, lying as white and straight through the meadows as the parting in Simon Lafleur's black, oily hair. The bride, still holding the diminutive bridegroom on her shoulder, burst out into song as she strode forward. The wedding guests followed. Some walked none too steadily. Griffo, the giraffe boy, staggered pitifully on his long, thin legs. Papa Copo alone remained behind.

"What a strange world!" he muttered, standing in the tent door and following them with his round blue eyes. "Ah, these children of mine are difficult at times—very difficult!"

III

A year had rolled by since the marriage of Mlle. Jeanne Marie and M. Jacques Courbé. Copo's Circus had once more taken up its quarters in the town of Roubaix. For more than a week the country people for miles around had flocked to the side-show to get a peep at Griffo, the giraffe boy; M. Hercule Hippo, the giant; Mlle. Lupa, the wolf lady; Mme. Samson, with her baby boa constrictors; and M. Jejongle, the famous juggler. Each was still firmly convinced that he or she alone was responsible for the popularity of the circus.

Simon Lafleur sat in his lodgings at the Sign of the Wild Boar. He wore nothing but red tights. His powerful torso, stripped to the waist, glistened with oil. He was kneading his biceps tenderly with some strong-smelling fluid.

Suddenly there came the sound of heavy, laborious footsteps on the stairs. Simon Lafleur looked up. His rather gloomy expression lifted, giving place to the brilliant smile that had won for him the hearts of so many lady acrobats.

"Ah, this is Marcelle!" he told himself. "Or perhaps it is Rose, the English girl; or, yet again, little Francesca, although she walks more lightly. Well, no matter—whoever it is, I will welcome her!"

But now the lagging, heavy footfalls were in the hall and, a moment later, they came to a halt outside the door. There was a timid knock.

Simon Lafleur's brilliant smile broadened. "Perhaps some new admirer who needs encouragement," he told himself. But aloud he said, "Enter, mademoiselle!"

The door swung slowly open and revealed the visitor. She was a tall, gaunt woman dressed like a peasant. The wind had blown her hair into her eyes. Now she raised a large, toil-worn hand, brushed it back across her forehead and looked long and attentively at the bareback rider.

"You do not remember me?" she said at length.

Two lines of perplexity appeared above Simon Lafleur's Roman nose; he slowly shook his head. He, who had known so many women

48

in his time, was now at a loss. Was it a fair question to ask a man who was no longer a boy and who had lived? Women change so in a brief time! Now this bag of bones might at one time have appeared desirable to him.

Parbleu! Fate was a conjurer! She waved her wand and beautiful women were transformed into hags, jewels into pebbles, silks and laces into hempen cords. The brave fellow who danced tonight at the prince's ball might tomorrow dance more lightly on the gallows tree. The thing was to live and die with a full belly. To digest all that one could—that was life!

"You do not remember me?" she said again.

Simon Lafleur once more shook his sleek, black head. "I have a poor memory for faces, madame," he said politely. "It is my misfortune, when there are such beautiful faces."

"Ah, but you should have remembered, Simon!" the woman cried, a sob rising in her throat. "We were very close together, you and I. Do you not remember Jeanne Marie?"

"Jeanne Marie!" the bareback rider cried. "Jeanne Marie, who married a marmoset and a country estate? Don't tell me, Madame, that you—"

He broke off and stared at her, open-mouthed. His sharp black eyes wandered from the wisps of wet, straggling hair down her gaunt person till they rested at last on her thick cowhide boots, encrusted with layer on layer of mud from the countryside.

"It is impossible!" he said at last.

"It is indeed Jeanne Marie," the woman answered, "or what is left of her. Ah, Simon, what a life he has led me! I have been merely a beast of burden! There are no ignominies which he has not made me suffer!"

"To whom do you refer?" Simon Lafleur demanded. "Surely you cannot mean that pocket edition husband of yours—that dwarf, Jacques Courbé?"

"Ah, but I do, Simon! Alas, he has broken me!"

"He—that toothpick of a man?" the bareback rider cried, with one of his silent laughs. "Why, it is impossible! As you once said yourself,

49

Jeanne, you could crack his skull between finger and thumb like a hickory nut!"

"So I thought once. Ah, but I did not know him then, Simon! Because he was small, I thought I could do with him as I liked. It seemed to me that I was marrying a manikin. 'I will play Punch and Judy with this little fellow,' I said to myself. Simon, you may imagine my surprise when he began playing Punch and Judy with me!"

"But I do not understand, Jeanne. Surely at any time you could have slapped him into obedience!"

"Perhaps," she assented wearily, "had it not been for St. Eustache. From the first that wolf dog of his hated me. If I so much as answered his master back, he would show his teeth. Once, at the beginning, when I raised my hand to cuff Jacques Courbé, he sprang at my throat and would have torn me limb from limb had not the dwarf called him off. I was a strong woman, but even then I was no match for a wolf!"

"There was poison, was there not?" Simon Lafleur suggested.

"Ah, yes, I, too, thought of poison; but it was of no avail. St. Eustache would eat nothing that I gave him and the dwarf forced me to taste first of all food that was placed before him and his dog. Unless I myself wished to die, there was no way of poisoning either of them."

"My poor girl!" the bareback rider said, pityingly. "I begin to understand, but sit down and tell me everything. This is a revelation to me, after seeing you stalking homeward so triumphantly with your bridegroom on your shoulder. You must begin at the beginning."

"It was just because I carried him thus on my shoulder that I have had to suffer so cruelly," she said, seating herself on the only other chair the room afforded. "He has never forgiven me the insult which he says I put upon him. Do you remember how I boasted that I could carry him from one end of France to the other?"

"I remember. Well, Jeanne?"

"Well, Simon, the little demon has figured out the exact distance in leagues. Each morning, rain or shine, we sally out of the house — he on my back, the wolf dog at my heels — and I tramp along the dusty roads till my knees tremble beneath me from fatigue. If I so much as slacken my pace, if I falter, he goads me with cruel little golden spurs, while, at the same time, St. Eustache nips my ankles. When we return home, he strikes so many leagues off a score which he says is the number of leagues from one end of France to the other. Not half that distance has been covered, and I am no longer a strong woman, Simon. Look at these shoes!"

She held up one of her feet for his inspection. The sole of the cowhide boot had been worn through; Simon Lafleur caught a glimpse of bruised flesh caked with the mire of the highway.

"This is the third pair that I have had," she continued hoarsely. "Now he tells me that the price of shoe leather is too high, that I shall have to finish my pilgrimage barefooted."

"But why do you put up with all this, Jeanne?" Simon Lafleur asked angrily. "You, who have a carriage and a servant, should not walk at all!"

"At first there was a carriage and a servant," she said, wiping the tears from her eyes with the back of her hand, "but they did not last a week. He sent the servant about his business and sold the carriage at a nearby fair. Now there is no one but me to wait on him and his dog."

"But the neighbours?" Simon Lafleur persisted. "Surely you could appeal to them?"

"We have no neighbours; the farm is quite isolated. I would have run away many months ago if I could have escaped unnoticed; but they keep a continual watch on me. Once I tried, but I hadn't travelled more than a league before the wolf dog was snapping at my ankles. He drove me back to the farm and the following day I was compelled to carry the little fiend until I fell from sheer exhaustion."

"But tonight you got away?"

"Yes," she said, with a quick, frightened glance at the door. "Tonight I slipped out while they were both sleeping and came here to you. I knew that you would protect me, Simon, because of what we have been to each other. Get Papa Copo to take me back in the circus, and I will work my fingers to the bone! Save me, Simon!"

51

Jeanne Marie could longer suppress her sobs. They rose in her throat, choking her, making her incapable of further speech.

"Calm yourself, Jeanne," Simon Lafleur said soothingly. "I will do what I can for you. I shall have a talk with Papa Copo tomorrow. Of course, you are no longer the same woman that you were a year ago. You have aged since then, but perhaps our good Papa Copo could find you something to do."

He broke off and eyed her intently. She had stiffened in the chair, her face, even under its coat of grime, had gone a sickly white.

"What troubles you, Jeanne?" he asked a trifle breathlessly.

"Hush!" she said, with a finger to her lips. "Listen!"

Simon Lafleur could hear nothing but the tapping of the rain on the roof and the sighing of the wind through the tree. An unusual silence seemed to pervade the Sign of the Wild Boar.

"Now don't you hear it?" she cried with an in articulate gasp. "Simon, it is in the house — it is on the stairs!"

At last the bareback rider's less sensitive ears caught the sound his companion had heard a full minute before. It was a steady *pit-pat, pit-pat*, on the stairs, hard to dissociate from the drip of the rain from the eaves; but each instant it came nearer, grew more distinct.

"Oh, save me, Simon, save me!" Jeanne Marie cried, throwing herself at his feet and clasping him about his knees. "Save me! It is St. Eustache!"

"Nonsense, woman!" the bareback rider said angrily, but neverthe-less he rose. "There are other dogs in the world. On the second landing there is a blind fellow who owns a dog. Perhaps it is he you hear."

"No, no — it is St. Eustache's step! My God, if you had lived with him a year, you would know it, too! Close the door and lock it!"

"That I will not," Simon Lafleur said contemptuously. "Do you think I am frightened so easily? If it is the wolf dog, so much the worse for him. He will not be the first cur I have choked to death with these two hands!"

Pit-pat, pit-pat — it was on the second landing. *Pit-pat, pit-pat* — now it was in the corridor, and coming fast. *Pit-pat* — all at once it stopped.

There was a moment's breathless silence and then into the room trotted St. Eustache. M. Jacques Courbé sat astride the dog's broad back, as he had so often done in the circus ring. He held a tiny drawn sword, his shoe-button eyes seemed to reflect its steely glitter.

The dwarf brought the dog to a halt in the middle of the room and took in, at a single glance, the prostrate figure of Jeanne Marie. St. Eustache, too, seemed to take silent note of it. The stiff hair on his back rose up, he showed his long white fangs hungrily and his eyes glowed like two live coals.

"So I find you *thus*, madame!" M. Jacques Courbé said at last. "It is fortunate that I have a charger here who can scent out my enemies as well as hunt them down in the open. Without him, I might have had some difficulty in discovering you. Well, the little game is up. I find you with your lover!"

"Simon Lafleur is not my lover!" she sobbed. "I have not seen him once since I married you until tonight! I swear it!"

"Once is enough," the dwarf said grimly. "The impudent stable boy must be chastised!"

"Oh, spare him!" Jeanne Marie implored. "Do not harm him, I beg of you! It is not his fault that I came! I —"

But at this point Simon Lafleur drowned her out in a roar of laughter.

"Ho, ho!" he roared, putting his hands on his hips. "You would chastise me, eh? *Nom d'un chien!* Don't try your circus tricks on me! Why, hop-o'-my-thumb, you who ride on a dog's back like a flea, out of this room before I squash you! Begone, melt, fade away!" He paused, expanded his barrel-like chest, puffed out his cheeks and blew a great breath at the dwarf. "Blow away, insect," he bellowed, "lest I put my heel on you!"

M. Jacques Courbé was unmoved by this torrent of abuse. He sat very upright on St. Eustache's back, his tiny sword resting on his tiny shoulder.

"Are you done?" he said at last, when the bareback rider had run dry of invectives. "Very well, monsieur! Prepare to receive cavalry!"

He paused for an instant, then added in a high, clear voice: "Get him, St. Eustache!"

The dog crouched and, at almost the same moment, sprang at Simon Lafleur. The bareback rider had no time to avoid him and his tiny rider. Almost instantaneously the three of them had come to death grips. It was a gory business.

Simon Lafleur, strong man as he was, was bowled over by the wolf dog's unexpected leap. St. Eustache's clashing jaws closed on his right arm and crushed it to the bone. A moment later the dwarf, still clinging to his dog's back, thrust the point of his tiny sword into the body of the prostrate bareback rider.

Simon Lafleur struggled valiantly, but to no purpose. Now he felt the fetid breath of the dog fanning his neck and the wasp-like sting of the dwarf's blade, which this time found a mortal spot. A convulsive tremor shook him and he rolled over on his back. The circus Romeo was dead.

M. Jacques Courbé cleansed his sword on a kerchief of lace, dismounted and approached Jeanne Marie. She was still crouching on the floor, her eyes closed, her head held tightly between both hands. The dwarf touched her imperiously on the broad shoulder which had so often carried him.

"Madame," he said, "we now can return home. You must be more careful hereafter. *Ma foi*, it is an ungentlemanly business cutting the throats of stable-boys!"

She rose to her feet, like a large trained animal at the word of command.

"Do you wish to be carried?" she said between livid lips.

"Ah, that is true, madame," he murmured. "I was forgetting our little wager. Ah, yes! Well, you are to be congratulated, madame—you have covered nearly half the distance."

"Nearly half the distance," she repeated in a lifeless voice.

"Yes, madame," M. Jacques Courbé continued. "I fancy that you will be quite a docile wife by the time you have done." He paused, and then added reflectively: "It is truly remarkable how speedily one can ride the devil out of a woman—with spurs!"

๛

Papa Copo had been spending a convivial evening at the Sign of the Wild Boar. As he stepped out into the street, he saw three familiar figures preceding him — a tall woman, a tiny man, and a large dog with upstanding ears. The woman carried the man on her shoulder, the dog trotted at her heels.

The circus owner came to a halt and stared after them. His round eyes were full of childish astonishment.

"Can it be?" he murmured. "Yes, it is! Three old friends! And so Jeanne carries him! Ah, but she should not poke fun at M. Jacques Courbé! He is so sensitive; but, alas, they are the kind that are always henpecked!"

Tiger, Tiger

Rio Youers

It was, once again, just a field. A stretch of green between Colin's estate and the road leading to town, where children played football and flew kites, and where they had fireworks every Bonfire Night (you'd always find a gaggle of kids—and Colin would be one of them—on the morning of November 6th, hunting for the blackened, ruptured tubes of spent rockets and Roman candles). Maybe one day they would build another housing estate here, or a factory, or one of those big shopping centres like they have in America. And that'd be where all the children would hang out, Colin thought, and they'd forget they ever used to play football and fly their kites. It was surely just a matter of time before the diggers and the workers in their high-vis vests appeared. But for now, on this crisp and golden morning in October, it was just a field.

The circus had left town.

Colin stood with his hands on his hips and looked around, appearing for all the world more adult than his eleven and a half years. It was hard to think that, just last night, this stretch of green had been crowded with people—with stalls, tents, and attractions. CIRCUS FANTASTICA, the sign over the midway had announced, and although Colin didn't know what "Fantastica" meant (and his father wasn't sure, either), he thought it the perfect word, and one he would apply to all things outlandish—and even a little bit scary—from now on.

Colin had only ever been to one circus before, a few years ago—a Big Top in the car park next to the Multiplex. There had been clowns and elephants and trapeze artists, all the usual stuff, and Colin had a great time ... but it was really *nothing* compared to Circus Fantastica, which had so much going on you really needed two nights — maybe even three — to see it all. The midway, which led toward a Big Top that appeared as light and large as a cloud, was lined with all manner of attractions. Magicians and fortune tellers. Fire breathers and sword swallowers. Carousels, coconut shies, dunk tanks. Colin had tried to make the "Human Statue" crack a smile (he couldn't) and had tested his strength on the High Stryker — had swung the mallet down as hard as he could. He didn't ring the bell, but the puck had climbed all the way to *Future Superhero,* which he thought was pretty good for an eleven-year-old.

Jugglers and shooting galleries. Knife throwers, contortionists, a strongman dressed in a leopard-print leotard. Barkers that colourfully promised to guess your weight or tried to lure you into various enter-tainments. *Arabian Wonderland,* one of them was called, and there had been pictures of belly dancers outside. *FREAKED OUT* another stated in oversized horror-film letters. Colin had been too afraid to go in that tent, but his friend, Billy Crisp, told him there was a four-legged woman inside. Crab-Girl, she was called. And a boy — The Human Unicorn — with a horn in the middle of his forehead.

Fantastica, indeed.

All this amid the aroma of popcorn and candy floss, beneath whorls of lights frantically flashing. So much laughter and the occasional thrilled scream, with mad calliope music swirling in the air.

Best of all was that Colin had been able to enjoy the circus with his father, just the two of them. His mum — his *step*mum — had stayed home with one of her migraines. Not surprising, given that she'd spent an hour shouting at him when he got home from school (which magically stopped when his father walked through the front door). Colin sometimes wondered how much noise and anger was inside his stepmother's head. He thought that one day the back of her skull would burst open and she'd fall to the ground, looking like one of the spent fireworks he found on November 6th. There'd be a single, sensational bang, a fountain of sparks, and that would be that.

Awesome.

Colin wasn't sure, but he thought his dad was happy it had just been the two of them, as well. He appeared relaxed—had laughed more than Colin had seen in a long time (certainly since Janice, stepmother from hell, arrived on the scene). A much-needed slice of father and son time, where the world outside the circus grounds could have broken away and drifted into space, and nothing mattered—only that moment in time and their precious togetherness. Colin wanted it to last forever, to float through eternity in Circus Fantastica, sharing gigantic hotdogs with his dad, knocking endless coconuts off their posts, laughing at the clowns. He'd felt sad when the Ringmaster closed the show, and as they walked home he kept looking back at the glow of lights above the trees and rooftops. Even when he went to bed—looking from his window at the soft patina of magic printed against the sky.

He stood now in the field that was just a field and closed his eyes. He thought, if he concentrated hard enough, he could recapture some of that magic . . . raise the Big Top once again and fill it with the spectacular, hear the drums roll and the elephants trombone, see the clowns tumble in fabulous colours while the trapeze artists twirled fantastic shapes through the air. Was that candy floss he could smell, and the syrupy tang of toffee apples? Could he hear the crack of the tiger tamer's whip, and the ghost of that calliope puffing out strange tunes?

"I wish."

The colour faded from his mind. He opened his eyes and the field seemed emptier than ever. The reddish tint of distant trees. Blocks of housing stacked at one end. The rush of a train and the insect-like buzz of traffic on the motorway. The field, though, was a sad, open space, with nothing to suggest that the circus had ever been there. Not even an empty nougat wrapper or the skin of a burst balloon.

Colin sighed and started walking. He'd already spent too long daydreaming in the field and would be late for school if he didn't get a move on. However, he'd taken only seven or eight steps before stopping again, all thoughts of school exiting his head.

"What the . . . ?"

There was something in the grass, mostly buried, with only a thin crescent winking in the morning light. Colin stepped closer, thinking it a coin or a ticket stub, but it was only when he hunkered down and pried it from the grass and dirt that he saw it was something *very* different.

"Oh, Jesus."

It appeared the field wasn't entirely cleared of Fantastica.

He dropped it at first—hurriedly, and with a little cry—then leapt to his feet. A reflex action. It took him a moment to recover his senses and realize that the thing he'd found couldn't hurt him. Uttering a nervous laugh (which made him sound about six years old, he thought), he stooped and picked it up again. He wiped dirt from its hard surface and tested the pointed end with the pad of his thumb.

Still sharp.

"Awesome."

He knew what it was. A tiger's tooth. *Had* to be a tiger's tooth because it was the only big cat at the circus. There'd been no lions or jaguars, and elephants didn't have teeth like this. Colin held it up, his breath caught high in his chest. It was easily three inches long, pale yellow and as thick as his dad's middle finger. He had no idea how it had fallen out—you certainly didn't *pull* out a tiger's tooth. It could have dropped out on its own, he supposed, but it didn't look rotten. It looked . . . *strong*.

Colin grabbed the fat end of the tooth and made a couple of slashing motions. He stalked forwards and roared, remembering how loud—how *powerful*—the tiger had been, muscles sliding beneath its coat, kept at bay by the tamer's whip. Colin had gripped his father's arm, trembling as the fierce animal prowled around the ring, very aware that only a thin set of bars separated it from the audience. It was a thrilling animal, no doubt, but Colin had been somewhat relieved to see it whipcracked back into its cage.

He grinned and stalked, imagining himself a tiger, with striking colours and brilliant eyes. He hunched his shoulders and roared, feeling his great tiger heart boom. An imaginary audience—smelling of popcorn and hotdogs and all things delicious—trembled in their seats.

Colin laughed, a boy of eleven and a half years once again, then slipped off his backpack and put the tiger's tooth into one of its deep side pockets. He pushed his P.E. socks down on top, to hide the tooth in case anyone should happen to look, then zipped the pocket, shouldered the pack, and went to school.

ॐॐ

He was late, of course. By thirteen minutes. Miss Bush shouted at him in front of the whole class, which was embarrassing, but he made himself feel better by imagining her trying to fend off a five-hundred-pound Bengal tiger with nothing but her chair and the blackboard ruler. Jimmy Gibbins saw him grinning to himself at the back of the class, flicked a pencil eraser at him, and called him a freak. Colin wondered what Jimmy would look like with his head in a tiger's mouth.

He didn't stop grinning.

He kept to himself at breaktime. All the other kids were in the yard, playing football or chatting in groups, but Colin found a quiet spot, sat down, and took out the tiger's tooth. He cleaned off the rest of the mud, inspected it carefully, and determined that it had broken off close to the root. Colin was not a boy who lacked imagination, yet he couldn't conceive a scenario in which the tiger—so powerful a beast—had its tooth snapped clean in two. And not just the tip, either, but at its thickest point.

He wondered where Circus Fantastica was now, and if the tiger was lying in its cage, in pain. "What happened to you?"

At lunchtime Colin went to the library and found some books about tigers. He read how, in some cultures, they were considered a sacred animal, and there were even tiger temples where people went to worship. He learned that the tooth—*his* tooth now—was called a canine, and its primary purpose was to tear through flesh. He also learned, somewhat alarmingly, that a tiger with broken or missing teeth could turn man-eater—an instinctive thing, it being harder for them to catch their usual prey. There were even photographs of people who had survived tiger attacks. He saw lots of scarred, mutilated body parts. Pretty gross, on the whole, and he flipped the pages quickly.

The afternoon was slow and Colin was glad when the final bell rang. He was also getting a headache. Perhaps not as bad as one of Janice's migraines, but he could feel it pulsing behind his eyes and thought he'd go home and crash for an hour. No such luck, though; his stepmother was doing her best dragon impersonation, breathing fire, hard as a sack of stones. To make matters worse, his school had called to inform her of his tardiness, and just happened to mention that his focus had been slipping of late.

"Are you *trying* to embarrass me, Colin?"

"No."

She had stopped breathing fire, but Colin was pretty sure he could see little puffs of smoke exiting her nostrils. She leaned over him, her teeth showing, eyes like burning matches. There were tiny bright flecks in her irises that, if you chiselled them out, Colin was sure would eat through skin.

"Do you think I enjoy getting calls from your school?"

"No," Colin replied, but he thought she enjoyed the opportunity to express displeasure, particularly in *him*. He shuffled back a step and she grabbed his arm and pulled him closer, shook him hard.

"You're a constant disappointment, do you know that?"

Colin winced, rubbing his arm where she had grabbed him.

"Constant!"

He nodded because he didn't know what else to do, how else to make this end. His head hurt, and his arm hurt now. All he wanted was to get away—run away. With Circus Fantastica, maybe. They couldn't be *too* far away. He could catch up with them, be a clown or learn how to swallow swords. Perhaps Crab-Girl and the Human Unicorn could be his new friends.

Janice showed her teeth and shouted something else but Colin didn't really hear; he was back at the circus, watching the acrobats tumble, hearing the tiger roar. This got him thinking about the tooth. The flesh-tearing canine in his backpack. He imagined Janice trapped in the ring and screaming, banging helplessly on the bars with the tiger watching, waiting to make its move. Colin and his dad were in the audience, cheering and clapping, spilling popcorn.

What a show!

Colin cracked a smile. He couldn't help it.

Big mistake.

Her hand was as quick as a knife-thrower's blade, but not designed to miss. She caught the left side of Colin's face. His head rocked sideways and he staggered, bright pain flaring in his cheek.

There followed a deep silence—what Colin thought was probably called a stunned silence. Janice pursed her lips and flexed her fingers; she'd hurt her hand. Colin held the left side of his face. It felt hot, as if she really had breathed fire on him, and he could taste blood in his mouth. He looked at her, tears prickling his eyes.

"I'm going to talk to your father about you," Janice said. Her face was a mask chipped from cold, grey stone. "Now go to your room."

Colin nodded, trying not to cry, but when he blinked the tears dropped onto his cheeks. He turned quickly, and on trembling legs started down the hallway.

"And if I hear one *peep* out of you," Janice snarled. There was a long pause, as if she were running through a long list of possible consequences. In the end—as if she couldn't decide—she simply said, "So help me God."

Colin trudged upstairs and into his room. He closed the door, fell onto his bed, and pressed his face into the pillow so that she wouldn't hear him crying.

వచ్

His headache got worse—maybe it *was* as bad as one of Janice's migraines—and now his mouth was hurting, too. The inside of his cheek was split and puffy, and it stung when he pressed his tongue against it. Colin lay on his bed and cried a little longer, then took the tiger's tooth from his backpack, clutched it and daydreamed.

His father came home at the usual time. Colin's heart sank when he heard his Clio pull up outside. He opened the front door and called out happily... and that was the last happy sound Colin heard that night. It was followed by terse murmuring and many periods of silence. Colin crept onto the landing at one point, trained his ear downstairs, and heard his stepmother say: "This isn't working, Mark. I don't know how much longer I can take this."

"Everything is still a little raw," his father said. "He misses his mum. It'll take time."

"She's been dead two years."

"They were extremely close."

Silence, except for the ITN news in the background, the buzz of the refrigerator.

"He's disruptive." Janice's voice, cold like the inside of that refrigerator. "He needs discipline."

"He's eleven years old," his father said. He never raised his voice to Janice — probably afraid to — but Colin sensed his words threaded with impatience. "He's just a boy."

"Your complacence isn't helping him," Janice said. Another silence. Colin imagined his father staring into space, jaw trembling, and Janice with the heel of her hand pressed to her forehead.

She spoke again: "I've been looking at boarding schools — "

"He's my *son*, Janice."

"Yes, and I'm your wife. A boarding school isn't a prison sentence, Mark. It will benefit his education no end, and he'll learn the values and principles essential to successful living. More importantly, we'll have the time together we need to make this marriage work."

Colin expected his father to reply immediately, with certain impatience, but he didn't. There was another heavy pause and finally he said: "Let's not talk about it now."

Colin slunk back to his room and softly closed the door. How he could move so quietly was beyond him, given how he trembled, and how his heart pounded so loud. He sat on the edge of his bed and tried to think, but couldn't concentrate because his head ached too much and his mouth had started bleeding again. He was *scared*, too—scared that his father wouldn't, or couldn't, stand up to Janice. His shoulders hitched and his chest made a dry sound. No tears left. He curled up on his bed, still clutching the tiger's tooth.

Muffled sounds from downstairs. They seemed so distant.

Colin closed his eyes and dropped, exhausted, into sleep.

જ⊸ક

A febrile, wild dream.

Wild . . . that was the word.

And the pain didn't go away.

The sound in his head was like the ocean. Crashing. Swaying. Constant. His mouth throbbed and he felt confused, angry—yearned for a place both dense and vast, his long back stroked by leaves and the perfume of flowers filling his lungs. A place where he *belonged*. Something jabbed him in the rump and he wheeled quickly—his movement felt different, as strong yet supple as rope—to see a man standing on the other side of the bars (*bars?*) holding a pointed stick. He was familiar, the man, with a bald head and shimmering clothes. He jabbed Colin with the stick again. "Get, now," he sneered, and Colin made a sound in his chest, full of force, that rumbled up and out of his aching mouth like thunder.

What's going on here? Colin thought. The bars on one side of his cage screeched up, giving him access to a narrow tunnel that led to a circle of light and sound. He started towards it because he knew he had to, and because the man with the stick jabbed him yet again, and this time hard enough to punch through his skin and draw blood. He roared and stalked forwards, his huge paws gripping the unnatural floor, and entered the ring to the threatening clash of applause.

"*Ladies and gentlemen,*" a voice announced over the loud speakers. "*From the mysterious depths of the Malaysian jungle . . . Ko, King of the Tigers.*"

He roared again and the audience applauded. Some of them took photographs. Their cameras flashed and confusing puddles of light filled Colin's aching head. He growled and skulked around the ring, tail flicking. Music boomed from the PA system—an old rock and roll song his father had said was called "Tiger Man"—and the tamer entered the ring to yet more applause. His bald head and shimmering suit reflected the bright lights. The pointed stick was gone but he had a whip instead, which he used now, snapping it an inch from Colin's rear leg.

Colin growled and circled away from him. *There aren't any bars between us now,* he thought.

A dream, it *had* to be, from having attended Circus Fantastica the previous night, finding the tiger's tooth, and spending the day in. . . well, *tigerish* reverie. His subconscious was processing the input and here was the result: a representation of his anger and frustration; a response to being bullied. He rolled his giant tongue and felt where Janice had slapped him, the stub of his broken tooth. *I am the tiger,* he thought, and roared, his claws digging into the soft floor. His nostrils flared and he smelled straw and dung and popcorn and man-sweat. Fear, too. So much fear. He showed his broken grin to the audience and felt them shudder. Just a dream, yes, but there was something deeper here—layers of realism not typical of a dream, from the minutia of the Big Top to the lean and limber way in which his body moved.

I am the tiger.

The tamer cracked his whip and Colin did the things he had to do: leap onto pedestals of various height and size (the last of them barely wide enough for all four paws), roll over and play dead, stand on his hind legs (he towered over the tamer, who was as small and breakable as a cheap toy), jump through hoops of fire. Throughout all of this his head thumped angrily, and he was relieved when the show was over and he was able to retreat from the mad light and sound. A small escape. He sometimes felt the same way when Janice sent him to his room. Four walls, a tight space, but at least he was alone.

He curled up on the floor of his cage, closed his eyes, and tried to sleep. To dream within a dream, perhaps, of a green, kind world where the birdsong was endless and the flora was as bright as his coat. He was aware of the circus sounds winding down, of people shouting and packing up around him. Trucks rumbling. The bang of a hammer. The cry of a drill. His massive body sighed and he longed to find his dream, his jungle. His tongue rolled over the stub of his broken tooth and he whimpered.

"Big. Stupid. Pussy cat."

Colin sat up at the sound of the voice. His tail twitched and he turned to see the tamer on the other side of the bars. His shimmering suit had been replaced by jeans and an old sweater. He twirled the pointed stick like a baton.

Colin growled, a fierce and menacing vibration from deep in his chest. He looked at the pointed stick and snarled.

"Time to show you who's in charge."

Another growl. Colin's heightened sense of smell detected dirt and alcohol. The tamer stepped towards his cage and ran the stick along the bars. The sound angered Colin and he roared, showed his claws.

"Stupid cat," the tamer slurred. He thrust the stick between the bars and stabbed Colin in the ribs. Colin felt his skin break and bleed. He hissed and retreated into one corner, the fur on his back lifting in a stiff orange and black brush.

Another jab, this time in the rear leg, drawing more blood. Colin's wild body heaved and he felt all of his emotion surface—a towering wave that could only crash hard and loud. His muscles flexed beneath his coat. His eyes were bright and wide.

When the tamer jabbed for a third time, he was ready.

His reactions, compared to the tamer, were so quick it felt as if he had slowed down time. He watched the pointed stick move towards him, and was not only able to jerk out of the way, but also whip out a paw and knock it from the tamer's hand. It clattered onto the cage floor. Colin placed one paw on top of it and looked at the tamer.

You want it, he thought. *Come and get it.*

He had no doubt the tamer would open the cage to retrieve his stick — his *weapon*. He was drunk and arrogant enough, and could not afford to show fear. Sure enough, he barked something, thrust out one hand like a policeman stopping traffic, and stepped towards the cage door. Colin took his paw off the stick and backed away, appearing compliant, head down but eyes up. His rear legs tensed, muscles tight.

The wave inside him swelled, ready to crash.

The tamer unlocked the cage door, lifted the catch, and Colin attacked.

Quick. Powerful. Furious.

It wasn't hard to analyze. The tiger was his emotion, and the tamer was everything and everybody that caused him woe. The emptiness his dead mother had left behind. His father's weakness. The threat of boarding school. Miss Bush shouting at him. Annoying bullies like Jimmy Gibbins. A staggering amalgamation of pain and sadness. But mostly, of course, he was Janice, with her hate and resentment. Janice, who shouted at him until her head was close to splitting open. . . and who hit him, made him bleed.

No wonder he attacked so viciously.

He lunged at the cage door and it burst open, pushing the tamer backwards. He staggered, hit the wall of the enclosure, and slumped to his knees. Colin was on him in a second, claws slashing, teeth tearing — and it didn't matter that one large tooth was missing. It didn't matter at all. He *ripped* and *swallowed* and the tamer managed half a scream then fell still. His days of taming were over. His cruel eyes stared nowhere.

Warm blood soaked Colin's mouth and ruff. A strip of meat dangled from between two molars.

The door to the enclosure creaked ajar. On the other side, the clear and open night.

Home, Colin thought, thinking not about the mysterious depths of the Malaysian jungle, but his three-bedroom house on Nutmeg Close. Once there, he would wake up. It was the way dreams worked, no matter how vivid. His headache would be gone and—hopefully—he'd feel a little better.

He tracked fat red paw prints across the floor, squeezed through the enclosure door, and stepped out into the night.

⇠❦⇢

Escaping the circus grounds was the hardest part. There were so many people around, working beneath blazing floodlights, dismantling tents and stalls, loading trucks. The advantage of the lights was that they created deep shadows, which Colin clung to, always vigilant. He passed the carousel, in pieces now, and the tent that had once been an Arabian Wonderland, but was now a canvas puddle on the ground. He saw one of the barkers, dressed not in his garish barker attire, but in dirty brown trousers and a flat cap, smoking a roll-up as thin as a toothpick. He saw the strongman, too, who looked decidedly ordinary without his leopard-print leotard and 180kg barbell. Colin started to wonder just how much "Fantastica" this circus really had, and then he spotted Crab-Girl. She spotted him, too. Her mouth fell open and she scampered away on all four legs, mostly sideways.

From the circus grounds into the thick foliage bordering the site, and from there into the open fields. He followed the sound of the traffic and came to the edge of the motorway. One of the big blue signs told him that he was forty-three miles east of his hometown.

He ran with wild speed, stopping only to drink from a river, or to wait until a road was clear of traffic before crossing. He slipped between shadows in urban areas, and ran for all his heart through forests and fields, scattering sheep and cows, causing birds to burst, startled, from the trees. Eventually he came to his hometown, and by the time he made it through the streets and into his back garden, the sky in the east had started to redden. He settled into the high grass behind his father's shed and closed his eyes.

Hard and fast breaths, growing slower, deeper, as he drifted into sleep.

He woke up when he heard Janice shouting.

๛

Colin blinked sleepy eyes, dragging himself from his deep and vivid dream. His head didn't ache anymore, but felt as if it were packed with lead. He hoisted it from the pillow with a groan and sat up, acclimating to the new day by tiny degrees, aware of Janice bellowing (such a wonderful morning sound) from the bottom of the stairs.

"... *get down here right now or* ..."

His right hand was curled into a tight fist. He opened it gingerly, wincing as his stiff fingers creaked and popped, and saw the tiger's tooth in his palm. He had clutched it all night, and so vehemently that the point had punctured his skin. Not deep, but enough to smear a crescent of blood between his index and middle fingers.

"... *late again your feet won't touch* ..."

The sight of the tooth, and the blood, broke his dream. He saw it all—*felt* it all—again, a rush of recollection that left him dizzy. He reeled to his bedroom window and pulled open the curtains, wiped the condensation from the glass and looked down at his back garden.

Are you out there? he thought.

He couldn't see behind his father's shed, but there was no mistaking the tracks in the dewy grass, too large and too far apart to have been made by a dog or a cat.

Well ... perhaps a *big* cat.

Colin's heart thudded high and hard in his chest. He clutched the tooth and looked towards his bedroom door. Janice was coming. He could hear her thudding up the stairs, still shouting.

"... *if you're still in bed, so help me God* ..."

He recalled going to Circus Fantastica with his father, just the two of them, how much fun it had been for them both, and how he had wanted it to last forever.

70

Just the two of them.

Janice threw open the bedroom door and snarled, but Colin heard something in the garden snarl even louder.

He looked into her mean, flinty eyes.

So help you God, he thought, and smiled.

Blind Voices

TOM REAMY

Sonny Redwine parked his father's Packard on the courthouse square across from the Majestic. He hastened around to open the door for Evelyn. Comfort had won out over fashion and he was in his shirtsleeves. Evelyn took his arm and they started across the street.

Suddenly Mr. Mier ran from the theater, a handkerchief pressed to his nose. Mrs. Mier followed him rapidly, still holding a box of salt. Evan Whittaker was right behind her. Caroline Robinson looked at them in astonishment from the cashier's booth. Then her nose wrinkled and she scrambled out, leaving the roll of tickets to unwind slowly onto the floor.

The crowd muttered and backed away and then scattered. Francine Latham and Billy Sullivan were among them, but they stopped when they reached Sonny and Evelyn standing dumbfounded in the middle of the street

"Did you hear?" Francine shrieked. "A skunk got in. Now I won't get to see Ronald Colman."

"They'll open up again—as soon as they get the smell out," Billy assured her, but a smile lurked around his mouth. Billy was nineteen, a year older than Francine, but he looked a year younger. He was slight and barely taller than she was. He worked at his father's ice house and hated it. He'd had no desire to go to college, so he was probably stuck there.

"But that could be *weeks!*" Francine complained.

"At least you don't have to make a decision anymore." Evelyn smiled. "Looks like it's gonna be Haverstock's old Traveling Wonder Show after all."

"That's where I wanted to go in the first place," Billy confided.

Francine drew herself up and fixed him with a steely stare. "If a lady has to buy the tickets, then the lady can choose what the tickets are *to*."

Evelyn and Sonny laughed and Billy shrugged helplessly.

"There's Rose and Harold," Francine cried, her pique disappearing. "Come on, Billy." She grabbed his arm and dragged him away. Sonny and Evelyn followed more slowly.

"Is it okay with you if we go to the tent show?" Sonny asked. "We don't have to go with them if you don't want to."

"Well," Evelyn laughed, "to tell you the truth, I'd much rather see the Minotaur than Ronald Colman. I was planning to go tomorrow night."

The warm stillness of the evening was suddenly shattered by the calliope. The metallic tones floated on the air, drawing people from their houses, pulling them in excited clumps down the street. Finney and Jack charged by, running as hard as they could toward the sound. Suppers were hurriedly finished, dishes were left unwashed, eggs were left ungathered. The sound was electricity, stirring the blood, flushing the face, a youth magic that sweetened the sour and smoothed the wrinkled and softened the crusty.

They gathered and stared curiously at the painted, lined-up wagons. In the center, with three wagons on either side, was a ticket stand with the playerless calliope beside it. A large canvas tent rose behind the wagons. Electric lights were strung over them, illuminating the paintings on their sides. A banner stretched across the entrance between two tall poles. HAVERSTOCK'S TRAVELING CUR-IOSUS AND WONDER SHOW it read in gold on black. Torches lined the street, adding more light and festivity. Insects flocked like a snowstorm. Moths and crickets, katydids and dragonflies, big brown beetles that buzzed like airplanes and got in the hair, shiny black beetles that scurried across the ground behind huge pincers, and three dozen kinds of bugs that could only be classified as unclassifiable.

The crowd converged and laughed and pointed and bought tickets and gossiped, what little they could over the noise of the calliope, and swatted bugs. The tickets were dispensed from a lofty perch by a plump lady rapidly approaching middle age. Her face was elaborately over made-up, causing her to look like an aging saloon girl. Her orange hair was haphazardly coiffed, erratically waved, amazingly curled, sloppily piled, and appeared on the verge of toppling around her.

She wore a low-cut satin ball gown of poisonous green. It had perspiration stains at the armpits and grime around the neckline. She received money and presented tickets with grandiloquent gestures, smiling and simpering and winking at the men. Every few moments she reached behind her neck and futilely patted stray strands of hair back into place.

Harold looked at the others and rolled his eyes. Francine poked Billy and slipped him her dollar. He quickly tucked it in his pocket.

"Remember to stay away from the Minotaur, Francine." Rose grinned.

Francine giggled. "Oh, Rose! Don't make me blush."

"What are you talking about?" Harold asked.

"Oh, nothing," Rose said airily.

They bought their tickets and moved with the crowd toward the entrance of the tent. "Boy," Harold groaned, "this better be worth fifty cents."

They gave their tickets to a young roustabout whose muscles rippled under his rolled-up sleeves as he tore tickets. Rose ogled him appreciatively and raised her eyebrows at Francine. Francine lowered her eyes. The man's eyes met Rose's and a faint smile flickered on his lips. She gave him an affronted glare and ducked under the tent flaps.

The interior was filled with rows of backless wooden benches, unpainted but polished by many backsides. Scattered on the benches were numerous cardboard fans imprinted with the Redwine Funeral

Home advertisement. Many of them were already in use. Sonny picked one up, fanned himself, grinned, and tossed it back on the bench.

An aisle down the center of the tent divided the benches into two sections. A wire ran the length of the tent above the aisle with a curtain bunched at the back, as if the audience were to be divided into two parts. Half a dozen naked electric light bulbs were strung in the upper reaches in a haphazard pattern. At the front, opposite the entrance, was a small stage raised about two feet above the trampled grass floor. A curtain ran across the back of the stage, fastened with metal rings to another wire. Otherwise, the interior of the tent was featureless.

They looked around doubtfully. The benches were only about half full. They finally found room enough to sit together near the front. Finney and Jack were on the front row, talking excitedly. Evelyn and the others looked a little depressed.

"This is a wonder show?" Harold asked the air and swatted a bug from his ear.

Most of the people still outside were standing around trying to make up their minds whether to go in or not. Louis Ortiz stepped onto a platform behind the calliope. He smiled and postured, letting the women get a good look at his white teeth and well-proportioned body. Then he held up his arms. The calliope fell silent. Louis waved his arms grandly and the murmur of the milling crowd died away.

"Ladies and gentlemen!" he said, relishing the rich sound of his own voice. He stood for a moment in a dramatic pose, his arms up and his legs apart. "The Wonder Show begins in five minutes. Get your tickets for the most wondrous sights your eyes have ever seen, more wondrous than your mind has ever imagined.

"Tiny Tim, a full-grown man, but only twelve inches tall.

"The Little Mermaid. She sits in her tank of water and dreams green dreams of the sea.

"The Minotaur, a man from the neck down, but a raging bull from the neck up.

"The Medusa. To look on her face means death. One glance and you turn to stone. But don't worry; you will see her only in a mirror, which makes it perfectly safe—just as the Greek hero Perseus saw her reflected in his shield and survived.

"The Invisible Woman. You won't believe your eyes. You won't believe what your eyes *don't* see.

"Electro, the Lightning Man. To him a million volts is nothing more than a firefly.

"Henry-etta. Half man, half woman. One of nature's most shocking mistakes. All of his . . . I mean, her . . . well, you know what I mean." Louis grinned erotically. "All the secrets will be revealed—if you're man enough to take it. And we promise not to embarrass the lovely ladies.

"The Snake Goddess. Is she woman or is she serpent? She's both, my friends, she's both. This ancient creature may be a million years old, a remnant of a forgotten race. Who knows?

"And the most astounding of all: Angel, the Magic Boy. If you've seen magicians before, forget them. Angel is not a magician. He pulls no rabbits out of hats. He does not make pink handkerchiefs out of blue ones. What Angel can do defies description. You have to see it for yourselves. It will shock and amaze you. It may even frighten you. They're all inside, ladies and gentlemen. They're all alive and they're all real."

He glanced over his shoulder at the roustabout collecting tickets. The man gave Louis a signal. "There are only thirty-seven seats left," he continued. "So hurry. If you don't get in to see this show, there'll be another in one hour. If you're skeptical, just ask your friends as they leave the first show." He smiled and bowed eloquently. "Thank you for your attention."

He hopped down from the platform and entered the tent. The calliope began to play once again. The citizens of Hawley rapidly bought tickets and the allotted thirty-seven were sold in a matter of seconds. At the sale of the thirty-seventh ticket, the woman with the orange hair plopped a sign over the front of the stand: "Next Show in

One Hour." She picked up the cash box, the roll of tickets, and left without a word or a backward glance, disappearing around the side of the tent. Those who hadn't made it to her in time murmured in disappointment.

The benches were filled. The people talked among themselves, but there was an air of tense anticipation. Louis walked up the aisle, letting his hips roll just the right amount, and stepped onto the stage. The lights dimmed slowly, leaving him in an illuminated island. Outside, the calliope stopped playing with a discordant wheeze. Louis held up his arms for silence and received it immediately.

"Good evening, ladies and gentlemen," he began with a white smile. "Welcome to Haverstock's Traveling Curiosus and Wonder Show, where you will see wonders you've hardly imagined. But I'm not going to tell you about them, I'm going to *show* them to you!"

He swept his arm to the curtains behind him. They parted, the metal rings rattling on the wire. A large doll house sat on a table. Two men rolled the table forward to the edge of the stage. The audience waited, hardly breathing.

Finney turned and whispered to Jack. "It's got to be Tiny Tim."

"I'm waiting for the Snake Goddess," Jack answered and squirmed nervously.

"Ladies and gentlemen," Louis bellowed, "Tiny Tim, the smallest man in the world!"

For a moment nothing happened, then the door of the doll house opened and Tiny Tim stepped out. A gasp fluttered through the audience. He was twelve inches tall, as promised, but the tiny figure was strangely misshapen. He was a hunchback and had a crooked leg. His face was like wax on the verge of melting. The crowd strained forward. They had known he was supposed to be twelve inches tall, but they hadn't really realized just how small that actually was. Some in the back stood up for a better look.

Finney grabbed Jack's arm and they stared, their eyes wide and their mouths open. The crowd began to murmur.

"How do they do it?" Rose hissed in amazement

"Probably with mirrors . . . or something," Harold answered and wished he could take off his sweater.

"Please keep your seats, ladies and gentlemen," Louis admonished. "You'll all have an opportunity to see Tim up close." He turned to the tiny man. "Tim, would you like to sing and dance for the nice people? They've come to see you and it would be unkind to disappoint them."

Tim looked up at Louis. "Yes," he said in a small whispery voice that could hardly be heard.

There was another gasp from the audience. Finney and Jack clutched at each other in excitement that could hardly be restrained.

"Sumbitch," Finney squeaked.

Rose stared and put her hand on Harold's arm. "Is the guy a ventriloquist too?"

Louis held up his hand for quiet. "Okay, Tim. These nice people are waiting."

The air in the tent rang with silence. Tim began to sing. His voice was tiny, but it was clear and melodious, and the song he sang was slow and sad. Then he danced, slowly, awkwardly, and grotesquely, his misshapen body unable to coordinate properly.

Evelyn frowned and looked away.

After a moment Louis leaned over and put his hand palm-up on the table. Tim stopped dancing and, still singing, stepped into Louis's hand. Louis lifted him up.

The houselights brightened. Louis stepped off the stage and walked slowly down the aisle to the rear of the tent. He turned and paused, holding the tiny singing man before him. Every head was twisted around and every eye was on his hand. Even though Tim's voice was very small, the inside of the tent was so hushed he could be heard clearly by everyone. Louis returned slowly to the stage.

He mounted the stage and put his hand on the table. Tim got off as the song ended and bowed to the silent faces. The silence continued for a moment and then was abruptly broken by frantic clapping from Finney and Jack. The others slowly picked it up. They laughed nervously. Then they cheered and laughed and slapped their hands together.

Tim bowed again, then turned and entered the doll house. The roustabouts came out and pushed the table to the rear of the stage, the curtains closing behind them. Louis held up his arms and grinned as the houselights dimmed. He waited a moment for the noise to die down.

Thank you, ladies and gentlemen. Tim appreciates your warm reception, but there are many more wonders to see." Shuffling and scraping sounds came from behind the curtain.

"Ladies and gentlemen," Louis continued, "there are many instruments of death used in the world to execute criminals and murderers. In France they use the guillotine. In the heathen countries of the East they use methods too terrible to describe before a good American, Christian audience. In this country several means are employed. In some states, murderers are hung, in others they are shot. The gas chamber is used and . . . " the curtains rattled open " . . . the electric chair, from which there is no escape!"

"Not too many recover from the guillotine either," Rose murmured.

Louis walked slowly behind the heavy wooden chair spotlighted on the stage. He put his hands on the back of it and paused dramatically. The audience leaned forward.

"There is no escape . . . except for one man!"

Louis turned and swung his arm toward the wings. A man stepped out. He was barefoot and shirtless, but a black hood was pulled over his head. He stood with his legs apart and his chest out. He turned his shrouded face toward the rows of people.

"Electro, the Lightning Man!" Louis's voice rang powerfully through the tent. Electro walked slowly to the chair. He was followed by the two men who had pushed forward the doll house. He sat stiffly, in an attitude of fearlessness, a sheen of perspiration on his chest. The roustabousts buckled heavy straps around his arms, legs, and chest and left the stage. Louis walked forward again. "Ladies and gentlemen, if Electro is ever executed in a state that uses the electric chair, there will be quite a few very surprised people."

He grinned and there was a slight laugh from the audience. "This electric chair, ladies and gentlemen, is one that was actually used to execute hundreds of criminals in one of this great country's state prisons. The electric current that will go through Electro's body when I pull this switch . . . " he placed his hand on a large knife switch mounted on a pole attached to the side of the chair ". . . will be exactly the same as used in that state prison."

The audience shifted expectantly.

"Are you ready, Electro?"

The black-covered head nodded. Louis closed his fingers slowly around the switch handle, paused to milk the last drop of suspense, and threw the switch. The chair hummed and crackled. Electro's body twitched and jerked. Louis turned off the switch and the man in the chair slumped back.

"Are you all right, Electro?"

The head under the hood nodded again. There was an almost inaudible release of breath from the audience.

"Are you ready, Electro?"

The hood dipped slightly and Louis pulled the switch again. The electric hum and crackle resumed. Electro trembled. Louis reached behind the chair and brought out an iron bar with a rubber handle. He held the bar over his head so the audience could see.

"As you can observe, this has a rubber handle because, unlike Electro, I am not immune to electricity."

Holding the bar by the rubber end, he reached out and touched the arm of the chair. A shower of sparks flew from the contact, filling the air with the smell of ozone. The audience inhaled loudly. He touched the chair again and again in many different places, each time producing a cascade of sparks.

Jack leaned over and whispered to Finney. "I think this is a trick."

Finney nodded. "Yes, but it's a very good trick."

Louis put the iron bar away and turned off the switch. Electro slumped in the chair again, his chest rising and falling rapidly. A drop of perspiration rolled over his stomach.

"Are you all right, Electro?"

The hooded head dipped forward. Louis turned to the audience with an expansive smile and spread his arms for applause. The two roustabouts came from the wings and unstrapped the man in the electric chair. Electro stood up, bowed to the applause, and walked from the stage as the chair was pushed behind the curtain.

"I hope the rest of it isn't as phony as that," Harold groaned.

"Tiny Tim wasn't a phony," Evelyn pointed out, arching her eyebrows.

Harold grunted. "Electro the Lightning Man certainly was."

There was once again shuffling and scraping behind the curtain. Louis walked to the edge of the stage and assumed a serious pose. The applause quickly subsided into silence.

"Many years before the fall of Troy," Louis intoned solemnly, "there were three wicked sisters called the Gorgons. They had snakes instead of hair on their heads, and anyone who gazed upon them was turned instantly into stone."

Behind him the curtain was slowly opening. Two panels about the size of doors, ornately decorated with fading paint and flaking gilt, stood side by side with one panel set slightly behind the other.

"Greek mythology tells us that one of these sisters, the one named Medusa, was killed by Perseus with the aid of magic sandals that let him fly and a magic cap that made him invisible. Perhaps this tale is true and perhaps it isn't. Maybe the Gorgon you are about to see isn't Medusa, but one of her sisters. I do not know, because she will not speak."

Louis stepped toward the panels. Jack grabbed Finney's arm. "Did you hear, Finney? He said it might not be Medusa."

"That's okay. It's okay if it's one of her sisters instead."

Louis put his hand on the farther panel and turned it slowly. There was a brilliant flash as the lights caught in the mirror on the reverse side. When the panel stopped moving, they could see, reflected in the mirror, the woman standing behind the forward panel. The audience hummed appreciatively.

The woman's reflection glared at them. She wore a dark robe that fell straight from her shoulders to the floor. Her arms were rigid at her sides. On her head, instead of hair, was a writhing mass of foot-long green snakes. They coiled and looped in agitation, as if trying to escape the bondage of the woman's skull.

Finney and Jack stared, transfixed.

Francine cringed. "Yaaah! Those snakes look *real!*" She shivered and put her knuckles against her mouth.

"That woman must be nuts, lettin' 'em put real snakes on her head," Rose said.

Louis looked speculatively at the audience, then turned the panel back to its original position. He walked to the front of the stage as the curtain closed. The applause was polite.

Harold looked at his sister. "Well? Medusa was just as phony as Electro, but I'll admit that was a pretty good touch, using real snakes instead of rubber ones."

Francine shivered again and made a little noise through her nose.

Louis held up his hands. "We stay with Greek mythology for the next part of the Wonder Show."

Rose reached over and poked Francine. "Here he comes, Francine. Watch out."

Francine put her hands over her face to hide her blushes. "Oh, Rose, you're so *wicked!*"

"The Greek god Poseidon," Louis said scholarly, "gave a wonderfully beautiful bull to Minos, the king of Crete, for Minos to sacrifice to him, but Minos could not bear to slay the beautiful animal and, instead, kept it for himself. To punish him for his betrayal, Poseidon caused Minos' wife, Pasiphaë, to fall madly in love with the bull. Do not be shocked, ladies." Louis smiled comfortingly. "This happened many thousands of years before Christianity. The son of Pasiphaë and the bull was a monster, half bull, half human—the Minotaur!"

The curtains swept open with a rattle. There were shocked, disapproving gasps from some in the audience, a rumble of excited comments from others, and titters of embarrassment from some of the girls at the sheer masculinity standing before them.

The Minotaur's resemblance to the painting on the caravan was only superficial. He was a tall, powerfully muscled man, wearing only a loincloth. He did not have the head of a bull, but had long, bushy hair and horns sprouting from either side of his head. His face was slightly elongated, with only a suggestion of bovine features.

He stepped forward. His muscles rippled like bronze satin. His cloven hoofs clumped loudly on the wooden stage. From the knees down, his legs were shaggy with brown hair, exactly like a bull's.

Rose looked at Francine and grinned. Francine was consumed by genuine blushes.

Finney and Jack stared. 'It's him," Finney breathed. "It's really and truly him."

"Sumbitch," Jack muttered.

"King Minos had a miraculous labyrinth built underneath his palace and there placed the Minotaur to live forever. Every year seven youths and seven maidens were sent into the labyrinth. What happened to them, we don't know, because none ever returned. Mythology tells us the Greek hero Theseus slew the Minotaur in the labyrinth, but there was only the word of Theseus—there were no witnesses.

"As you can see, standing before you, Theseus was prone to exaggeration." He smiled at his little joke. "You all know of the fabulous strength of the Minotaur."

A roustabout brought two straight-backed wooden chairs onto the stage. He placed one on either side of the Minotaur, who ignored him, standing placidly, seeming to ignore the whole affair.

"Haverstock's Traveling Curiosus and Wonder Show will now demonstrate that strength for you. I need two volunteers from the audience . . . "

Finney and Jack immediately sprang up.

"Thank you, boys." Louis grinned. "But I need someone with a little more meat on their bones."

Finney and Jack sat back down, limp with disappointment.

Louis looked over the audience. They shifted this way and that, waiting for someone to volunteer. Louis suddenly pointed at a man about halfway back. "You, sir. What is your name?"

The man looked around him with embarrassment. "Uh . . . Jakey Dunlap," he said and grinned.

"What is your occupation, Mr. Dunlap?" Louis asked.

"Oh, I work at the feed store," Jakey said, warming up to being the center of attention.

"And how much do you weigh, Mr. Dunlap?"

"Oh, about two hundred and forty pounds, give or take."

"Thank you, sir. Is there anyone in the audience who weighs more?"

"Here!" a voice brayed near the rear of the tent

"Oh, no," Sonny moaned dramatically and hunched over with his hands on the back of his head.

"The name's Baby Sis Redwine and I weigh two hundred and forty-one pounds," the voice bellowed. Everyone twisted around to look. There was laughter and a scattering of applause.

Louis was momentarily rattled. He had never had a woman volunteer before and he was taken by surprise, but it took only a few seconds for him to regain his rhythm. "This demonstration might be a bit too . . . strenuous for a lady, ma'am," he said smoothly and flashed his teeth.

"Oh, hell!" Sis Redwine said. "I can out drink, out shoot, and out cuss any man in this place. And I ain't scared of no hairy man wearin' drawers!" The crowd guffawed with delight. Sis was a popular character in Hawley, and Sonny's first cousin. Some said she wasn't quite right in the head, but she owned the blacksmith shop and the Sinclair station and didn't hurt for money. She was thirty-four years old and unmarried, and the pet of the Redwine family, though smiles were sometimes strained when her escapades got too rambunctious.

Louis bowed and smiled. "I bow to your wishes, ma'am. Will you and the gentleman come up on the stage? You will be perfectly safe. There is no danger."

Jakey and Sis left their seats and grinned at the crowd. Sis was shorter than Jakey and almost as wide as she was tall. Her turgid body rolled with soft fat. Jakey had considerable fat on him, but it was hard and underlain with solid muscle. Even so, the Minotaur towered over him, and his chiseled muscular definition and slimmer body made Jakey look bloated.

"Give 'em what for, Sis!" someone yelled.

Sis and Jakey raised their eyes to the Minotaur critically and unconsciously edged away. The Minotaur looked at them with his big, soft bovine eyes without interest.

"Will you please be seated in the two chairs?" Louis asked politely.

Jakey and Sis looked at each other and grinned, then Sis made a belligerent face at the Minotaur and turned to the audience for approval. The audience responded with the expected laughter. They sat tentatively in the chairs. The Minotaur squatted between them, reached out his massive arms full-length and grasped one leg of each chair. After some shifting and getting into position, he stood slowly, the muscles in his arms and shoulders bulging. He held the two chairs at arm's length.

Surprised, Jakey and Sis gasped and grabbed at the chairs for support, then laughed at their own nervousness. The audience laughed with them and applauded mightily. The Minotaur squatted again and lowered the chairs lightly to the stage, then stood up. Perspiration sparkled on his chest and shoulders.

Jakey and Sis grinned in embarrassment and hurried back to their seats. Smiling broadly, Louis held up his hands. 'Thank you, Mr. Dunlap and Miss Redwine. If any of you think what you have just seen is a trick, I invite you to try it when you get home tonight — with empty chairs. Is there anyone in the audience who would like a closer look at the Minotaur?"

Finney sprang to his feet like a jack-in-the-box. The Minotaur moved to the front of the stage as the houselights went up. He turned toward Finney, then stepped off the stage and went to him. He bent over so his head was level with Finney's and looked at him from brown, liquid, kindly eyes. Finney tentatively reached out his hand and touched one of the horns lightly. He ran his finger to the point, then to the base surrounded by hair. He pulled his hand back quickly and grinned at the wonder of it all. The Minotaur smiled and softly stroked Finney's hair with his large hard hand. Finney's arm prickled with goosebumps. The Minotaur straightened and moved to the front of the aisle. Finney sat down slowly. Jack grabbed his arm.

"Is there anyone else?" Louis asked.

The Minotaur walked carefully down the aisle, looking around him, smiling slightly. The silent audience watched him nervously.

Harold stood up when the Minotaur reached the bench on which he sat. "Yes, I would," he said.

"Harold," Rose hissed.

The Minotaur stopped walking and stepped toward him, leaning over slightly. Harold sat fourth from the aisle. He reached over Rose, Billy, and Francine and grasped one of the horns. He tugged at it with moderate force, then felt around the base, pushing the hair aside to examine the juncture. The Minotaur, apparently accustomed to such liberties, made no objection.

The Minotaur's leg touched Francine's knee. She jerked it away with a little gasp. The contact was like an electric shock, adding fuel to the heat already enclosing her body. The Minotaur shifted his gaze from Harold to her, looking into her eyes. He smiled. Francine quickly looked away, fleeing his eyes, pulling her head down.

Then she was looking at the protruding fabric of the Minotaur's loincloth, only a foot from her face. She could smell the odors of his body and see the fine hairs glistening on his stomach. Her throat constricted and her face began to tingle. She forced her eyes shut, but her eyelids seemed made of glass. Tears squeezed from her compressed eyes and rolled down her cheeks.

The Minotaur watched her, still smiling.

Harold finished his examination. "Uh . . . thank you," he said timorously and sat down. The Minotaur took a step backward and continued toward the rear of the tent.

Billy leaned across Rose. "Well?" he asked excitedly.

Harold shrugged. "It's a great makeup job. I couldn't tell how they were fastened. They didn't budge a bit when I pulled on 'em. If I didn't know better, I'd think they were real." He looked thoughtful for a moment "I wish I could examine the hoofs."

Billy turned back to Francine and saw her closed eyes and pinched face. "What's the matter with you?" he asked, half-concerned and half-amused.

The others turned to look at her. None of them had noticed her reaction; they had been watching Harold and the Minotaur. Francine quickly wiped the wetness from her face with her fingers and sniffled. "Nothing," she said quietly. "Nothing's the matter."

Billy gave her his handkerchief and she daubed at her eyes with it.

"Are you sick?" Harold asked. "Do you want to leave?"

"No," Francine said tensely, twitching her head. "I'm not sick. I don't want to leave. I said nothing's the matter." She gave Billy his handkerchief and wouldn't look at them. Rose watched her with a little ghost of a smile and a twinkle in her eye.

The houselights went off and applause rose around them, drawing their attention to the stage where the Minotaur bowed as the curtains slithered together and blocked him from view. There were more grating sounds as something heavy was moved behind the curtain.

Louis stepped forward. "Thank you, ladies and gentlemen." He paused until there was complete silence.

There are many strange stories of the sea and the marvelous creatures who dwell there. One of the most awesome of these sea-creatures is the mermaid—half woman and half fish. Are they one of nature's mistakes? One of nature's experiments that didn't work? Or are they one of nature's secrets? Ladies and gentlemen, decide for yourselves."

He gestured grandly and the curtain opened on a large water-filled glass tank. A slight rustle swept the tent as the audience strained forward to get a better look.

The creature floated in the tank, her body rotating slowly with the movement of the water. She was a fish from the waist down, but barely human from the waist up. Her body was greenish-gray and leathery. Her small breasts were like deflated bladders. Her arms were small and her fingers stubby and webbed. Her head was bald and scaly; her mouth very small with horny lips; her eyes round and lidless like a fish. Her ears were tiny holes. She had the look of being half-finished.

Rose leaned across Harold, bracing herself with a hand on his thigh, and whispered to Evelyn. "What did I tell you? It's just an old dead fish."

Then the Little Mermaid moved. She swam around in a tight circle, gracefully undulating her tail fins. She stopped and put her hands against the glass, looking at the people with eyes like pearl buttons. The gasps and murmurs gradually turned to applause.

"The poor horrible thing," Evelyn said.

There she is, ladies and gentlemen: the Little Mermaid," Louis called. "What secrets does she hold? What does she think about? We'll never know because she does not speak."

The curtain closed and the applause died.

"How did they *do* that, Hal?" Rose asked.

Harold shrugged. "I'm not sure. It's probably somebody in a costume."

"Ladies and gentlemen, our next guest is already here. She's been standing right beside me for the last five minutes." He looked around furtively and then laughed. "At least, I *think* she's standing beside me. Are you there, invisible woman?"

"Yes, I'm here." The voice was musically feminine and seemed to originate in the air beside Louis. Laughter rippled from the audience.

"Don't you think it would be a good idea if you got dressed so the people can see where you are?" Louis asked, laughing with the audience.

"Oh, very well," the voice pouted. "But it's been such a dreadfully warm day and this tent is so stuffy. It's so cool and comfortable without clothes." There was more laughter from the audience.

89

"Please!" Louis gasped with mock indignation that managed to be half leer. "You'll shock these nice people. There are children in the audience."

"But I don't have a thing to wear," the voice complained.

"I'll fix that," Louis said with a flourish.

A roustabout came through the curtains, disinterest on his good-looking face and a red dress over his arm. He held gloves, a hat, and a pair of shoes in the other hand.

"Will these do?" Louis asked with a little bow to the empty air.

"Ooh, those are lovely," the disembodied voice cooed.

The dress suddenly lifted from the man's arm, contorted through the air, and slipped down as if someone had pulled it over her head. It settled and stood there as if it were on a well-proportioned female body. The audience cheered and laughed as the dress turned and bent, the skirt swirling.

"Will you hook me please?" the voice asked sweetly. There was thunderous applause. Finney and Jack could hardly contain themselves. Louis reached over, as the dress turned its back to him, and fastened the hooks and eyes.

"Thank you," the voice said pleasantly.

The gloves went into the air and onto invisible hands; the shoes were slipped onto invisible feet; the hat went atop an invisible head. The gloves lifted the hem of the skirt slightly and the invisible woman curtsied. She turned and sashayed toward the rear of the stage, swinging her hips. A glove parted the curtain and the dress twirled through the opening.

"Boy!" Harold shook his head as he applauded. "You gotta give 'em credit. They're really good. Of course," he said complacently, "it's either done with wires or mirrors."

"I'm proud of you, Harold," Evelyn said with feigned awe. "It's amazing what three years of college can do."

"What do you mean?" he asked, looking at her with lowered brows. "You don't believe all this stuff is *real*, do you?"

"It's as easy to believe in an invisible woman as it is to believe they could do all that with wires."

"Okay." He shrugged. "They do it with mirrors. I'll explain how when we get home."

"Thank you . . . Hal," she said, smiling sweetly. He looked at her with a suspicious frown.

Louis ended the applause. "Thank you, ladies and gentlemen. You've seen some wondrous sights tonight, but what you will see next is perhaps the strangest of all. Stranger than the Minotaur, stranger than Tiny Tim, stranger than the Little Mermaid, stranger even than Medusa."

Jack grabbed Finney's arm and stared at the closed curtain with round eyes. 'It's the Snake Goddess — it's finally the Snake Goddess."

"There have been many legends of a race of snake people who dwelt on Earth before the dawn of civilization. Legends of the lost continents of Mu and Lemuria where the snake people lived. How can we doubt these legends when we have the living proof before our very eyes?" He gestured dramatically and stepped to the side of the stage. "The Snake Goddess!"

The curtains rustled open, revealing a low platform on which rested the giant coils of a snake, coils as thick as the Minotaur's thigh. Propped in the nest of coils was the torso of a woman. Silver hair crested on her head like the feathers of a jungle bird. Her skin was white and mottled with patches of light brown. She had the startled face of an idiot.

Her small hands rested on the pile of coils. She looked nervously about, with quick, jerking movements of her head. A leather collar encircled her neck. A chain attached to the collar lay across the coils. A roustabout held the other end.

The audience drew in its collective breath and leaned forward tensely.

"Don't be alarmed, ladies and gentlemen," Louis said quickly, smiling and holding up his hands. "The Snake Goddess is not dangerous. She is at least a million years old and senile. The collar and chain are merely to keep her from wandering off and injuring herself."

Harold made a sour face of disbelief.

Finney looked at Jack anxiously. "How do you like her? Is she everything you wanted her to be?" he whispered.

"Sumbitch," Jack answered softly, not taking his shining eyes from the creature on the stage.

"Come along," Louis said to the snake woman. "Let the folks get a better look at you."

The roustabout gave the chain a casual jerk and stepped toward the front of the stage. The pale torso slowly rose up on its serpent body. The coils shifted, gleaming dully under the lights. The snake woman slid off the platform and undulated across the stage, her body uncoiling behind her. The audience stirred nervously, the muttering growing in volume.

The man led her off the stage as the houselights came up. The reptilian body flowed over the edge until it stretched twenty feet down the aisle. The people rose to their feet, trying to see but only managing to get in one another's way. Those on the aisle shrank back against those straining forward. The roustabout held the chain with a practiced hand, not letting her get too close to either side, but he could not control her slithering body. A woman screamed as the Goddess brushed against the bench on which she sat, then giggled in embarrassment.

The snake woman turned at the rear of the tent and drew her body around her, then flowed back toward the stage. She held her small arms out slightly as if keeping her balance. Her eyes darted from one side of the aisle to the other as she seemed to hurry back to her platform.

"Which is it, Harold? Wires or mirrors?" Evelyn asked with a wry smile. Harold gave her an annoyed glance and held Rose's hand as she huddled against him.

Francine watched the snake woman's scaly body glide by her feet with little reaction. She felt that she probably should be carrying on like the others, but it was just some sort of trick and she couldn't get excited over it. She felt numb and wished she were home.

Billy gave Francine an occasional worried glance but said nothing.

Louis had some trouble quieting the audience as the Snake Goddess gathered her coils around her on the platform. But they finally settled down as the houselights dimmed and the curtain closed.

"Thank you, ladies and gentlemen," Louis said over the fading murmurs. "Now, I would like to introduce the man who made the Wonder Show possible, the man who brought all these oddities of nature and legend together for your amusement and edification. Ladies and gentlemen, may I present: the Curator."

Haverstock stepped from between the curtains, wearing flowing black robes. He walked to the front of the stage, ignoring Louis, who ducked through the curtains. There was expectant applause.

"I was wondering when he was gonna show up," Harold said from the side of his mouth.

"Doesn't look very much like his picture, does he?" Sonny whispered.

"He looks too much like it to suit me," Rose said.

"I am not a magician," Haverstock began. "I do not do card tricks, saw ladies in half, or pull paper flowers from my sleeve."

He spoke in a perfunctory voice, using none of Louis's theatrics. He seemed confident his performance would stand on its own, without razzle-dazzle.

"Nor am I a mentalist," he continued. "I do not identify keys or pocket watches concealed by an assistant. I do not use sleight of hand nor legerdemain in any way. I am here to reveal to you the powers of the Ancients, the race that ruled the Earth before Man. The Ancients were the masters of the elements, but perished because they used their powers unwisely. In a cataclysm that sank whole continents beneath the seas, they perished, leaving no trace of their great works. I, and I alone, have rediscovered a small fragment of their incredible powers.

"Before we go further, I would like to introduce my assistant Angel the Magic Boy."

The interior of the tent went suddenly and totally dark. There was a nervous rustle in the audience as they heard the curtains parting.

A single light sprang into being over the stage near the top of the tent. A face floated there, pale and beautiful, topped by slightly unruly white hair. The light spread gradually until the entire figure was illuminated, floating six feet above the stage.

Angel wore a robe similar to Haverstock's, but white. He floated upright, his arms outstretched, his face calm and bland.

He began to move. He floated out over the wide-eyed faces, his robes billowing around him like a slow-motion wraith, like a ghost ship sailing on moonbeams. The light stayed with him as if he were radiating it himself. The startled faces looked up at him, illuminated by his warm glow.

He reached the rear of the tent and turned in a fantasy of swirling robes. He returned to the stage and turned again, facing the audience. Then he slowly lowered to the stage. The audience applauded madly. Angel's glow waned as the stage lights came up. He stood looking vaguely at the audience as Haverstock held up his hands for silence.

"The Ancients recognized only four elements: air, earth, fire, and water. They knew complete mastery of them all. Tonight I will demonstrate these powers for you." He lowered his eyebrows sternly. "I must caution you, however, to remain in your seats during this demonstration. What you see may frighten you, may even terrify you. There will be apparitions and manifestations in the air over your heads and in the ground under your feet, but there is no danger if you remain in your seats and do not panic!"

Finney and Jack trembled in anticipation and looked at each other in delicious fright.

Harold rolled his eyes. "Oh, brother," he groaned.

"Remember," Haverstock admonished, "no matter what you see, no matter what you hear, there is no danger if you remain seated. I cannot be responsible for your safety otherwise. Do not leave your seats!"

He pulled a wand from his robes as the audience sat, barely breathing. He held it above his head and the tent was again pitched into total darkness.

"Fire!" Haverstock bellowed.

The tip of the wand burst into flame, illuminating the stage and creating ruby reflections in the wide eyes of the spectators. Angel stood where he had, calmly, his arms at his sides, his eyes partially closed, his head moving faintly side to side. Haverstock reached downward with the wand and touched the flaming end to Angel's robes.

Angel burst into flame as though the robes had been soaked in gasoline. The audience screamed and jumped to its feet. Evelyn gasped and involuntarily clutched her throat. Haverstock held up a cautionary hand.

Angel was completely obliterated by the fire. No trace of him remained, only a raw flame that burned with no source. Then the flame shrank, pulled into itself, became not a fire but a ball of light, a chunk of the sun a yard across that rose from the stage and convoluted in the air. Haverstock stood beneath it, his arms outstretched, his head thrown back, staring intensely at it.

Suddenly feathery extensions of flame stretched from either side of the fireball. The flickering appendages coalesced, shaped themselves, became wings of fire. The fireball shifted, transmuted, shrank further, and took form.

The fiery swan flapped its wings of blazing feathers and took flight over the audience. It reached the rear of the tent, stretched its wings, banked, turned gracefully, and returned toward the stage. It repeated the maneuver, circling the tent, leaving behind it stray little flames that died in the air.

The audience followed it with reddened faces, swiveling heads and bodies. They crouched in their seats, hardly breathing.

"Water!" Haverstock shouted.

The air in the center of the tent darkened. Wisps of fog appeared from nowhere and rushed to the center of the darkness, swirling around it, and then were drawn into the cauldron of roiling air. The firebird continued to circle, now trailing feathers of steam as it flew through the damp air. The darkness grew light, became a whirlpool of mist. The walls of the tent billowed inward, though there was no wind. The mist thickened swiftly, rounding its shape.

Then a six-foot globe of clear water floated high in the tent. The surface rippled and trembled as if trying to disintegrate. The tent walls settled back and the swirling turbulence in the air died away.

The people watched in amazement, craning their necks, too far into shock to make a sound.

The swan of fire plunged suddenly into the sphere. Steam hissed and billowed, obscuring the globe of water for a moment. When the steam cleared, Angel was inside it, naked and unharmed. He lay curled in the center of the globe, seen as if through a fogged window, his pale, slim body gleaming although no lights were on. The air itself seemed illuminated.

Then his body uncurled and he swam in the globe of water, executing graceful turns and flourishes, slow, dreamlike movements which belied the limited space in which he floated.

Evelyn watched, lost in a reverie, overwhelmed by the beauty of what she saw. Only when she couldn't see any longer did she realize that her eyes had filled with tears.

"Earth!" Haverstock called, though it is doubtful if anyone heard him.

The hard-packed earth that was the floor of the tent trembled. The people looked away from the globe of water, looked at the ground, held their breaths, waiting for the next onslaught on their senses. The earth moved again and they screamed. They heard a grumbling, a grinding, a rending. They were frozen, afraid to move. Then there was a new sound, a sharp crack like gunfire and a fissure opened down the center of the aisle, exposing raw earth and stones. It started at the stage as a mere crack, then widened to about a foot and dwindled away to a crack again at the rear of the tent. Loose earth and small stones broke away from the sides and fell with small clattering sounds. The people drew back, away from the miniature chasm.

Then there was a sound above them, a huge sigh of suddenly rushing water. The globe collapsed like a punctured water-filled balloon, the water streaming into the fissure. For a moment, the audience was divided by a shimmering curtain. Then when the water had stopped falling, with a rumble and more trembling the ground closed, leaving no mark where the fissure had been.

An exhalation filled the tent and all eyes shifted upward. Angel floated where the water globe had been, his naked body still making its own light, still obscured by a haze.

"Air!" screamed Haverstock.

The haze around Angel grew heavier. His body became tenuous, out of focus, vaporous, vague, until finally it was indistinguishable. The haze darkened, became a mist that gradually spread until it filled the top of the tent. It grew darker still, thickening into a storm cloud. There was a faint rumble of thunder and heat lightning played over the surface of the darkness. The thunder grew louder and broke through the tent. The lightning grew in intensity until it singed the air.

All eyes were on the electrical display. No one saw a roustabout walk onto the stage, carrying a robe. He stood beside Haverstock and held it in readiness. Haverstock stared at the cloud intently, deep in concentration.

Suddenly a bolt of lightning lanced from the cloud. It crackled through the air and struck the stage with an ear-rattling crash. Heads twisted toward Haverstock.

Angel was standing on the stage, tying the sash of the robe around his waist. The roustabout walked away, unconcerned, and the storm cloud dissipated almost instantly.

Angel bowed to the silent audience. A whisper rustled over the benches. A babble shook the air. Laughter escaped from tense throats. The applause became deafening. Cheers and whistles added to the bedlam. Angel bowed again, his face composed and empty, then turned and went through the curtains. Haverstock bowed slightly and followed him.

Louis emerged and held up his hands for quiet. He was slow in getting it.

"The last item on the program is Henry-etta, half man, half woman," he said as if he had lost interest in the whole affair. "Because of the delicate biological nature of this performance, we must request that all children under the age of eighteen please leave the auditorium. Also, any ladies who might be offended are urged to leave also. Thank you." He departed through the curtains.

Finney and Jack looked at each other in horror, then reluctantly got up to leave. The children and a number of women, as well as a few men, rose and left, their eyes still a bit glassy.

Evelyn sat in deep contemplation. Francine was dazed. Rose still clutched at Harold's arm. The boys looked at each other and grinned at their own seriousness.

"Boy," Harold exhaled, "they really put on a show."

"How did they *do* that?" Billy Sullivan squeaked. "There was no way they could *do* that!"

"I don't know," Harold said, shifting on the bench. "It must have been mass hypnotism."

"I almost wet my drawers when he set Angel on fire." Rose shivered deliciously.

"Do we stay and see Henry-etta?" Sonny asked with a grin. "Or are you girls too refined for this delicate biological exhibition?"

"If it's as good as the rest," Rose said flatly, "I wouldn't miss it for the world."

"Evie?" Sonny asked.

"Huh?" She looked up, coming out of her reverie. "Oh. Yeah. We might as well."

Louis stepped from between the curtains and waited impatiently for the remaining audience to settle down.

"Because we have no desire to embarrass anyone," he said over the noise, "we must ask that all the ladies move to this side of the auditorium." He gestured to his right. "And all the gentlemen move to the other side. Thank you." He once more left the stage.

"Henry-etta must be a dilly," Rose grimaced as she stood up.

"Are you sure you girls want to stay for this?" Harold asked, wrinkling his forehead.

"Sure," Rose said. "Sounds like it might be the closest I'll ever get to a smoker at the Grange Hall."

"Okay." He grinned and waved his hand. "Good-bye, ladies."

The girls moved to the other side, as did the other women. The men already on that side shifted, creating a lot of confusion and conversation in the aisle. A few more people, unnerved by this latest request, left the tent.

A roustabout, the same one who had been collecting tickets, came from the stage and loosened the curtain bunched by the exit.

He pulled it, stretching it down the aisle, closing off each sex from the sight of the other. He caught Rose's eye as he passed and winked at her.

"Well, *really!*" she huffed and then grinned behind her hand. "Isn't he the cutest thing?" she whispered to Evelyn. "Have you noticed? This place is absolutely crawling with gorgeous men. The ticket-taker, that Latin hot tamale . . . "

"He's not quite as gorgeous as he thinks he is," Evelyn said wryly.

". . . Angel, all those stage hands." She leered at Francine. "The Minotaur. Hotcha!" But Francine didn't rise to the bait. Rose frowned at her and then smiled wistfully. "I wonder if I could get a job with this outfit."

"If you did, you wouldn't have any competition," Evelyn said. "There don't seem to be any women with the show."

"That woman selling tickets."

"Oh, yeah," Evelyn said frowning. "I forgot about her."

Louis stepped onto the stage so he could be seen by those on both sides of the curtain.

"Thank you, ladies and gentlemen. Now, I would like to introduce Henry-etta, as strange in his . . . I mean, her . . . " He grinned. "You know what I mean, *its* own way as anything you've seen tonight. Henry-etta!"

The curtain opened and the houselights went down. The fat lady in the poisonous green dress stepped coquettishly onto the stage.

Harold looked at Sonny and Billy and groaned.

Rose snickered. "Well, you were half right when you said there were no women with the show," she whispered to Evelyn.

"Thank you, Louis, you darling boy," Henry-etta said in a thin, reedy voice, pursing her lips and simpering. "Ladies and gentlemen, your master of ceremonies was Louis Ortiz. Isn't he the handsomest thing you ever saw, ladies?" Her mouth twisted into a provocative smile, but her eyes remained flat. "Give him a big hand for doing a wonderful job."

Henry-etta applauded and the audience half-heartedly joined in, feeling uncomfortable but not wanting to appear unsophisticated. Louis smiled and bowed and left the stage. Henry-etta watched him leave, then turned to the audience.

"Ladies and gentlemen, my real name is Claude Duvier. I was born in Tours, France, in 1887. My parents moved to America when I was four years old. We lived in New Orleans until I was fourteen, when my poor mama and papa died of fever. Desperate and alone, I was placed in an orphan asylum. It was there, shortly after—" she touched her breasts "—that the female half of my body began to emerge. Up until that time I had assumed I was a normal boy. I later discovered, thanks to some older boys, that I was female as well as male in every way.

"I have been married twice—once to a man and once to a woman. I am the mother of two children and the father of three. I am at present unmarried." She touched the hair at the back of her neck.

Harold rolled his eyes and Billy put his hand over his mouth to keep from laughing out loud.

"My body has confounded the greatest doctors and scientists in the world," Henry-etta continued. "Because of the delicate and shocking nature of the rest of my performance, I must request the ladies to leave."

The young man pushed the curtain back to the rear of the tent. As he passed, Rose held her head at what she imagined to be a sophisticated angle, not looking at him.

Evelyn laughed. "Rose, if the judge could see you..." The consequences were too dire to put into words.

The women began moving out, looking embarrassed. Several more of the men joined them.

"Thank you for attending Haverstock's Traveling Curiosus and Wonder Show," Henry-etta called over the departing conversation. "I hope you had an entertaining and enlightening evening. Thank you and good night. Don't forget to tell your friends that there will be two performances tomorrow night."

The girls stopped for a moment to talk to the boys.

"Rats!" Rose snarled.

"This is stupid." Harold stood up. "We'll leave with you."

"You'll do no such thing!" Rose put her hand against his chest. "You'll stay right here and tell me everything that happens. I want to know exactly why Henry-etta's body has confounded medical science the world over."

Harold laughed. "Hold it down. She'll hear you."

Rose *humphed*.

"We'll wait for you outside." Evelyn waved and smiled. They moved away, whispering and giggling.

Henry-etta waited patiently until everyone who wanted to leave had left. Only a very small group remained.

"Good," she said and smiled. "Now that the ladies have left, we can get down to business. My, what a handsome group you are. There will be an additional charge of ten cents for the remainder of my perform-ance," she stated flatly.

Is she kidding?" Harold spread his hands in disbelief.

"Come on, let's stay," Billy urged gleefully. "This ought to be good."

"You've got a dirty mind," Sonny said, grinning.

"Isn't it the truth?" Billy smirked.

A few more left as Henry-etta passed among them collecting their dimes.

"I thought you were broke," Sonny said.

"Well, I've got a dime." He shrugged. "Besides, Rose'll be mad if we don't stay so we can tell her all about it."

Henry-etta reached them and held out her hand. They placed their dimes in it and tried not to meet her eyes. She continued down the row of benches.

"Boy, is Henry-etta a phony," Harold whispered.

"Why?" Billy asked.

"I just looked down the front of *his* dress. All that frontage is pure cotton."

"Really?"

Henry-etta climbed back onto the stage with a grunt. "Would all you lovely gentlemen move up closer, please? I am about to show you exactly what it means to be half man and half woman."

Henry-etta bent over and pulled the long skirt up to her waist. She wore nothing underneath.

"Good Lord," Sonny croaked.

"I was bigger than that when I was five years old," Harold snick-ered.

"You can see my male sex for yourselves," Henry-etta continued, a little bored with it all. "The female part is more difficult to see — but it's easy to feel. Would any of you gentlemen like to come up and feel for yourselves?"

Henry-etta looked around questioningly, but she had no offers. Some of the men shifted nervously and others did their best not to laugh. Suddenly a man rose from the rear of the tent and walked to the stage.

"Who's that?" Sonny asked. "I never saw him around here before."

"Me neither," Billy agreed.

"Of course not," Harold said with a superior tone. "He's with the show. He's a shill."

"What's a shill?" Billy asked.

The man stepped up onto the stage. Henry-etta moved to him and he very matter-of-factly stuck his hand between her legs. "Ooooh," she moaned and squirmed. "Don't stick it in too far," she said wryly. "You might lose it. Are you satisfied? Is it the real thing?"

The man leered and nodded.

"Okay. That's enough. Don't get carried away."

The man dropped his hand, stepped off the stage, and walked back down the aisle. Harold turned and watched him leave the tent.

"As you can see, I am fully equipped as a man and as a woman. For an additional ten cents, you can watch me screw myself."

"Let's get out of here," Harold grunted. They left, as did all the others.

Henry-etta watched them leave, standing there with her skirt ridiculously around her waist before the rows of empty benches. She sighed and let her skirt drop. "We really had an adventurous crowd tonight," she said in a deeper voice. "Thank goodness." She sighed again and pulled off the orange wig, then turned and walked through the curtains at the rear of the stage.

Harold, Sonny, and Billy joined the girls outside the tent. There were more people gathered around the lined-up circus wagons than there had been earlier. Those who had seen the show were excitedly telling all about it to those who hadn't.

"What happened?" Rose asked excitedly.

"It was very tacky," Harold grimaced. "I'll tell you later."

Finney and Jack ran up to them, their bare feet pounding on the hard ground, their chests heaving in excitement.

"Did you see Henry-etta?" Finney gasped. "What did she do? Tell me. I want to know. I want to know everything."

"Oh, Finney, you can't know everything," Jack said. "There just isn't time."

"But you can try, Jack. You gotta at least try."

"Henry-etta's a phony and his act wouldn't interest you, believe me," Harold said seriously.

Finney looked at him a moment, then nodded, accepting his word. He and Jack ran to get in the rapidly growing line for tickets to the next show. The word had spread like a grass fire. Those who had missed the first show weren't about to miss the second. There was suddenly cheering and applause as Henry-etta came around the side of the tent, the cash box and roll of tickets under her arm.

Rose shook her head, staring at Finney. "I swear. That kid gets stranger by the minute."

Evelyn also looked at Finney, but she smiled and understood.

Mister Magister

THOMAS F. MONTELEONE

Mister Magister was not his real name.

He was tall and skeleton thin, enhanced by the dark clothing he wore. He fancied a sweeping black cape that hung upon him like a scarecrow's rag, fastened by a single silver clasp in the shape of a bird's taloned claw. His face was pale, gaunt, accented by sunken cheeks, a pointed nose, thin bloodless lips, and dark eyes that seemed to glow faintly like the coals of a dying fire. His hair was black and thick and greased against his skull, although it was mostly concealed by his broad-brimmed, drooped-down black hat.

Mister Magister had come from a faraway place to perform his appointed tasks. To accomplish this, he was forced to pretend to be something he was not: a traveling road-showman.

And so he was Mister Magister, the proprietor of a most unusual wagon, a portable carnival shooting gallery. It was a magnificent affair: gingerbread paneling, filigreed ironwork, polished brass, and shining paint with pinstripe. The folks of a small Midwestern town were righteously impressed when he appeared one early autumn evening, upon the heels of a dusty carnival of loud barkers and gypsy workers. They assumed he was but a straggler from the main troupe, and they patronized his wagon with no great suspicion.

There were others among us at that time, all of them conducting their own specialized tests upon our species, but we are concerned only with Mister Magister's test.

It went something like this:

At one end of the carnival wagon was a section of boards that hinged down to form a countertop where several BB guns were anchored with generous lengths of chain. Past the counter was an open space, an emptiness, that suggested a gulf far greater than the mere length of the wagon, beyond which there was a dimly lit stage where targets seemed to float effortlessly.

The targets were the important things.

On the first evening, when the townspeople lined up at the counter and squinted down the thin barrels of the rifles, the target they saw was the half-grinning face of one of the town's Negroes—a young man who ran deliveries for the grocer. Although the people thought this odd, it did not stop them from taking careful aim at the familiar black face.

But they were stunned the next morning when news spread through the streets that the young Negro had been found shot to death in the alley behind the grocery store. The sheriff was prevailed upon to investigate the death, but there was a strange feeling in the town. It was as though everyone understood what had happened, but chose not to talk about it.

The next evening, a different face appeared under the shrouded light of the gallery. Mister Magister quietly took their coins as they all took their turns squeezing off rounds at the melancholy face of the town shoemaker—an old Jewish man who spoke with a funny accent.

And it was really no surprise when they found the Jew slumped over his cobbler's bench shortly after sunrise. But still they pretended not to know. And still they would not talk. Much less would they look oddly toward the southern end of town where Mister Magister had set up his wrinkled canvas tent alongside his magnificent wagon.

The next evening brought a steady stream of people to his counter, where the shifting target now became the familiar features of a big immigrant auto mechanic—a well-intentioned Swede who spoke so little English so poorly that most people laughed at him. Coins were dropped. The guns were fired.

106

And in the morning the Swede was dead.

In the evenings that followed, the business was brisk at Mister Magister's wagon. The townspeople each secretly wondered who would be next at the wrong end of the gallery.

Most of their wonderings eventually came to pass: an Indian who pumped gas at the Texaco; another Negro, who was the janitor at the boiler factory; the addled, cross-eyed boy who did gardening in the summer and snow shoveling in winter to earn his meager keep at a boarding house in the north end; an Italian immigrant who washed dishes in the hotel cafe.

All targets; all now dead.

And the strangest part of this story was that the remaining towns-people went about their business as if nothing were amiss. Perhaps they knew—of course they knew!—that Mister Magister and his wagon were to blame, but no one said a word against him.

No one, until a young girl of thirteen named Stella. She was wiry-lean, with reddish-blonde hair that fell down her back in a thick braid. She had green-gray eyes, full pouting lips, a turned-up nose. She came to the wagon after dinner, watching the dark road-showman set up for the evening's entertainment.

"I know who you are," she said, looking into those cold dark eyes.

"You *do?*" he said in his low, solemn voice.

Stella nodded as she continued to stare at the tall thin man. "Yes. You're *Death*, aren't you?"

"Death?" Mister Magister smiled and shook his head.

"Yes, you know . . . the one that takes us. The Reaper."

"I know of whom you speak, little girl," said Mister Magister. "But I must confess that I am not . . . that person."

"Then who *are* you? Why're you killing us like this?"

"It is not I who is killing you. You are killing yourselves."

Stella stared at him for a moment. A wind touched her neck coolly and there was the sound of scuttling leaves. The sunlight was almost a memory now. "But we wouldn't be doing it . . . if you and your shoot-ing gallery wasn't here. Don't you see what I mean?"

"Oh, I see what you mean. But you are wrong, child . . . " Magister paused, turning over that last word—"child"—in his mind. She *was* a child, but she spoke with the directness, the power, and the maturity of someone far older, far stronger. "It seems to me," he continued once again, "that your people were killing them long before I came along. Only much more slowly."

Stella considered the dark one's words. She understood what he said. She was not so young that she had not already noticed the hate in the world, the mindless dislike for things that people did not understand, for things that were *different*.

But another question occurred to her. "There's something else, though . . . "

"And what is that?" he said, as he began carefully to lay out the shooting gallery rifles, make small adjustments to the wagon's trappings.

"How long are you going to let this go on?"

"It could go on for a very long time. I really don't know." Mister Magister shook his head slowly, then turned his back on the little girl. She knew that he was finished with her, and so she wandered off, seeking a deeper meaning to his words.

Later that evening, the customers came to play at Magister's game. The faces seemed to change in the swirling half-light of the gallery stage. But they did not seem to care.

The new deaths were no longer the feared, the foreign, and the hated. News spread each morning of violent passings: neighbors, cousins, councilmen, and brothers. The little girl, wise Stella, having spoken so openly to Mister Magister, stood apart from the rest of the town and its trancelike attraction to the strange and terrible gallery. She thought she knew now what was really happening, and she went again to see the master of the black wagon.

It was late and he was lowering the flaps, hinging the boards that would lock away the rifles and the counters for the night. "So," he said upon seeing her in the light of an almost full moon, "you have come back."

"You're not going to ever stop, are you?" she said, trying to hate this strange man, but failing.

Magister smiled. Yes, *this child knows*, he thought. "That's correct," he said. "It is not my decision to stop this thing. I am only a tool, a means to an end, not the agent."

"We *are* the agents," said Stella. "And we must stop it."

Mister Magister nodded slowly; the fire behind his dark eyes seemed momentarily to flare.

Stella tried to smile. There was something about this man that made her feel, almost *know*, that he was not of her familiar world. There was a coldness about him, a detached aspect, that, while it was not good, was not evil either.

"We would all keep coming," she said. "All of us who were left . . . until there was no one left at all."

Mister Magister could only nod his head, and she thought she caught a hint of sadness in this gesture.

"It's always been our way, I think," said Stella, the words now rushing out of her. "As long as it's somebody else, it doesn't seem to matter. But I want to stop it. I want to stop it right now!" The dark, thin man looked down at her and she shuddered. He threw hard the bolt that locked up the wagon and said, "You already have, little one. You already have. I will leave you now. My business here is done."

"You're leaving?" Stella was shocked indeed to hear such words.

"Yes, I have discovered what I came here to know."

"And what is that?" she asked.

"That there is hope for this race of beings, for this tiny world of selfish creatures." He paused and walked to the front of the wagon. "Know this, child, and never wonder why I came here: I have come for *you*."

As Stella heard these words, the moon slipped behind a passing cloud and darkness settled upon them. The wind grew suddenly chillier, and the thought of being swept away in the shadowy wagon passed icily through her.

But Mister Magister turned away from her and climbed upon the wagon. He rattled the black reins and slowly rolled away from that place. As the distance grew between himself and the town, Mister Magister found himself alone with waving fields of wheat. It shimmered like a ghostly sea in the moonlight. Looking up into the starry sky, Magister smiled. Somewhere, out among the stars, there would be another race of beings, another town, another role for him to play.

He wondered if the next world would be so lucky as to have a Stella in their midst. If they did not, he felt truly sorry for them.

Twittering from the Circus of the Dead

Joe Hill

WHAT IS TWITTER?

"Twitter is a service for friends, family, and co-workers to communicate and stay connected through the exchange of quick, frequent answers to one simple question: *What are you doing?*... Answers must be under 140 characters in length and can be sent via mobile texting, instant message, or the web."

— from twitter.com

TYME2WASTE

TYME2WASTE I'm only trying this because I'm so bored I wish I was dead. Hi Twitter. Want to know what I'm doing? Screaming inside.
8:17 PM February 28th from Tweetie

TYME2WASTE My didn't that sound melodramatic.
8:19 PM February 28th from Tweetie

TYME2WASTE Lets try this again. Hello Twitterverse. I am Blake and Blake is me. What am I doing? Counting seconds.
8:23 PM February 28th from Tweetie

TYME2WASTE Only about 50,000 more until we pack up and finish what is hopefully the last family trip of my life.
8:25 PM February 28th from Tweetie

TYME2WASTE It's been all downhill since we got to Colorado. And I don't mean on my snowboard.
8:27 PM February 28th from Tweetie

TYME2WASTE We were supposed to spend the break boarding and skiing but it's too cold and won't stop snowing so we had to go to plan B.
8:29 PM February 28th from Tweetie

TYME2WASTE Plan B is Mom and I face off in a contest to see who can make the other cry hot tears of rage and hate first.
8:33 PM February 28th from Tweetie

TYME2WASTE I'm winning. All I have to do to make Mom leave the room at this point is walk into it. Wait, I'm walking into room where she is now . . .
8:35 PM February 28th from Tweetie

TYME2WASTE She's such a mean bitch.
10:11 PM February 28th from Tweetie

TYME2WASTE @caseinSD, @bevsez, @harmlesspervo yay my real friends! I miss San Diego. Home soon.
10:41 PM February 28th from Tweetie

TYME2WASTE @caseinSD Hell no I'm not afraid Mom is going to read any of this. She's never going to know about it.
10:46 PM February 28th from Tweetie

TYME2WASTE After she made me take down my blog, it's not like I'm ever going to tell her.
10:48 PM February 28th from Tweetie

TYME2WASTE You know what bitchy thing she said to me a couple hours ago? She said the reason I don't like Colorado is because I can't blog about it.
10:53 PM February 28th from Tweetie

TYME2WASTE She's always saying the net is more real for me and my friends than the world. For us, nothing really happens till someone blogs about it.
10:55 PM February 28th from Tweetie

TYME2WASTE Or writes about it on their Facebook page. Or at least sends an instant message about it. She says the internet is 'life-validation.'
10:55 PM February 28th from Tweetie

TYME2WASTE Oh and we don't go online because it's fun. She has this attitude that people socially network 'cause they're scared to die. It's deep.
10:58 PM February 28th from Tweetie

TYME2WASTE She sez no one ever blogs their own death. No one instant messages about it. No one's Facebook status ever says 'dead.'
10:59 PM February 28th from Tweetie

TYME2WASTE So for online people, death doesn't happen. People go online to hide from death and wind up hiding from life. Words right from her lips.
11:01 PM February 28th from Tweetie

TYME2WASTE Shit like that, she ought to write fortune cookies for a living. You see why I want to strangle her. With an Ethernet cable.
11:02 PM February 28th from Tweetie

TYME2WASTE Little bro asked if I could blog about him having sex with a certain goth girl from school to make it real but no one laughed.
11:06 PM February 28th from Tweetie

TYME2WASTE I told Mom, no, the reason I hate Colo-rado is 'cause I'm stuck with her and it's all waaaaay too real.
11:09 PM February 28th from Tweetie

TYME2WASTE And she said that was progress and got this smug bitch look on her face and then Dad threw down his book & left the room.
11:11 PM February 28th from Tweetie

TYME2WASTE I feel worst for him. A few more months and I'm gone forever but he's stuck with her for life and all her anger and the rest of it.
11:13 PM February 28th from Tweetie

TYME2WASTE I'm sure he wishes he just got us plane tickets now. Suddenly our van is looking like the setting for a cage match duel to the death.
11:15 PM February 28th from Tweetie

TYME2WASTE All of us jammed in together for 3 days. Who will emerge alive? Place your bets ladies and germs. Person-ally I predict no survivors.
11:19 PM February 28th from Tweetie

TYME2WASTE Arrr. Fuck. Shit. It was dark when I went to bed and it is dark now and Dad says it's time to leave. This is so terribly wrong.

6:21 AM March 1st from Tweetie

TYME2WASTE We're going. Mom gave the condo a careful search to make sure nothing got left behind, which is how she found me.

7:01 AM March 1st from Tweetie

TYME2WASTE Damn knew I needed a better hiding place.

7:02 AM March 1st from Tweetie

TYME2WASTE Dad just said the whole trip ought to take between thirty-five and forty hours. I offer this as conclusive proof there is no God.

7:11 AM March 1st from Tweetie

TYME2WASTE Writing something on Twitter just to piss Mom off. She knows if I'm typing something on my phone I'm obviously engaged in a sinful act.

7:23 AM March 1st from Tweetie

TYME2WASTE I'm expressing myself and staying in touch with my friends and she hates it. Whereas if I was knitting and unpopular . . .

7:25 AM March 1st from Tweetie

TYME2WASTE . . . then I'd be just like her when she was 17. And I'd also marry the first guy who came along and get knocked up by 19.

7:25 AM March 1st from Tweetie

TYME2WASTE Coming down the mountain in the snow. Coming down the mountain in the snow. 1 more hairpin turn and my stomach's gonna blow . . .
7:30 AM March 1st from Tweetie

TYME2WASTE My contribution to this glorious family moment is going to come when I barf on my little brother's head.
7:49 AM March 1st from Tweetie

TYME2WASTE If we wind up in a snowbank and have a Donner Party, I know whose ass they'll be chewing on first. Mine.
7:52 AM March 1st from Tweetie

TYME2WASTE Of course my survival skilz would amount to Twittering madly for someone to rescue us.
7:54 AM March 1st from Tweetie

TYME2WASTE Mom would make a slingshot out of rubber from the tyres, kill squirrels with it, stitch a fur bikini out of 'em and be sad when we got saved.
7:56 AM March 1st from Tweetie

TYME2WASTE Dad would go out of his mind because we'd have to burn his books to stay warm.
8:00 AM March 1st from Tweetie

TYME2WASTE Eric would put on a pair of my pantyhose. Not to stay warm. Just cause my little brother wants to wear my pantyhose.
8:00 AM March 1st from Tweetie

TYME2WASTE I wrote that last bit cause Eric was looking over my shoulder.
8:02 AM March 1st from Tweetie

TYME2WASTE But the sick bastard said wearing my panty-hose is the closest he'll probably come to getting laid in high school.
8:06 AM March 1st from Tweetie

TYME2WASTE He's completely gross but I love him.
8:06 AM March 1st from Tweetie

TYME2WASTE Mom taught him to knit while we were snowed in here in happy CO and he knitted himself a cocksock and then she was sorry.
8:11 AM March 1st from Tweetie

TYME2WASTE I miss my blog which she had no right to make me take down.
8:13 AM March 1st from Tweetie

TYME2WASTE But Twittering is better than blogging because my blog always made me feel like I should have interesting ideas to blog about.
8:14 AM March 1st from Tweetie

TYME2WASTE But on Twitter every post can only be 140 letters long. Which is enough room to cover every interesting thing to ever happen to me.
8:15 AM March 1st from Tweetie

TYME2WASTE True. Check it out.
8:15 AM March 1st from Tweetie

TYME2WASTE Born. School. Mall. Cell phone. Driver's permit. Broke my nose playing trapeze at 8—there goes the modeling career. Need to lose 10 lbs.
8:19 AM March 1st from Tweetie

TYME2WASTE Think that covers it.
8:20 AM March 1st from Tweetie

TYME2WASTE It's snowing in the mountains but not down here snow falling in the sunlight in a storm of gold. Goodbye beautiful mountains.
9:17 AM March 1st from Tweetie

TYME2WASTE Hello not so beautiful Utah desert. Utah is brown and puckered like Judy Kennedy's weird nipples.
9:51 AM March 1st from Tweetie

TYME2WASTE @caseinSD Yes she does have weird nipples. And it doesn't make me a lesbo for noticing. Everyone notices.
10:02 AM March 1st from Tweetie

TYME2WASTE Sagebrush!!!!!! W00t!
11:09 AM March 1st from Tweetie

TYME2WASTE Now Eric is trying on my pantyhose. He's bored. Mom thinks its funny but Dad is stressed.
12:20 PM March 1st from Tweetie

TYME2WASTE I dared Eric to wear a skirt in the diner to get our takeout. Dad says no. Mom is still laughing.
12:36 PM March 1st from Tweetie

TYME2WASTE I promised him if he does it I'll invite a certain hot goth to the pool party in April so he can see her in her tacky bikini.
12:39 PM March 1st from Tweetie

TYME2WASTE Theres no way he'll do it.
12:42 PM March 1st from Tweetie

TYME2WASTE ZOMG hes doing it. Dad is going into the diner with him to make sure he isn't killed by offended Mormons.
12:44 PM March 1st from Tweetie

TYME2WASTE Eric came back alive. Eric saves the day. I'm actually glad to be in the van right now.
12:59 PM March 1st from Tweetie

TYME2WASTE Dad says Eric sat at the bar and talked football with this big trucker guy. Trucker guy was fine with the skirt and pantyhose.
1:03 PM March 1st from Tweetie

TYME2WASTE He's still wearing it. The skirt. He's probably a total closet tranny. Sicko. Course that would be fun. We could shop together.
1:45 PM March 1st from Tweetie

TYME2WASTE @caseinSD Yes we do have to invite a certain goth to the pool party now. She probably won't even come. I think sunlight burns her.
2:09 PM March 1st from Tweetie

TYME2WASTE Every time I start to fall asleep the van hits a bump and my head falls off the seat.
11:01 PM March 1st from Tweetie

TYME2WASTE Trying to sleep.
11:31 PM March 1st from Tweetie

TYME2WASTE I give up trying to sleep.
1:01 AM March 2nd from Tweetie

TYME2WASTE Oh fuck Eric. He's asleep and he looks like he's having a wet dream about a certain goth chick.
1:07 AM March 2nd from Tweetie

TYME2WASTE Meanwhile I'd have a better chance of sleeping if there were only steel pins inserted under my eyelids.
1:09 AM March 2nd from Tweetie

TYME2WASTE I'm so happy right now. I just want to hold this moment for as long as I can.
6:11 AM March 2nd from Tweetie

TYME2WASTE I just want to be home. I hate Mom. I hate everyone in the van. Including myself.
8:13 AM March 2nd from Tweetie

TYME2WASTE Okay. This is why I was happy earlier. It was 4 in the morning and Mom pulled into a rest area and then she came and got me.
10:21 AM March 2nd from Tweetie

TYME2WASTE She said it was my turn to drive. I said my permit is only for driving in Cali and she just said get behind the wheel.
10:22 AM March 2nd from Tweetie

TYME2WASTE She told me if I got pulled over to wake her up and we'd switch and everything would be all right.
10:23 AM March 2nd from Tweetie

TYME2WASTE So she went to sleep in the passenger seat and I drove. We were down in the desert and the sun came up behind us.
10:25 AM March 2nd from Tweetie

TYME2WASTE And then there were coyotes in the road. In the red sunlight. They were all over the interstate and I stopped so I wouldn't hit them.
10:26 AM March 2nd from Tweetie

TYME2WASTE Their eyes were gold and the sun was in their fur and there were so many, this huge pack. Just standing there like they were waiting for me.
10:28 AM March 2nd from Tweetie

TYME2WASTE I wanted to take a picture with my cell phone, but I couldn't figure out where I left it. While I was looking for it they disappeared.
10:31 AM March 2nd from Tweetie

TYME2WASTE When Mom woke up I told her all about them. And then I thought she'd be mad I didn't shake her awake to see them so I said I was sorry.
10:34 AM March 2nd from Tweetie

TYME2WASTE And she said she was glad I didn't wake her up, because that moment was just for me. And for like three seconds I liked her again.
10:35 AM March 2nd from Tweetie

TYME2WASTE But then in the place we ate breakfast I was looking at my e-mail for a sec. & I heard Mom saying to the waitress, we apologize for her.
10:37 AM March 2nd from Tweetie

TYME2WASTE I guess the waitress was standing there waiting for my order and I didn't notice.
10:40 AM March 2nd from Tweetie

TYME2WASTE But I didn't sleep all night and I was tired and zoned out and that's why I didn't notice, not 'cause I was looking at the phone.
10:42 AM March 2nd from Tweetie

TYME2WASTE And Mom had to trot out her stories about being a waitress herself and that it was demeaning not to be acknowledged.
10:45 AM March 2nd from Tweetie

TYME2WASTE Just to rub it in. And she can be completely right and I can still hate the way she makes me feel like shit at every opportunity.
10:46 AM March 2nd from Tweetie

TYME2WASTE I napped but I don't feel better.
4:55 PM March 2nd from Tweetie

TYME2WASTE Dad of course has to go the slowest possible route by way of every back road. Mom says he missed a turn and added 100 miles to the trip.
6:30 PM March 2nd from Tweetie

TYME2WASTE Now Mom and Dad are fighting. OMG I want out of this van.
6:37 PM March 2nd from Tweetie

TYME2WASTE Eric I am psychically willing you to find some reason for us to get off the road. Put on the pantyhose again. Say you have to pee.
6:49 PM March 2nd from Tweetie

TYME2WASTE Anything. Please.
6:49 PM March 2nd from Tweetie

TYME2WASTE No no no Eric, no. When I was sending you psychic signals, I was not signaling to you to pull over for this.
6:57 PM March 2nd from Tweetie

TYME2WASTE Mom doesn't want to pull over either. Write it down, kids, first time in two years we've agreed on anything.
7:00 PM March 2nd from Tweetie

TYME2WASTE Oh Dad is being a prick now. He says there was no point in taking backroads if we weren't going to find some culture.
7:02 PM March 2nd from Tweetie

TYME2WASTE We are driving up to something called the Circus of the Dead. The ticket guy looks really REALLY sick. Not funny sick. SICK sick.
7:06 PM March 2nd from Tweetie

TYME2WASTE Sores around his mouth and few teeth and I can smell him. He's got a pet rat. His pet rat dived in his pocket and came out with the tickets.
7:08 PM March 2nd from Tweetie

TYME2WASTE No it wasn't cute. None of us want to touch the tickets.
7:10 PM March 2nd from Tweetie

TYME2WASTE Boy, they're really packing them in. Show starts in 15 min. but the parking lot is 1/2 empty. The big top is a black tent with holes in it.
7:13 PM March 2nd from Tweetie

TYME2WASTE Mom says to be sure to keep doing whatever I'm doing on my phone. She wouldn't want me to look up and see something happening.
7:17 PM March 2nd from Tweetie

TYME2WASTE Oh that was shitty. She just said to Dad that I'll love the circus because it'll be just like the internet.
7:18 PM March 2nd from Tweetie

TYME2WASTE Youtube is full of clowns, message boards are full of firebreathers and blogs are for people who can't live without a spotlight on them.
7:20 PM March 2nd from Tweetie

TYME2WASTE I'm going to tweet like 5 times a minute and make her insane.
7:21 PM March 2nd from Tweetie

TYME2WASTE The usher is a funny old Mickey Rooney type with a bowler and a cigar. He also has on a hazmat suit. He says so he can't get bitten.
7:25 PM March 2nd from Tweetie

TYME2WASTE I almost fell twice on the walk to our seats. Guess they're saving $ on lights. I'm using my iPhone as a flashlight. Hope there isn't a fire.
7:28 PM March 2nd from Tweetie

TYME2WASTE God this is the stinkiest circus ever. I don't know what I'm smelling. Are those the animals? Call PETA.
7:30 PM March 2nd from Tweetie

TYME2WASTE I can't believe how many people there are. Every seat is taken. Don't know where this crowd came from.
7:31 PM March 2nd from Tweetie

TYME2WASTE They must've had us park in a secondary parking lot. Oh, wait, they just flipped on a spotlight. Show-time. Beating heart, restrain yourself.
7:34 PM March 2nd from Tweetie

TYME2WASTE Well that got Eric and Dad's attention. The ringmistress came out on stilts and she's practically naked. Fishnets and top hat.
7:38 PM March 2nd from Tweetie

TYME2WASTE She's weird. She talks like she's stoned. Did I mention there are zombies in clown outfits chasing her around?
7:40 PM March 2nd from Tweetie

TYME2WASTE The zombies are waaay gross. They have on big clown shoes, and polka dot outfits, and clown makeup.
7:43 PM March 2nd from Tweetie

TYME2WASTE But the makeup is flaking off, and beneath it they're all rotted and black. Yow! They almost grabbed her. She's quick.
7:44 PM March 2nd from Tweetie

TYME2WASTE She says she's been a prisoner of the circus for six weeks and that she survived because she learned the stilts fast.
7:47 PM March 2nd from Tweetie

TYME2WASTE She said her boyfriend couldn't walk on them and fell down and was eaten his first night. She said her best friend was eaten the 2nd night.
7:49 PM March 2nd from Tweetie

TYME2WASTE She walked right up to the wall under us and begged someone to pull her over and rescue her, but the guy in the front row just laughed.
7:50 PM March 2nd from Tweetie

TYME2WASTE Then she had to run away in a hurry before Zippo the Zombie knocked her off her stilts. It's all very well choreographed.
7:50 PM March 2nd from Tweetie

TYME2WASTE You can totally believe they're trying to get her.
7:51 PM March 2nd from Tweetie

TYME2WASTE They rolled a cannon out. She said here at the Circus of the Dead we always begin things with a bang. She read it off a card.
7:54 PM March 2nd from Tweetie

TYME2WASTE She walked up to a tall door and banged on it and for a minute I didn't think they were going to let her out of the ring, but then they did.
7:55 PM March 2nd from Tweetie

TYME2WASTE Two men in hazmat suits just led a zombie out. He's got a metal collar around his neck with a black stick attached.
7:56 PM March 2nd from Tweetie

TYME2WASTE They're using the stick to hold him at a distance so he can't grab them.
7:57 PM March 2nd from Tweetie

TYME2WASTE Eric says he has fantasies about a certain

goth girl putting him in a rig like that.
7:58 PM March 2nd from Tweetie

TYME2WASTE This show would be a great date for the two of them. It's got a hint of sex, a whiff of bondage, and it's really really morbid.
7:59 PM March 2nd from Tweetie

TYME2WASTE They put the zombie in the cannon.
8:00 PM March 2nd from Tweetie

TYME2WASTE Auuuughhh! They pointed the cannon at the crowd and fired it and fucking pieces of zombie went everywhere.
8:03 PM March 2nd from Tweetie

TYME2WASTE The guy in the row in front of us got smashed in the mouth with a flying shoe. He's bleeding and everything.
8:05 PM March 2nd from Tweetie

TYME2WASTE Fucking yuck! There's still a foot inside the shoe! It's totally realistic looking.
8:08 PM March 2nd from Tweetie

TYME2WASTE The guy sitting in front of us just walked off w/his wife to complain. Same dude who laffed at the ringmistress when she asked for help.
8:11 PM March 2nd from Tweetie

TYME2WASTE Dad had a zombie lip in his hair. I am so glad I didn't eat lunch. Looks like a gummy worm and it smells like ass.
8:13 PM March 2nd from Tweetie

TYME2WASTE Naturally Eric wants to keep it.
8:13 PM March 2nd from Tweetie

TYME2WASTE Here comes the ringmistress again. She says the next act is the cat's meo.
8:14 PM March 2nd from Tweetie

TYME2WASTE OMG OMG that was not funny. She almost fell down and the way they were snarling.
8:16 PM March 2nd from Tweetie

TYNIE2WASTE The men in hazmat suits just wheeled in a lion in a cage. Yay, a lion! I am still girl enough to like a big cat.
8:17 PM March 2nd from Tweetie

TYME2WASTE Oh that's a really sad sick looking lion. Not fun. They're opening the cage and sending in zombies and he's hissing like a housecat.
8:19 PM March 2nd from Tweetie

TYME2WASTE Roawwwwr! Lion power. He's swatting them down and shredding them apart. He's got an arm in his mouth. Everyone cheering.
8:21 PM March 2nd from Tweetie

TYME2WASTE Eeeuuuw. Not so much cheering now. He's got one and he's tugging out its guts like he's pulling on one end of a tug rope.
8:22 PM March 2nd from Tweetie

TYME2WASTE They're sending in more zombies. No one laughing or cheering now. It's really crowded in there.
8:24 PM March 2nd from Tweetie

TYME2WASTE I can't even see the lion anymore. Lots of angry snarling and flying fur and walking corpses getting knocked around.
8:24 PM March 2nd from Tweetie

TYME2WASTE OH GROSS. The lion made a sound, like this scared whine, and now the zombies are passing around organ meat and hunks of fur.
8:25 PM March 2nd from Tweetie

TYME2WASTE They're eating. That's awful. I feel sick.
8:26 PM March 2nd from Tweetie

TYME2WASTE Dad saw I was getting upset and told me how they did it. The cage has a false bottom. They pulled the lion out through the floor.
8:30 PM March 2nd from Tweetie

TYME2WASTE You really get swept up in this thing.
8:30 PM March 2nd from Tweetie

TYME2WASTE The Mickey Rooney guy who led us back to the seats just showed up with a flashlight. He says we left the headlights on in the van.
8:31 PM March 2nd from Tweetie

TYME2WASTE Eric went to turn them off. He has to pee anyway.
8:32 PM March 2nd from Tweetie

TYME2WASTE The fireswallower just came out. He has no eyes and there's some kind of steel contraption forcing his head back and his mouth open.
8:34 PM March 2nd from Tweetie

TYME2WASTE One of the men in the hazmat suits is FUCK ME.
8:35 PM March 2nd from Tweetie

TYME2WASTE They shoved a torch down his throat and now he's burning! He's running around with smoke coming out of his mouth and
8:36 PM March 2nd from Tweetie

TYME2WASTE fire in his head coming out his eyes like a jack o lante
8:36 PM March 2nd from Tweetie

TYME2WASTE They just let him burn to death from the inside out. Realest thing I've ever seen.
8:39 PM March 2nd from Tweetie

TYME2WASTE What's even realer is the corpse after the hazmat guys sprayed it down with the fire extinguishers. It looks so sad and shriveled and black.
8:39 PM March 2nd from Tweetie

TYME2WASTE The ringmistress is back. She's really weaving around. I think something is wrong with her ankle.
8:40 PM March 2nd from Tweetie

TYME2WASTE She says someone from the audience has agreed to be tonight's sacrifice. She says he will be the lucky one.
8:41 PM March 2nd from Tweetie

TYME2WASTE He? I thought the sacrifice was usually a girl in this sort of situation.
8:41 PM March 2nd from Tweetie

TYME2WASTE Oh no he did not. They just wheeled Eric out, cuffed to a big wooden wheel. He winked on the way past. Psycho. Go Eric!
8:42 PM March 2nd from Tweetie

TYME2WASTE They hauled out a zombie and chained him to a stake in the dirt. There's a box of hatchets in front of him. Don't like where this is going.
8:43 PM March 2nd from Tweetie

TYME2WASTE Everyone's laughing now. The lion scene was a little grim, but we're back to funny again. The zombie threw the first hatchet into the crowd.
8:45 PM March 2nd from Tweetie

TYME2WASTE There was a thunk, and someone scream-ed like they got it in the head. Obvious plant.
8:45 PM March 2nd from Tweetie

TYME2WASTE Eric is spinning around and around the wheel. He's telling the zombie to kill him before he throws up.
8:46 PM March 2nd from Tweetie

TYME2WASTE Eeeks! I'm not as brave as Eric. A knife just banged into the wheel next to his head. Like: INCHES. Eric screamed too. Bet he wishes now
8:47 PM March 2nd from Tweetie

TYME2WASTE OMGOMGO
8:47 PM March 2nd from Tweetie

TYME2WASTE Okay. He must be okay. He was still smiling when they wheeled him out of the ring. The hatchet went right in the side of his neck.
8:50 PM March 2nd from Tweetie

TYME2WASTE Dad says it's a trick. Dad says he's fine. He says later Eric will come out as a zombie. That it's part of the show.
8:51 PM March 2nd from Tweetie

TYME2WASTE Yep, looks like Dad's right. They've promised Eric will reemerge shortly.
8:53 PM March 2nd from Tweetie

TYME2WASTE Mom is wigging. She wants Dad to check on Eric.
8:54 PM March 2nd from Tweetie

TYME2WASTE She's being kind of crazy. She's talking about how the guy who sat in front of us never came back after he got hit by the shoe.
8:55 PM March 2nd from Tweetie

TYME2WASTE I don't really see what that has to do with Eric. And besides, if I got hit by a flying shoe . . .
8:55 PM March 2nd from Tweetie

TYME2WASTE Okay, Dad is going to check on Eric. Sanity restored.
8:56 PM March 2nd from Tweetie

TYME2WASTE Here comes the ringmistress again. This is why Eric agreed to go backstage. With the fishnets and black panties she's very goth-hot.
8:56 PM March 2nd from Tweetie

TYME2WASTE She's being weird. She isn't saying any-thing about the next act. She says if she goes off script they don't let her out of the ring.
8:57 PM March 2nd from Tweetie

TYME2WASTE But she doesn't care. She says she twisted her ankle and she knows tonight is her last night.
8:58 PM March 2nd from Tweetie

TYME2WASTE She says her name is Gail Ross and she went to high school in Plano.
8:59 PM March 2nd from Tweetie

TYME2WASTE She says she was going to marry her boy-friend after college. She says his name was Craig and he wanted to teach.
9:00 PM March 2nd from Tweetie

TYME2WASTE She says she's sorry for all of us. She says they take our cars and dispose of them while we're in the tent.
9:01 PM March 2nd from Tweetie

TYME2WASTE She says 12,000 people vanish every year on the roads with no explanation, their cars turn up empty or not at all and no one will miss us.
9:02 PM March 2nd from Tweetie

TYME2WASTE Creepy stuff. Here's Eric. His zombie makeup is really good. Most of the zombies are black and rotted but he looks like fresh kill.
9:03 PM March 2nd from Tweetie

TYME2WASTE Still got the hatchet in the neck. That looks totally fake.
9:03 PM March 2nd from Tweetie

TYME2WASTE He's not very good at being a zombie. He isn't even trying to walk slow. He's really going after her.
9:04 PM March 2nd from Tweetie

TYME2WASTE oh shit I hope that's part of the show. He just knocked her down. Oh Eric Eric Eric. She hit the dirt really, really hard.
9:05 PM March 2nd from Tweetie

TYME2WASTE They're eating her like they ate the lion. Eric is playing with guts. He's so gross. He's going totally method.
9:07 PM March 2nd from Tweetie

TYME2WASTE Gymnastics now. They're making a human pyramid. Or maybe I should say an INhuman pyramid. They're surprisingly good at it. For zombies.
9:10 PM March 2nd from Tweetie

TYME2WASTE Eric is climbing the pyramid like he knows what he's doing. I wonder if they gave him backstage training or
9:11 PM March 2nd from Tweetie

TYME2WASTE He's up high enough to grab the wall around the ring. He's snarling at someone in the front row, just a couple feet from here. Wait
9:13 PM March 2nd from Tweetie

TYME2WASTE no lights fuck thta was stupid whyd they put out the
9:14 PM March 2nd from Tweetie

TYME2WASTE someones screaming
9:15 PM March 2nd from Tweetie

TYME2WASTE this is really dangerous its so dark and lots of people are screaming and getting up. im mad now you don't do this to people you don't
9:18 PM March 2nd from Tweetie

TYME2WASTE we need help we areacv
9:32 PM March 2nd from Tweetie

TYME2WASTE gtttttgggtttggtttttttttgggbbbnnnfrfffgt
9:32 PM March 2nd from Tweetie

TYME2WASTE I cant say anything theyll hear, were beinb ver y qiuet wevegot a plas
10:17 PM March 2nd from Tweetie

TYME2WASTE were off i70 mom says it was exit 331 but we drove a long way the last town we saw was called ucmba
10:19 PM March 2nd from Tweetie

TYME2WASTE cumba
10:19 PM March 2nd from Tweetie

TYME2WASTE the people in the stands were all dead except for us and a few others and they were roped together tethered
10:20 PM March 2nd from Tweetie

TYME2WASTE please someone send help call UT state police not making this up
10:22 PM March 2nd from Tweetie

TYME2WASTE @caseinSD lease help you know me you know I wouldnt isnta joke
10:23 PM March 2nd from Tweetie

TYME2WASTE have to be quiet so I can't call got the ringer is turned off
10:24 PM March 2nd from Tweetie

TYME2WASTE AZ state police mom says its arizona not UT our van is a white econlein
10:27 PM March 2nd from Tweetie

TYME2WASTE its quiet less screaming now less growling
10:50 PM March 2nd from Tweetie

TYME2WASTE theyre dragging people into piles
10:56 PM March 2nd from Tweetie

TYME2WASTE eating theyre eating them
11:09 PM March 2nd from Tweetie

TYME2WASTE the man who got hit by the shoe earlier walked by but he isn't like he was he hes dead now
1:11 PM March 2nd from Tweetie

TYME2WASTE just mom and me i love my mom shes so brave i love her so much so much i never ment it none of the bad things not one i am with her i am
11:37 PM March 2nd from Tweetie

TYME2WASTE imso csared
11:39 PM March 2nd from Tweetie

TYME2WASTE theyresearching to see if anyone is left with flashlights the men in hazmat soups i say go out mom says no
11:41 PM March 2nd from Tweetie

TYME2WASTE were here were waiting for help please forward this to everyone on twitter this is true not an internet prank believe believe believe pleves
12:03 AM March 3rd from Tweetie

TYME2WASTE ohgod it was dad went by mom sat up and said his name and mom and dad and mom and dad
12:09 AM March 3rd from Tweetie

TYME2WASTE notdad oh my oh bnb nnnb ;;/'/.,/;'././/
12:13 AM March 3rd from Tweetie

TYNIE2WASTE /'/.
12:13 AM March 3rd from Tweetie

TYME2WASTE Were you SCARED by this TWITTER FEED???!?!?
9:17 AM March 3rd from Tweetie

TYME2WASTE The FEAR—and THE FUN—is only just BEGINNING!
9:20 AM March 3rd from Tweetie

TYME2WASTE 'THE CIRCUS OF THE DEAD' featuring our newest RINGMISTRESS the SEXY & DARING BLAKE THE BLACKHEARTED.
9::22 AM March 3rd from Tweetie

TYME2WASTE Watch as our newest QUEEN OF THE TRAPEZE introduces our PERVERSE & PERNICIOUS performer...
9:23 AM March 3rd from Tweetie

TYME2WASTE ...while DANGLING FROM A ROPE ABOVE THE RAVENOUS DEAD!
9:23 AM March 3rd from Tweetie

TYME2WASTE A CIRCUS so SHOCKING it makes the JIM ROSE CIRCUS look like THE MUPPET SHOW!
9:25 AM March 3rd from Tweetie

TYME2WASTE Now touring with stops in ALL CORNERS OF THE COUNTRY!
9:26 AM March 3rd from Tweetie

TYME2WASTE Visit our Facebook page and join our E-MAIL LIST to find out when we'll be in YOUR AREA.
9:28 AM March 3rd from Tweetie

TYME2WASTE STAY CONNECTED OR YOU DON'T KNOW WHAT YOU'LL MISS!
9:30 AM March 3rd from Tweetie

TYME2WASTE 'THE CIRCUS OF THE DEAD' . . . Where YOU are the concessions! Other circuses promise DEATH-DEFYING THRILLS!
9:31 AM March 3rd from Tweetie

TYME2WASTE BUT ONLY WE DELIVER! (Tix to be purchased at box office day of show. No refunds. Cash only. Minors must be accompanied by adult.)
9:31 AM March 3rd from Tweetie

The Pilo Family Circus: The Velvet Bag

Will Elliott

There was not one among them that did not cast an eye behind
In the hope that the carny would return to his own kind.

"The Carny", Nick Cave

Jamie's tyres squealed to a halt, and the first thought to pass through his head was *I almost killed it*, rather than, *I almost killed him*. Standing in the glare of his headlights was an apparition dressed in a puffy shirt with a garish flower pattern splashed violently across it. It wore oversized red shoes, striped pants and white face paint.

What immediately disturbed Jamie was the look in the clown's eyes, a bewildered glaze which suggested the clown was completely new to the world, that Jamie's car was the very first it had ever seen. It was as though it had just hatched out of a giant egg and wandered straight onto the road to stand as still as a store mannequin, its flower shirt tucked in at the waist, barely holding in a sagging belly, arms locked stiff at its sides, hands bunched into fat round fists stuffed into white gloves. Sweat patches spread out under both armpits. It stared at him through the windshield with ungodly boggling eyes, then it lost interest and turned away from the vehicle that had nearly killed it.

The dashboard clock ticked over the tenth second since Jamie's car had stopped. He could smell burnt rubber. His time as a motorist had cost the world two cats, one pheasant, and now very nearly one absolute fool of a human being. Flashing through his mind was all that could have gone wrong had his foot hesitated *at all* on the brake: law suits, charges, sleepless nights and guilt attacks for the rest of his life. Road rage came on fast and murderous. He rolled down the window and screamed, "Hey! Get off the fucking *rooooad!*"

The clown stayed put—only its mouth moved, opening and shutting twice, though no words came out. Jamie's fury brought him to the verge of a seizure; did this guy think he was being *funny?* He gritted his teeth and slammed on the horn. His little old Nissan wheezed with all her might, a piercing sound in the 2am quiet.

At last he appeared to have made an impression. The clown's mouth flapped open and shut again, and it held its white-gloved hands to its ears as it turned to face Jamie again. Its gaze hit him like a cold touch and sent a shiver up his spine. *Don't beep that horn again, sport*, said its ungodly eyes. *A guy like me's got problems, wouldn't you say? You'd like me to keep my problems to myself, wouldn't you?*

Jamie's hand hesitated above the horn.

The clown turned back towards the footpath and took a few drunken steps before coming to a halt once more. If a car came the other way at speed, it would do what Jamie had almost done. Oh well, Mother Nature knew best—it was just the natural course of the stupid gene, streaming its way out of the species like the letting of poisoned blood. Jamie drove off, shaking his head and laughing nervously. "What the hell was that about?" he whispered to his reflection in the rear-view mirror.

He would know all too soon—the next night, in fact.

❧

"Where's me fuckin' UMBRELLA?"

Jamie groaned to himself. It was the fourth time the question had been roared at him, with each word now having had its turn at the emphasis. Standing before him was none other than Richard

Peterson, sob sister from one of the national rags, *Voice of the Taxpayer*. He'd bustled through the doors of the Wentworth Gentlemen's Club in a storm of Armani and shoe polish. As concierge, Jamie was getting eighteen bucks an hour to politely endure the tirade.

There was a pause in shouting. Peterson stared at him in baleful silence, moustache twitching.

"I'm sorry, sir, I haven't seen it. Could I offer you a com-plimentary—"

"That umbrella was a fuckin' HEIRLOOM!"

"I understand, sir. Perhaps—"

"WHERE'S me fuckin' umbrella?"

Jamie grimaced as two attractive women walked past the doors, smiling in at the commotion. For the next two minutes he repeated "I understand sir, perhaps—" as Peterson threatened to resign his membership, to sue, to get Jamie fired... *Didn't he know who he was dealing with?* Finally, one of Peterson's associates wandered through the lobby and lured him up to the bar in the manner of someone luring a Doberman with a bloody steak. Peterson backed away growling. Jamie sighed, feeling not for the first time like he was the guest star on some British sitcom.

The 6pm rush came and went. Through the doors came a stampede of beer-gutted Brisbane Personalities, from law firm partners to televi-sion news readers, AFL head honchos, retired test cricketers, members of State Parliament, and suits of all descriptions, bar young and female. Quiet descended on the lobby; the only sounds to permeate the granite walls were the muffled honking of traffic, the quieting bustle of the city's working day filing out, and its night life waking. The lobby was deserted, the peace sporadically interrupted by club members leaving drunker and happier than when they'd arrived. Once the last of them had staggered off, Jamie descended into his science fiction novel, stealing furtive glances over his shoulder occasionally in case his boss or a stray Brisbane Personality caught him at it. This, by contrast, wasn't such a bad way to earn eighteen bucks an hour, either.

The clock struck two. Jamie started from a kind of trance and wondered where the last six hours had gone. The club was silent; the rest of the staff had gone home, all members were tucked into bed, comfortably full of beer, with their hired escorts asleep beside them.

Jamie walked through the city to the Myer Centre, a tall redheaded young man taking long jerking strides with thin legs, polished shoes tapping crisply on the pavement, hands shoved into the pockets of his slacks, where his thumb and forefinger played with a dollar coin. A beggar had learned his shift times and for weeks had been making an effort to intercept him on his way to the car park. On cue, the old man met him outside the Myer Centre, smelling of cask wine and looking like Santa Claus gone to seed. He muttered something about the weather then acted surprised and delighted when Jamie handed him the dollar, as though it were the last thing in the world he'd expected, and so Jamie's shift ended in profuse thanks, which was gratifying in a small way.

Wondering not for the first time why the hell he'd done an arts degree, he started his little Nissan. Its engine rasped like an ailing lung. On the drive home he saw another clown.

☙❧

His headlights swept past the closed shops in New Farm and there it was, standing out front of a grocery store. This clown was not the same as last night's; it had dark clumps of black hair sticking like bristles out of a head as round as a basketball. Its clothes were different too—it wore a plain red shirt that looked like old-fashioned cotton underwear, clinging tightly to its chest and belly, and pants of the same fashion, with a button-up seat. Its face paint, plastic nose and big red shoes were the only things "clown" about it; otherwise it might have been any fifty-something booze hound lost on his way home, or in search of back-alley romance.

As Jamie's car passed, the clown looked to be in the throes of despair, throwing its arms up in exasperation and mouthing some complaint to the heavens. In his rear-view mirror he saw it ducking between the grocer and a garden supply store, disappearing from view.

Jamie would have happily left it at that — there were psychos loose in the neighbourhood, no surprise in New Farm. He'd have driven home, crept up the back steps to shower, put out some cat food for the legion of local strays, slunk back to his room, masturbated to some internet porn then collapsed into bed, set to repeat it all tomorrow. But his car had other ideas. There was the grinding noise of a big metal belly with indigestion, then the smell of oil and smoke. Halfway down the street his little Nissan died.

He thumped his hand on the passenger seat, sending cassette tapes scuttling in all directions like plastic cockroaches. Home was four streets away and up a hill. He was stretching his calf muscles to begin pushing the mutinous wreck home when he heard a strange voice say, "Goshy!"

Jamie's heart skipped a beat. The voice came from behind him again. "Goshy?"

He'd forgotten about the clown. It was a clown's voice all right, a silly voice with exaggerated worry and a childish whine, from the throat of a middle-aged man. In Jamie's mind the tone conjured an image of the village idiot pounding his own foot with a hammer and asking why his foot hurt. The clown called out again, louder: "Gosh-*eeeeeeee*?"

Goshy? Was that some kind of swearword? Jamie about-faced and headed back towards the grocery store car park. The streets were silent and his footsteps seemed very loud. Obeying some instinct that told him to stay hidden, he crept behind a hedge next to the car park and, through the leaves, he saw the clown standing outside the gardening shop, staring at the roof and going through the motions of a distressed parent, running a hand over its scalp, tossing its arms to the sky, now making an extravagant swooning gesture like a stage actress: hand to the forehead, a backward step, a moan. Jamie waited until its back was turned before darting from the hedge and crouching behind an industrial garbage bin for a closer look. The clown called out that word again: *"Gosh-eeeeeeeeee!"*

A thought occurred: *"Goshy" is a name. Maybe the name of the clown I nearly ran over. Maybe this one is out looking for it, because Goshy is lost.* It seemed to fit. And, as he watched, the clown found its friend. The clown from last night was standing on the roof of the plant shop, still as a chimney. The suddenness with which it caught Jamie's eye almost made him cry out in alarm. On its face was the same look of naked bewilderment.

"Goshy, it's not *funny!*" said the clown in the car park. "Come down from there. Come on, Goshy, you come down, you *just* gotta! Goshy, it's not *funny!*"

Goshy stood motionless, up on the roof, his fists bunched at his sides like a petulant child, eyes wide, lips pursed, gut sagging like a bag of wet cement under his shirt. Goshy stared unblinking down at the other clown; he wasn't coming down, that was for sure. He seemed to be throwing some kind of passive tantrum. He gave one mute flap of the lips then turned away.

"Goshy, come down, *pleeeeeease!* Gonko's comin', he's gonna be *soooo maaaaad . . . "*

No reaction from the rooftop.

"Goshy, come *onnnnn . . . "*

Goshy turned back to the other clown, gave another mute flap of the lips, and without warning took three stiff-legged paces towards the roof's edge, then over it. The drop was about twelve feet. He plummeted to the concrete headfirst, with all the grace of a sack of dead kittens. There was a loud sickening *crack-thud* as he landed.

Jamie sucked in a sharp breath.

"Goshy!" The other clown rushed over. Goshy lay face down with his arms locked stiff at his sides. The clown patted Goshy on the back, as though Goshy were having a mere coughing spell. No good— Goshy would probably need an ambulance. Jamie looked uneasily at the payphone across the street.

The other clown patted Goshy's back a little harder. Still lying face down, Goshy rolled from side to side like a felled ninepin; he looked to be having some kind of fit. The other clown grabbed his shoulders. Goshy began making a noise like a steel kettle boiling, a high-pitched squealing: "*Mmmmmmmmm! Mmmmmmmmmm!*"

The other clown pulled Goshy upright. Once on his feet, still making that awful noise, he stared at the other clown with wide star-tled eyes. The clown held his shoulders, whispered "Goshy!" and embraced him. The kettle kept squealing, over and over, but with each burst the volume lowered until the noise ceased altogether. When the other clown released him, Goshy turned to the plant shop, pointed a stiff arm at it and silently flapped his mouth. The other clown said, "I know, but we gotta hafta go! Gonko's comin', and—" The clown patted Goshy's pants, then dug into his pockets and pulled something out. Jamie couldn't see what it was, but it sent the other clown into throes of distress again. "Oh! Oh oh! Jeez, Goshy, what're you *thinking*? You're not meant to, not s'posed to have this here. Oh, oh oh, Gonko's gonna . . . the boss'll be *øoo* . . . "

The clown paused and looked around the empty car park before tossing the small bundle away. It landed with a sound like a wind chime striking a single note, and slid into the hedges by the footpath before Jamie could get a good look at it. "Come *on* now, Goshy," the clown said. "We gotta hafta *go.*"

He grabbed Goshy by the collar and started to lead him away. Jamie stood up, unsure if he should follow the pair or run for the public phone—one of these idiots was going to get himself killed if they were left to their own devices. Then something caught his eye: a *third* clown. This one stood by the door of a copy centre two doors down from the plant shop, arms folded across its chest. Jamie shook his head in disbelief and crouched back down out of sight. He knew immediately that whatever maladies affected the brains of the first two clowns did not affect this one; there was a sharp awareness in its face, staring with narrowed eyes at the other two as they shuffled across the car park. Goshy and his com-panion halted. Goshy's face didn't change, but the other looked at the new clown with something near terror. He stammered, "Hi . . . Gonko."

The new clown didn't move or react. It was thin, dressed in a full uniform of oversized striped pants held by suspenders, a bow-tie, white face paint, a shirt decorated with pictures of kittens, and a huge puffy hat. It squinted at the other clowns like a gangster from a Mafia movie; if it had ever intended to make people laugh, it may well have done so at gunpoint. It glanced around the car park, as though for witnesses, and Jamie found himself crouching further behind the industrial bin, suddenly convinced it was a very good idea not to be seen. The sound of Goshy smacking into the concrete echoed in his ears, *crack-thud*, and he shuddered.

The new clown beckoned the others with a single finger. They stumbled over. "I just gotta, had to find him, Gonko," said the clown who wasn't Goshy. "I just *had* to, he can't look after himself out here, he just can't . . . "

The new clown answered in a harsh voice, "Shut your fucking trap. Let's go." Its gaze swept over the car park again, from the footpath right over to the industrial bin. Jamie ducked out of sight, holding his breath. He stayed down for a minute, worried his heart was beating loud enough for the clowns to hear—yet he couldn't pinpoint what it was exactly that he feared. Finally he risked a glance over the top of the bin. They were gone. He stepped gladly away from the stale reek of garbage. Over by the gardening shop there was a small white smear where Goshy the clown had fallen. Face paint. He touched it, rubbed it between his fingers to confirm the last ten minutes had actually happened.

The night-time city sounds hummed in the near distance, as though being switched on again after a short break. A dog barked, a car alarm beeped somewhere far away. Jamie shivered with sudden cold and looked at his watch: 2.59am. It was going to be a long walk home.

As he passed the footpath something in the hedge caught his eye. He remembered the clown reaching into the other's pocket, pulling something out and throwing it away. He picked it up, a small velvet bag about half the size of his fist, tied at the top with white string. It felt like it was full of sand. Or, maybe, a different kind of powder. And judging by the way the clowns had acted, just maybe it was the kind of powder Wentworth Club members occasionally left little traces of on hand-held mirrors, in their rooms along with bloody tissues and straws. Interesting. He stuffed the velvet bag in his pocket, where it bumped against his thigh with each step.

Now for the fun part. He put his Nissan in neutral and started pushing it to the service station two streets away. A passing motorist informed him with a scream: "That's what you get for driving Jap shit, mate."

"*Arigato, gozaimasu,*" Jamie muttered.

Later, looking back on this night, Jamie would marvel that he'd believed his worst trouble was the car and the ache in his back from pushing it, that never for a moment did his mind turn in alarm to the little velvet bag in his pocket, which felt like it was full of sand.

Face of the Circus

LOU MORGAN

There's space for three hundred souls on the train: living quarters and kitchens and communal spaces for when life on the rails gets lonely. There are carriages for the animals—for the horses and lions and even the elephants—and for the clowns' car; there are carriages for the folded canvas of the tents.

All this space, and only one man aboard.

Well. Only one man . . . and his cat.

They sit side by side on the old musty velvet of a banquette in the dining car, both of them staring at the world which creeps past outside the window. Winter is biting hard, and the snow lies thigh-deep beyond the tracks with the promise of more to come. Clusters of houses slide out of white fog and vanish again.

And still, man and cat sit with their faces toward the window.

The man with his tattered red coat (which some will tell you isn't red, but "pink"—although it makes you think of fire and roses and blood, and if that's not red, you ask, then what is?) and his top hat of shining black silk, he drums his fingers on the table in front of him; tapping out the rhythm of the wheels. His face is hidden by the shadow of the brim, but the coat has seen better days and his finger-nails are ragged and torn. Only the hat has kept its lustre.

The cat beside him has fared little better. Its fur is dusty and dishev-elled, hinting at mange. One of its eyes is moonstone-milky, while the other is as black as its master's hat.

Alone together in the fog, the Ringmaster and his cat rattle on into the dusk.

രൂപ

Franklin had always known that he would be the Ringmaster when he grew up, and the circus had known it too. Even when he was small, the animals would quiet in their cages as he passed; would shy away from him and press themselves against the far walls of their pens. The clowns—always so friendly with the circus children—would watch him with wary eyes when he came near, never quite meeting his gaze. Even Marcel the Nine-Fingered Master of Magic never offered to pull a coin from Franklin's ear or teach him the African three-rope trick.

He had always been seen as "different" from the rest of them— which, coming from the crew around him, was saying something. But he was in tune with the circus more than anyone there, man or boy . . . with the exception of Monsieur Loyal.

A giant of a man with a barrel chest and a booming voice which easily carried to the back of the Big Top, Loyal was the heart of the circus. He ran the rings with long-practiced ease: genial host, showman, lord of all before him—and Franklin would watch the man from the shadows with marvellous envy.

But when the crowd had drifted away and the lights had faded, and the last of Franklin's tasks were done—the sweeping and the tying and the folding and the litter-picking that falls to every circus after a show—and Loyal would allow him to sit in his dressing room, that was when he saw the Ringmaster *really* at work. One by one, each of the acts would come in procession for benediction or beration. And, one by one, they bowed their heads and listened to what Loyal had to say as he reclined in his chair and cradled a glass of rotgut, still caked in the dust and greasepaint of the evening. It was Franklin's favourite part of the day, watching Loyal pass judgement on the performance, and Loyal indulged him; letting Franklin crawl behind his chair, opening the trunk full of costumes for him to play with—and, as he grew older, giving him the task of pouring his drink.

However, for all that Loyal indulged him, Franklin was never allowed to touch the box on the dressing table.

It was a square box carved from heavy, dark wood and its hinges — once silver — had tarnished to a dingy greenish grey. There was only one key to the lock: the one Loyal kept on a chain around his neck. Over the years, Franklin wondered what could be in the box, and at first he thought it might be a gun, a knife — something dangerous and valuable. As time passed and Loyal's shock of black hair faded to grey, he began to suspect it was nothing more than his prized chewing tobacco and a handful of old photographs . . . pictures, perhaps, of the man he had been before he had become Monsieur Loyal.

Franklin had been sixteen when, the night's show done, Loyal explained it: that no man is born Loyal; that the name belongs to the circus and only to the circus. It is the name the Ringmaster takes when he becomes the face of the circus, for better or worse. "There's a weight to it, you see. You have to know the circus, to know it without seeing. You have to *feel* it," he said, breathing bourbon and sawdust at Franklin from beneath his hat. "If Loyal fails, the circus fails. And if the circus fails . . . " He held up his hands.

And that was how Franklin's apprenticeship began. From that night on, he clung to Loyal like a shadow: he followed him across the pitches, half-skipping to keep pace with the taller man's stride. He slept on a mattress on the floor outside Loyal's compartment on the train as it hurtled from one town to the next, lulled by the sound of the tracks and the Ringmaster's snores. He polished his boots, and brushed the silk of his top-hat until it glowed. He watched the way Loyal moved in the ring: how the slightest gesture would draw the crowd's eyes one way or another, to accent or to distract. He would stare at himself in the mirror, mouthing the same words every night, hoping to find the same grace and power in his own voice as that in Loyal's.

"Ladies and gentlemen! Boys and girls! Children of all ages . . . "

By eighteen, Franklin was as good a roustabout as any. He knew his way around the circus better than anyone (except, perhaps Loyal himself, whose hair by now was the shade of snow kicked from the kerb). He could do everything that the Ringmaster should do, and more.

It was the night of his nineteenth birthday, and he knew the time had come. For weeks, Loyal had been slipping away. The giant man was now shrunken and weak, his great voice reduced to a whisper. From his mattress on the floor of the train, Franklin heard him coughing through the night and understood. Loyal was dying.

But Loyal never dies.

The night of his nineteenth birthday, and already he knew. After the show, when the audience was nothing but an echo in the air, the circus would come together in the ring for Franklin's death, and Loyal's birth.

And in the meantime, Franklin would sit and hand out tickets.

He never enjoyed working the ticket booth. It took him away from the circus; pushed him out onto the edge, far away from the life of the Big Top. Out here there was nothing but darkness. Nothing but strangers and headlights and slips of paper they could trade for a look at his world. It was cold and lonely, until he saw *her*.

She looked like Snow White. Long, dark hair and lips as soft and red as petals. She stood behind the others, a crowd of seven or eight of them all bundled together — come straight from the football field for a night at the circus; piling into cars in a tangle of laughter to come here. To his circus, or as good as. He took their money and passed them their tickets — but still she hung back. Her eyes met his through the glass screen, and he knew she felt it too. She *had* to. How could she not feel the ground beneath them as it tipped and turned? How could she not see the light growing brighter, the dark growing deeper? How could she not catch the scent of fresh sawdust and candy apples on the air where before there was nothing? They looked at each other through the screen . . . and she smiled, and then she was gone, her hand twined into another man's.

Franklin shook his head, tossing the money into the cashbox. He didn't see the girl look back at him, nor did he see her pull her hand away from the one who held it. By the time he did look up, the group had ducked into the tent and were hidden inside the warm folds of the canvas.

Time ticked on. Loyal's last show was entirely without incident, and none of the audience knew that they were watching the passing of a master; of a Ringmaster. As the crowd cleared, Franklin watched for her—the girl, Snow White—but he didn't see her again. His heart sank as he realised he must have missed her, but it was too late now. She was gone.

The crowd had left. There was only the circus left. Only the circus.

He locked the ticket booth behind him and started his walk across the field to the Big Top. The clowns were waiting for him, still wearing their face-paint, smudged now and running; blurring their features in the gloom. They were a guard of honour leading to the canvas and beyond, to the ring. A guard of honour that closed behind him and turned their backs on the rest of the world. Pushing the canvas aside, Franklin stepped into the tent.

Loyal was waiting for him in the ring. He was sitting on one of the lion tamer's stools, his back straight and his hands resting easily on his knees—and for a second, Franklin saw the Loyal he knew, the Loyal through whose dressing room he had crawled so many times. But then something happened: a shift in the light, perhaps, and Loyal was no more than a hunched old man in a black silk top hat, a man whose health was fading. Already the rust had begun to nibble at the edges of the circus; the guy ropes were fraying and the holes in the tent would not stay patched. The Ringmaster was failing. The circus would follow.

There were others in the ring with Loyal: behind him, the Strong Man and the Painted Lady watched Franklin with serious faces. Marcus, the Clown-King, rested his hand on Loyal's shoulder while tiny Lucinda, the girl who danced on the horses' backs, sat at his feet and leaned her head against his knee.

Franklin barely saw them.

He saw the box. Loyal's box, on a rickety wooden table which stood in the centre of the ring.

The key was in the lock.

As he stepped into the ring, Loyal rose to greet him — more slowly than he once had.

"My boy."

"Monsieur Loyal."

"Not for much longer. But you know that better than any of them, I think." He clapped his hand on Franklin's shoulder. "Come. Walk with me. There are things which must be said, choices which must be made."

"You know I've made my choice. I — "

"Allow an old man to be heard one last time, boy. You were always so keen! No-one keener, I'd wager: not even me, when I was young." Loyal chuckled quietly. "Oh, yes. I was just like you. I knew what I wanted, knew where I'd find it. My mother, she did not ... understand."

They were walking now, arm in arm around the ring. The others watched from the middle where Loyal had left them.

"I left. More precisely, I ran away. Barely twelve, I was, when I came to the circus. And now ... " He broke off and Franklin tried to read his face — but it was lost in the dark beneath his hat.

"Forgive me, Franklin. I have allowed you to grow into this life. Perhaps I've damned you." He sounded troubled.

Franklin shook his head. "How can you say that? The circus is ... "

"Everything to you? Yes. Everything and more." They had completed their circuit of the ring now, and Loyal was steering them towards the table. His arm around Franklin's shoulder felt heavier and harder than any arm should.

There was something on the table beside the box. Franklin couldn't quite make it out, but it was long, and thin. Wooden ...

"It takes so much. I told you once: it's a great weight, being the face of the circus. So much rides on the Master of the Rings. So much. The circus: she demands it. And I allowed you to dance after me into damnation without ever once questioning what it is that she will take from you."

Franklin felt a surge of panic. Was Loyal changing his mind? Now, of all times? "Monsieur, you know how much this means to me — how much it's always meant. It's my life . . . "

"And she might well be. But Loyal is hers." Loyal stopped in front of the table.

It was a knife. Beside the box. A knife: its blade thin and slick and whisper-sharp; its wooden handle stained with age — just like the wood of the box. And for the first time, Franklin's growing unease began to taste like fear. He looked again at Loyal, who only nodded. "Open the box, boy. See what the circus will take to make you hers."

Franklin's fingers closed around the key and he hoped that no-one could see him trembling. It turned, the latch popping open with well-oiled ease. All he had to do was to lift the lid.

"You could be the greatest Loyal the world has ever seen," Loyal said, seeing him hesitate. "But you must know what it is that the circus asks of you."

Franklin felt the world contract around him in a rush. There was nothing else, nothing beyond the walls of the tent. He felt the breeze that swam along the canvas, he smelled the sweat and the sawdust on the air. There was nothing beyond the ring. And he would be its master.

He opened the box.

At first, he could see nothing inside . . . and then, as though it rose out of dark water, he saw it. A patch of pale surrounded by black velvet; blue jewels at its heart. It drew closer and closer, clearer and clearer . . . and he felt the bile rise in his throat. His heart crashed against the bars of his ribs as the world grew ever smaller and all the air was sucked out of it. There was nothing now but Loyal and his box.

He stumbled back and must have tripped or lost his balance, his legs turning to mist beneath him, as he was suddenly on the sawdust, looking up. Loyal loomed above him, raising his hand to his hat — and even though Franklin scrabbled with his hands and his feet to put distance between them, still Loyal stood over him, close enough to whisper. Franklin shook his head, mute, his mouth hanging open as Loyal swept off his hat . . . *and the Ringmaster had no face.*

There was nothing there, beneath the shadows of hat brim — nothing more than a mask made of greasepaint and Franklin's own admiration. The white paint, streaked now, hung in mid-air above Loyal's collar. Even his eyes were an illusion: how could they be anything else, when his real eyes lay in the box — when they had blinked up at him from the blackness inside? And blinked they had; he was sure of it. Franklin would have staked his soul on it at that moment, that when he looked inside Loyal's box and realised what it contained, the face within had smiled.

"Now you know what she asks, my boy. To be Loyal, you must give her all she asks . . . "

Franklin didn't understand how Loyal could speak. There were no lips to form the words, no tongue . . . but speak he did, and all Franklin wanted to do was to run. So that's what he did; his arms and legs windmilling wildly as he ran for the canvas. And the others . . . they followed. Chased him as Loyal stood in the ring at the heart of the circus and laughed and laughed and laughed.

The opening to the tent had been closed: the lacing pulled tight. There was no way out there. In desperation, Franklin dropped to his knees and hauled at the bottom edge of the canvas, heaving it over his shoulders. It weighed more than it had any right to, but he wriggled and slid his body forward, inching beneath it and out into the cool night air — and he was almost free when a hand clasped around his ankle. With a shout, he kicked back as hard as he could — all the time thinking of the face in the box and the long, sharp knife beside it. Moments passed: moments which felt like forever, and then he was free, dragging his feet clear of the canvas and running, stumbling . . . wildly, blindly tumbling through the field and clear of the tents and the booths and the animal pens. Away from the life he had known, the future he'd thought he wanted. Away from the circus and Loyal and the black top hat that shone in the lights and hid an emptiness with its shadow.

He ran into the darkness.

And he ran.

And he ran.

And then there were lights and a high-pitched howl, and a scream. A solid, meaty sound, and a sudden pain. Then nothing.

అఅ

When he opened his eyes, the first thing he saw was Snow White, eating an apple.

Not Snow White.

The girl. The girl from the circus.

The circus . . .

He sat upright so fast that a thin grey veil slipped across his vision and his ears rang. Hands on his shoulders guided him back down onto the bed just as he faded out again.

The next time he opened his eyes, she was gone. There was only an empty chair beside his bed. He stared at it for a moment, as though staring might make her materialise. A magic trick of sorts.

She did not appear. He passed out again.

They told him, when his fever finally broke, that he had spent three days that way: waking and sleeping and wandering the space between the two—and talking of the man who had no face. "They" were the Whittles, and Snow White was their daughter, Jenny. It was her friend, Max, who was driving the car he had run out in front of, his face as white as death and his eyes already rolling in their sockets. Max had swerved, turned the car off the road and—by only clipping Franklin as he came from nowhere in the dark—had saved him. The same could not be said for the car.

Franklin had three broken ribs and a cracked hip, among other things, and would walk with a limp for the rest of his life. The Whittles took him in and cared for him, fed him and put a roof over his head. As he healed, he did what he could to help them—he groomed the horses, he fed the chickens; he peeled potatoes and scrubbed floors and helped with the harvest as best as he could. And as the spring turned to summer, which turned to autumn, he came to love pretty Jenny Whittle more than he had loved anything in his life . . . and the circus was all but forgotten until the day the flyers appeared.

It was not his circus, of course. How could it have been? Months had passed since that night. This one was nothing but a pale imitation: a single ring filled with piss-soaked sawdust and shabby costumes. The ringmaster wore a gaudy waistcoat that glittered as it caught the light, but he was not a Loyal: there was no grace to him, no presence, no *command*.

The Whittles chattered amongst themselves as they left the tent; their eyes ablaze with fire and wonder—but Franklin did not say a word. His heart felt suddenly empty, and although he saw Jenny looking back at him, he felt completely alone. He did not know that Jenny's hand was reaching for his—or perhaps he did not care—but when her fingers were within a heartbeat of his, he snatched his hand away and thrust it into his pocket.

She curled her fingers in on her palm and didn't say a word.

It was soon after the trip to the circus that Max began to call at the house. It had taken time, but he had mended his car, and he would take Jenny out driving in the gathering dusk. Franklin was never invited.

Something changed, right around then. Whether it was the Whittles, or whether it was Franklin himself was hard to say. But a chill settled between them: the little family with their happy daughter, and the quiet young man they had accepted as one of their own. Max called him "cuckoo-boy", and Jenny giggled behind her hand, and still Franklin stayed until the day that Jenny came home with a smile on her face and a ring on her finger.

Franklin slipped out of the back door without so much as a goodbye—walking off into the world with only the clothes on his back.

క్రు-్ర

He found the circus where he had left it—and although he had passed that empty field a hundred times and more, the tents were pitched as though he had never been away, as though no time had passed at all.

And yet . . . the circus that waited for him was only a shell. There were tents, yes—but no people. No animals. No music; none of the scents or sounds that make the magic of the circus.

The circus was dead and he wandered its corpse, looking for answers. He found none until he entered the Big Top. There, in the centre of the ring, was the table. And on it, the knife and the box, the key still in the lock. His stomach churned at the memory of it.

But something was different. Loyal's stool was empty now, save for a black silk top hat.

So it was true. Loyal was dead, and the circus with him.

Franklin was about to pick up the hat when he heard it: a faint whisper of music. He cocked his head to one side, and caught it again—the sound of a barrel organ. He turned, about to go searching for its source, and as he did so he saw the cat.

It had not been there when he came in: he was sure of that much, but now it sat almost directly behind him with its paws folded neatly beneath it, watching him with one clear eye, one milky. As soon as it was sure it had his attention, it yawned and stretched, then sashayed towards the curtain that led backstage. He watched it go—but as it reached the edge of the ring, it stopped and looked back at him, and Franklin knew he was meant to follow it. So he did.

Behind the curtain, everything was just as he remembered: the crates of equipment, the discarded costumes flung over chairs. The water for the animals. The shotgun for the lions. But still there were no people. The cat wove between the stacks of detritus to the furthest edge of the tent where the crates were stacked four or five rows deep. There were no markings on them, and the lids were sealed tight, giving no clue as to what they contained. They were simply wooden crates, perhaps half as high as a man and as wide again.

The cat hopped onto the lowest stack and sat, folding its tail around its feet. It made a knowing "mew" sound and blinked at him.

"What? You want me to open it?"

"Mew."

"Sure." Franklin shook his head and smiled. "They leave your food in there or something?"

"Mew."

"You're a chatty little thing," he said as he scratched it behind one of its ears. It purred loudly and leaned into his hand.

"Don't suppose you know where to find a crowbar . . . "

"Mew." The little cat hopped straight down from its perch and padded round the corner of the crate, disappearing into the dark. With a laugh, Franklin stuck his head around after it, and was only half-surprised to find it standing next to a crowbar. A hammer and a handful of nails lay scattered on the ground next to it, along with what looked like packing straw.

"Well, now. I'll be damned." Franklin picked up the crowbar and passed it from hand to hand, testing its weight.

With the cat following him closely, he moved back around to the front of the crate. The end of the crowbar slid under the edge of the lid and Franklin heaved . . .

The lid popped open with no protest, tightly-packed straw spilling from the open top. The cat circled his feet, purring, and Franklin was hit by the sudden urge to walk away. To leave the circus as he had found it — empty and rotten and lost. But the crate was open, and it would take no more than a moment . . .

His hands were clearing the straw before he knew what they were doing.

There, in the box, lay the Painted Lady. And beside her, Lucinda the horse-runner. And Marcus the Clown-King . . . all of them, folded in on one another like puppets. As though they were coats packed away for the winter, waiting for a body to fill them again.

Waiting.

Waiting for him.

Franklin opened another case, and another, and another. They were all the same: filled with faces he knew, people he recognised. All of the circus save one.

And there, surrounded by packing straw and with the strange little cat rubbing at his feet, he knew.

He was always meant to be the Ringmaster, and the circus knew it too. That's why it had waited.

His steps had purpose as he made his way back to the ring. He had been wrong, that night. He had not understood. When he had seen Loyal's face — his real face — he thought the circus would take his away, but that wasn't it at all. The circus was offering him a new one instead; she would *give* him a face. The face she needed him to have. There was nothing beneath Loyal's hat because he had no need of it: his shining black hat and his coat the colour of broken hearts were the only face he would ever wear.

The cat was still beside him as he reached the table, always beside him. Even as he pulled up the stool, the cat was there, watching. His hands were steady as he turned the key in the lock and this time he did not hesitate.

The box was empty and Franklin picked up the knife... but it was Loyal who set it down again: set it down and, fingers still tacky with blood, lifted the top hat and placed it upon his head.

Escardy Gap

PETER CROWTHER & JAMES LOVEGROVE

Clem Stimpson reached for his bottle of Jack Daniel's. Numbly he unscrewed the cap and brought the neck of the bottle up to his mouth. The whites of his eyes were crazed with blood vessels and flecked with chips of yellow. The scrub of stubble around his jaw and chin glistened with raindrops, spittle, and spilled whisky. His wet clothes sagged limply off of him, as if his body had shrunk dramatically overnight. He stank like an outhouse in high summer. The rain had tried to wash away the smell, but it had its work cut out for it, what with the booze breath, the body odor ingrained into the fabric of his clothing, and the dried boy-gore spattering his boots.

"Oh, yeah!" said Clem as the liquor hit his belly and danced a soft-shoe shuffle all around his innards. "Oh, boy, that's better."

Clem was sheltering in the waiting room of the railway station. The entire day had passed in a garish, phantasmagorical haze, images of blood and trees and severed heads flitting madly batlike through his head as he staggered from street to street beneath the beating heat of the sun. In Poacher's Park he had briefly come to his senses, enough to recover from his secret hiding place in the bandstand the two emergency bottles he had purchased with the last of his week's welfare money, and then he had sat there and he had drunk and drunk until he was drunker than drunk, so drunk he was in danger of going right through to the other side and becoming sober again.

When the storm had started to brew, his first instinct had been to find shelter and warmth. He had tried the Bar & Grill (closed), then the Merrie Malted (also closed), then the library (closed on Sundays), then the Reverend King's chapel (locked). Then, beginning to panic, he had hurried over to Belvedere Way, where his one and perhaps only friend, Walt Donaldson, lived. But there had been nobody home. Clem had swung and swung the knocker as though he meant to smash a hole in the door. Not a peep from inside. Not even a tirade from Miss Ohllson. He had tried the handle. Locked. Just his luck that the Ohllson woman was the only person in Escardy Gap who locked the damn front door.

Clem had been getting pretty desperate by the time he reached the station. The first fat raindrops had been splashing down, darkening the road dust. The thunder had been cackling and crackling right overhead. Casting a last glance up at the glowering sky, he had darted inside like a hunted animal going to earth.

It was dark in here, and drafty because there were no doors, only wide-open entrances, and Clem was hunkered down on one of the benches, shivering, hugging his legs to his chest for warmth and cuddling the bottle at his crotch. It had just turned six, according to the clock that he could see through the window that gave onto the platform. The hands divided the face into two semicircles. Beyond the platform awning the rain streamed down in a shimmering curtain, the over-flowing gullies spilling their loads in long trickles and loud spatters.

Tonight, it seemed, the whole world was trying to drown its sorrows along with him.

Clem had an abhorrence of water in any shape or form: water in baths, water in drinks, water from the sky—he particularly loathed water from the sky. When you didn't have a roof regularly over your head, the last thing you wanted was Mother Nature reminding you of that fact, soaking you to the skin, trying to give you pneumonia and bronchitis and God knows what else.

He sneered and cursed the rain, and took another slug of Jack Daniel's. Then, in a rare fit of self-denial, he screwed the cap back on. The bottle was two-thirds empty and would have to last the whole night—

CRACK THERRUMPH!!!

"Jesus H. Christ!" Clem hissed, flinching. There hadn't been a storm like this since longer than he could remember. Which wasn't all that long, owing to the parlous state of his memory cells. All over Escardy Gap, however, people with better memories than Clem Stimpson were coming to the same conclusion. These people—good people, concerned people, worried people, even frightened people, people cowering in their living rooms and dens, people huddling in loved ones' embraces and people soothing alarmed toddlers—kept casting upward glances and wondering out loud if anyone could recall a storm quite like this one, lightning quite so bright, thunder quite so terrible. The suddenness and ferocity of it had caught everyone by surprise. This, coupled with the suspicions and rumors that were flying around, the reports of peculiar disappearances, the firsthand and secondhand accounts of murders, the silence in certain neighboring houses, and the presence of the strangers who had threaded themselves into the community, latching on like some kind of parasitic virus, led these people to fear not just for their lives but for the continued existence of everything they held dear and true.

From the platform entrance to the waiting room there came a loud throat-clearing, a voluble and peremptory "Har-rumph!"

Clem nearly redecorated the interior of his pants.

The figure standing there was tall and lean and silhouetted in black. He had his hands on his hips and from the angle of his hatted head Clem could tell the man was looking right at him. Clem lost his grip on the bottle. It slithered from his grasp, down his chest, to land unbroken on the bench. From there—cruel irony—it rolled onto the floor, where it shattered.

Clem didn't notice, didn't care, didn't think he would ever have need for a bottle of anything ever again.

For Death was standing in the doorway.

Death had come for him.

A split-second blitz of lightning lit up the angular contours of Death's face, throwing knife-shaped nose and sickle smile into sharp relief. Then the face was lost in darkness again, and from the aftermath of the ensuing *CRACK THERRUMPH!* Death's voice emerged, low and precise and ringing out as clear as a knell.

"You're not supposed to be here," Death said. "No one's supposed to be here. Haven't you a home to go to?"

"N-n-no," said Clem.

"Ah, it's Stimpson, isn't it?" said Death. "Very much the wild rover you are, Clem, old fellow. Here one moment, somewhere else the next. Such an irritating habit. I like to know where people are. It makes everything so much less complicated. I like people to be in places and stay there."

"P-please leave me alone. I ain't done nothing."

"A common cry," said Death. "'I ain't done nothing so I don't deserve nothing to be done to me.' Of course 'I ain't done nothing' means quite the opposite from what you intend it to mean. Those double negatives can be so-o-o tricky, can't they?"

"But I ain't ready yet. Please don't take me."

"Take you? What would I want to take you *for*, Clem? And *where* would I take you?"

"Please. I don't want to die."

"Naturally you don't. Few of us do. But Death comes for all of us in the end, Clem. Whether we like it or not, he swoops down and plucks us up from the ground in his talons and carries us off to the Forever Hereafter. You should learn not to fear him. Learn to appreciate him. Learn to *love* him. That way, when he comes for you, it won't be a parting, but a meeting."

Death strode into the waiting room, the swish of his clothing like a scythe cropping through good corn. Clem scuttled backward along the bench until his shoulder blades met wall and he could go no further. Death came to a halt. Lightning fluttered in his eyes, two tiny flames dancing in the abyss. *CRACK THERRUMPH!*

"Oh, good God, oh, sweet Jesus . . ." murmured Clem. "Don't ask *them* for help, Clem," Death advised. "They've got better things to do than waste time on a miserable sinner like you. They've got holy men and saints and nuns and monks to look after. Do you fall into any of those categories? Heavens, no, Clem. You're a disgrace. You're a walking, shambling pile of shame. You're Escardy Gap's greatest embarrassment. All those fine upstanding people just look the other way when they see you come staggering toward them, don't they? Just turn up their noses and pretend you don't exist. But you do! Oh, you do! And how marvelous that you *do*! You've spent your life reminding them that this is what they could become, these are the depths to which they could descend, should things go wrong, should the Good Lord turn a blind eye for a moment, should His grip on them slacken. In a way, you know, I admire you, Clem Stimpson."

Through the fog, understanding dawned. "You . . . you ain't Death!" Clem exclaimed. Then, less sure: "Are you?"

"In a sense, yes. In a sense, no," said Jeremiah Rackstraw (for it was he). "Death and I have what you might call an arrangement. I'm certainly a major contributor to Death's fund. However, I can assure you I didn't come here to kill you, Clem."

"Oh, praise be." Relief came over Clem in cooling waves, and he offered up a short vote of thanks to whichever lucky star had smiled on him today.

"No," said Rackstraw, "that sordid little task I will leave to others." He found a switch and illuminated the two overhead bulbs that hung unshaded from the ceiling on lengths of cord. Clem was dazzled.

Hitching up his pants so as not to ruin the creases, Rackstraw sat down on the bench beside Clem. He doffed Grampa's hat and smoothed his dark hair into place. "Honestly, Clem," he said, "I meant it just now when I told you I admired you. I do. You've been a perpetual thorn in Escardy Gap's side, a permanent blot on the landscape. Some say that beauty can be gauged only by contrasting it with ugliness. You are the imperfection, Clem, that makes Escardy Gap all the more beautiful. The mole on Marie Antoinette's cheek. It's not a desirable role by any means, not one anybody would willingly have played, but you took it on nevertheless, Clem, and you have played it to the hilt. For that, I think, you deserve some kind of reward."

"Reward?"

"Reward. Clem Stimpson, what you are about to see is a rare behind-the-scenes glimpse of the Company. It will also be the last thing you ever see, but, honestly, what a way to go!" A thrill shivered through the last five words. "I hope you appreciate the honor I am conferring on you, Clem. I hope you will be properly grateful, and show that gratitude by not struggling or resisting when the time of your death comes." Dumbly, Clem Stimpson nodded.

"Then sit back!" said Jeremiah Rackstraw cheerfully. "Relax! Make yourself comfortable! And let this little sideshow commence."

~~~

A few minutes later, they began to arrive.

Mr. Olesqui was first, coming through the entrance in a whirl of pipe smoke. This smoke cloud had surrounded him all the way across town from the Chisholms' residence on Furnival Street. It had kept him completely dry, deflecting the rain as efficiently as any umbrella.

Mr. Olesqui bowed to Rackstraw and passed through to the platform. Rackstraw turned to Clem and told him the midget's name and described his penchant for a particular kind of tobacco grown only on the slopes of a certain remote mountain in Peru, the soil of which local tribesmen fertilized once a month with semen and menstrual blood, thereby imbuing it with magical properties. Clem nodded his head without taking any of this in.

Then came the Boy. He was not wearing his gloves. Where his hands should have been there was a lambent glow that sometimes took the shape of hands and sometimes transformed into hideous malformities. The Boy fascinated himself with these creations. Without even acknowledging the presence or existence of anyone else, he passed through the waiting room.

"A princeling," Rackstraw explained. "Although his ancestry is not entirely clear, it is believed that his grandfather or great-grandfather is none other than the Count of the Undead."

"Um, yeah," said Clem.

"He was born without hands. In their place there are two fields of eldritch energy. No one is exactly sure how they work, but it seems they have the ability to twist and alter reality. They can make new the old, make old the new, bring chaos to order."

Zzzzzzap!

Thus did Buzz Beaumont signal his arrival, accompanied by an almighty flash, a hail of sparks, and the smell of ozone.

He stood there, blue fireballs whizzing up and down the length of his solenoid suit, a halo of flickering blue sizzling around him like St. Elmo's fire. When he spoke, Clem saw miniature arcs of blue light leaping across the back of his mouth from molar to molar.

"My kinda weather!" Buzz informed Rackstraw.

"I'm very happy for you," replied Rackstraw. "A showman born and bred," he whispered aside to Clem. "His act was banned in several states after spectators began to be killed accidentally. Accidentally!" he repeated with a wink and a nudge.

After Buzz came Agnes Destiny, clad shambolically in items of clothing pilfered from Hannah Marrs's closets and chests of drawers. She threw Rackstraw a contemptuous look and waltzed haughtily past, trailing several limp phalli along the floor behind her.

Rackstraw nudged Clem and said, "The lady is a tramp."

Next up was Walt Donaldson.

Clem gasped. "Walt?" he said. "Walt, old buddy, what are *you* doing here?"

Walt didn't even glance at Clem. He crossed the waiting room, and as he did so his body began to thin. He began to shrink. He began to change. Clothing, hair, eyes, nose, mouth, all shifted fluently, until, by the time he had reached the entrance to the platform, Walt Donaldson was no more and in his place strode Ingrid Ohllson.

Clem gulped hard, then turned to Rackstraw. "That wasn't Walt, was it?" he said, and an amused Rackstraw gently shook his head.

"There aren't many of Clarence's kind left in the world," he said. "Most of his race have made one change too many and have forgotten who they really are. Now they lead lives as boring animals or ordinary humans, in forests and towns, working and playing, melding in with their surroundings. It's really rather tragic."

Now Felcher ran in, dripping wet, puffing and panting, his bottles glittering and chinking around him. He stood there shaking the water from his hair, cursing the weather and cursing God and cursing Escardy Gap hardest of all. He uncapped one of his little bottles and took a restorative sip.

"Felcher," said Rackstraw, and indicated Clem. "Our friend here is also something of a connoisseur of intoxicating beverages. Perhaps? . . . "

Felcher regarded Clem with what can only be described as naked contempt and reluctantly proffered him the bottle. Clem hesitated before accepting. He sniffed the chalky white liquid inside. It smelled of things he vaguely remembered, things from distant days, faded souvenirs from the far-flung country of the past: a hint of aniseed, a tinge of sarsaparilla, a touch of vanilla, a notion of bubblegum, a wisp of cotton candy, a suggestion of peppermint, a proposition of popcorn, a soupçon of buttermilk, a shade of chocolate, a tincture of cough linctus, a breath of lemonade, and much more besides.

Clem only pretended to take a sip, then handed the bottle back. He vowed right there and then that if he ever got out of this alive, he would never touch a drop of the hard stuff again. Oh, no. From this day on — should the Lord see fit to preserve him — it would be milk and orange juice for Clem Stimpson.

Felcher grouched and grumbled off, joining the others on the platform beneath the awning.

"Memories are the grape and grain," said Rackstraw, "from which he distills his exotic concoctions."

A large fly came fizzing through the open doorway, swerved sideways and buffeted against the bulletin board with a mildly metallic clonk. Before Clem's very, very startled eyes, the fly assumed human shape, its jeweled joints lengthening into limbs, its muscid body becoming muscle and bone, its fly features flowering forth into a face.

"Jeremiah Rackstraw!" cried Neville N. Nolan. "Joyous rapture! Genial regards! Genuine respect!"

"Nice of you to notice me, Neville."

"Notice? Nothing is nimble enough to evade my eye."

"And you've done your job right, I trust."

"Job right, Jeremiah Rackstraw? How arrogant of you to ask! Big Ben is a burden no more. Earl Evett has entered the eternal ever-after. Both men have met their Maker."

"Brilliant. Excellent."

Neville N. Nolan and Jeremiah Rackstraw exchanged a few more purple pleasantries, and then the werefly walked through to the platform.

Clem hadn't followed a word that was said, and figured these guys were talking in some kind of fancy code known only to members of the Company. "Is that it?" he asked Rackstraw.

"Oh, no," came the reply.

Clem didn't know whether to be glad or worried. And on and on they came, the storm announcing each new arrival with a thunderous drumroll.

Most of them Clem recognized. He had seen them come out of the carriages of the train yesterday. He did not know their names or anything about them, but Rackstraw conscientiously filled him in.

Here was Mort Carroway, a cadaverous anatomy of a man with a fondness for creeping through small holes, penetrating crevices, lurking in crawl spaces, and lingering in crannies, watching through knotholes, spying through cracks, and seeing everything.

CRACK THERRUMPH!!!

Here was Gypsy Zelda, headscarved and hoop-earringed, who made predictions of imminent mortality which, strangely enough, always proved true.

CRACK THERRUMPH!!!

Here was a man known only as the Mayfly, who had over the past twenty-four hours forcibly impregnated three of Escardy Gap's youngest and prettiest females. The seed of his loins, Rackstraw explained to Clem with a zestful smacking of lips, had the unusual characteristic of growing to full size within a matter of minutes, and then eating its way out, and then, alas, dying on contact with air. The Mayfly was in many ways a tragic figure, a desperate philoprogenitive who could never father any offspring that lasted for more than a few precious moments. The Mayfly's eyes were red and swollen from crying.

CRACK THERRUMPH!!!

And this was the diabolical Nick St. Nicholas, who wasn't interested in bargaining for your soul as long as he could control your body for an hour or so and have you perform acts of self-mutilation, which he watched with childish, demonic, cackling glee.

CRACK THERRUMPH!!!

And the Crone, an awesomely wrinkled hag who always carried a spare set of lovingly tooled and sharpened dentures for those awkward meals, the ones that involved biting through living flesh and bone.

CRACK THERRUMPH!!!

And Dr. Canker, who had once been a real doctor, and still made housecalls, leaving each home with the heavy slopping carpetbag he toted a few growths and tumors lighter.

CRACK THERRUMPH!!!

And Titus Nonesuch, an expert with pencil and ink brush, the artist responsible for the playbills all over town, who had drawn Andy Gallagher into his own version of an EC Comics horror anthology and had flipped the young fellow from story to story, making sure he met with a grisly end in the closing panel of each.

And on and on they came.

And Clem watched this parade of human and not-so-human monsters pass by, and he listened to Rackstraw's brief descriptions of their needs and deeds, and he grew numb, and number, and number still.

"And that," Rackstraw said finally, dusting off his palms, "is everybody. Come on, Clem. There's one last thing you ought to see."

Clem let himself be helped to his feet and ushered out onto the platform, pliable as an etherized patient.

The gathered Company were chatting idly to one another, comparing notes. Through the plummet of rain and ripples of thunder Clem caught snatches of their conversations.

". . . their screams, music to my ears . . . "

". . . down and down, like a shower of red petals . . . "

". . . and he said to me, 'That's a funny pouch you've got yourself there'. . . "

". . . tasted good, if a little too sweet for my palate . . . "

". . . job's worth doing, it's worth doing well . . . "

". . . was, I may say, a moment of egregious ecstasy and eternal embarrassment . . . "

". . . David Copperfield . . . "

". . . made 'em sing, made 'em dance, made 'em pop their fingernails back one by one . . . "

". . . boiled his eyeballs in their sockets like hard-boiled eggs . . . "

". . . baked a fine pecan pie, though . . . "

". . . heh heh heh . . . "

". . . my sweet children, my poor little babies . . . "

". . . lamb to the slaughter. . . "

". . . blood . . . "

". . . vomit . . . "

". . . strings of intestine . . . "

". . . Freaks . . . "

". . . waited for them to die before I closed them up again . . . "

". . . there's nothing nasty about cancer cells, they're just cells that grow too well . . . "

". . . *lead* the way, ho ho! . . . "

Leading Clem away from the hubbub, Rackstraw said, "Our Angel should be arriving shortly. Really, Clem, you are the most privileged man I know. I can't remember when was the last time that one of our victims actually got to meet our Angel."

Angel? Was he saying something about an angel? It didn't make any sense to Clem. He thought these people must be in league with the devil, not with an angel. It must be said, though, that right then nothing much was making any sense to Clem.

Rackstraw led him right to the edge of the platform. He turned and peered along the track, trying to discern movement through the rain. Finally he said, "Ah. Here we are."

There was a short, shrill scream. The tracks began to whine on their ties. Clem heard a huffing and puffing, a laborious clanking and churning. Then he became aware of a huge shape moving through the air toward them, silhouetted in the rain. Gradually it came closer, the huffing and puffing and clanking and churning grew louder, and the air was filled with a fizzing noise—the sound of raindrops striking piping-hot metal and turning to steam.

The train drew up to the platform and squealed to a halt. The three women Clem remembered from yesterday danced over the boiler, their hair plastered down in tangled rattails and their gossamer gowns clinging wetly to their bodies to reveal everything beneath—*everything*—in pornographic detail, from the pink concentric O's of their nipples to the dark pubic triangles at the base of their taut bellies. Their triple chitter-clack was audible above the rain, above even the thunder.

The carriage doors flew open, but nobody made a move to climb in. Clem became aware that a hush had fallen over the assembled Company. They were no longer talking to each other. A quick look over his shoulder confirmed his worst suspicions. They were watching him. Every pair of eyes was trained on him.

"Uh, Mr. Rackstraw... What happens now?"

"Now, Clem," said Rackstraw, laying a gentle hand on Clem's neck, "you die."

"Oh, p-please, Mr. Rackstraw! Please! I ain't ready. I ain't ready to die. I've got a few good years left in me. A *lotta* good years. I swear I'll be a better person from now on. I swear it! Won't drink, won't cuss, won't look at ladies in a bad way—"

174

"Clem," said Rackstraw, shaking his head sadly. "Clem, if I had a heart, it would be touched. It might even be moved to forgiveness. If I had a merciful bone in my body, I'd let you go, let you run out into the street as free as a bird. But of course, the quality of mercy is something I find a bit of a strain."

Tears spilled down from Clem's yellowy red eyes, seeping into his scrubby beard. He clutched the lapels of Rackstraw's jacket and he begged, he implored the leader of the Company to spare him. Rackstraw merely regarded Clem's grubby mitts with disdain and then plucked them, left, then right, from his lapels.

"It's no use, Clem. Save your tears. Use the last few moments of your life wisely. Make your peace with God, if you have to."

"Ohhhhhh . . . " Clem groaned, and slumped against Rackstraw, a sack of a man. Rackstraw pushed him brusquely away.

Between blubbering sobs Clem managed to ask, "Will it hurt?" Not wanting to hear the reply, he stared miserably down at his boots.

"Yes, it'll hurt, Clem," said Rackstraw. "I cannot tell a lie. It will hurt like hell."

"Can't you make it quick?"

"No, Clem. All the same, I think you'll find your particular death a not altogether unpleasant experience. In fact, the pain will be so intense and dizzying as to be all but indistinguishable from an orgasm."

So saying, Rackstraw stepped back. The Company had formed a tight circle around Clem. Clem's back was to the locomotive, from which were coming deep murmurs and gurgles like the sounds of a digestive system working hard in anticipation of a meal. Clem had always thought he would die alone, silently slip away in the night in an alley somewhere. He didn't think his last moments would be so public, with a ring of onlookers around him, watching, waiting.

Clem glared at them all with his rheumy eyes, a mad dog, a cornered fox. He snarled and spat at them defiantly.

The chitter-clack was coming from right behind his head. With an air of desperate resignation. Clem turned to meet his fate.

175

As if obeying some unspoken cue, the Man-eaters raised their gowns and pulled them neatly over their heads, baring their pale bodies to the rain. The gowns fell in three crumpling piles around Clem's feet.

Clem gawked up at the naked beauty before him. He ran his eyes over each and every inch of those smooth-skinned, light-fleshed frames, his gaze coming to rest at each well-sprung pair of breasts, each scooped navel, each matted pubic thatch—honey brown, bear black, fire red. Clem felt the first stirrings of the lust worm that nestled at his crotch, dormant all these years but welcoming resurrection like a soul on Judgment Day and swelling, steepening, stretching its neck.

"Oh, my sweet Lord . . . " Clem sighed.

He barely listened as Rackstraw spoke to him, telling him about the Man-eaters with the air of a museum curator explaining an exhibit to a gaggle of eager schoolchildren. "Predators since before the dawn of history, men—and I refer directly to the male of the species here— have given women such as these three names like Furies, Fates, Hesperides, maenads, succubae, and many other things besides. Men have always regarded them as the foe and have always been afraid of them, for they represent everything that the masculine sex do not and cannot know, and they wield an influence that holds sway over the very root of a man's being. These three are among perhaps the most fearsomely rapacious examples of the breed, and have been our Angel's guardians and fellow travelers since before even I joined the Company. They are, in a literal sense, Man-eaters."

The women descended from the engine, portions of their flesh jouncing resiliently, exquisitely, and Clem watched them in awe and rapture. They approached him, still chitter-clacking madly, and ran their hands over him, fondling his sodden clothing, stroking his bristly cheeks, gazing at him adoringly, avariciously.

Before Clem realized what they were doing, they had stripped him bare—quickly, dexterously, in fewer movements than he would have thought possible. Gooseflesh puckered all over his bare skin, arching the lank hairs on his chest and forearms. He shivered. He shivered with cold and delight and cold delight. How absurd that he had mistaken the man in the waiting room entrance for Death. Death was quite clearly a lady. Three ladies. Death was a beauty and a delight and a joy.

The Man-eaters caressed him. They brought his penis to twitching tumescence until it felt bigger than a flagpole, bigger than a grain silo, bigger than the whole damn Empire State Building. It felt like a nuclear missile, primed and ready to explode.

Then the three women joined hands and came together, giggling and chitter-clacking. It was then that Clem noticed the way their navels seemed to be moving around, dilating and contracting like . . . well, for all the world like *nostrils*.

Then their nipples opened.

Blinked.

Glistening eyeballs shone.

Three pairs, matching the blue, brown, and green of the eyes of the blond, brunette and redhead.

Eyes, nose . . .

And Clem knew now where that dental chitter-clack was coming from, but somehow that knowledge didn't instill terror in his heart or cause his rivet-hard cock to droop so much as a degree from vertical. Somehow that knowledge filled him with a deeper yearning, a profounder need for the touch and caress and, oh, yes, the sweet sinking into the warmth of these three women. If the Man-eaters had been shallow lagoons with jagged rocks lurking just beneath the surface. Clem would still have wanted nothing on earth so much as to dive into them from a great height.

He spread out his arms. He gave them his body. He surrendered to them willingly.

Some time later — he didn't know how much later — Clem died writhing, his spine arching and his jaw clenched in agony and bliss.

The Circus of Dr Lao

CHARLES G. FINNEY

The widow Mrs. Howard T. Cassan came to the circus in her flimsy brown dress and her low shoes and went direct to the fortune-teller's tent. She paid her mite and sat down to hear of her future. Apollonius warned her she was going to be disappointed.

"Not if you tell me the truth," said Mrs. Cassan. "I particularly want to know how soon oil is going to be found on that twenty acres of mine in New Mexico."

"Never," said the seer.

"Well, then, when shall I be married again?"

"Never," said the seer.

"Very well. What sort of man will next come into my life?"

"There will be no more men in your life," said the seer.

"Well, what in the world is the use of my living then, if I'm not going to be rich, not going to be married again, not going to know any more men?"

"I don't know," confessed the prophet. "I only read futures. I don't evaluate them."

"Well, I paid you. Read my future."

"Tomorrow will be like today, and day after tomorrow will be like the day before yesterday," said Apollonius. "I see your remaining days each as quiet, tedious collections of hours. You will not travel anywhere. You will think no new thoughts. You will experience no new passions. Older you will become but not wiser. Stiffer but not more dignified. Childless you are, and childless you shall remain. Of that suppleness you once commanded in your youth, of that strange simplicity which once attracted a few men to you, neither endures, nor shall you recapture any of them any more. People will talk to you and visit with you out of sentiment or pity, not because you have anything to offer them. Have you ever seen an old cornstalk turning brown, dying, but refusing to fall over, upon which stray birds alight now and then, hardly remarking what it is they perch on? That is you. I cannot fathom your place in life's economy. A living thing should either create or destroy according to its capacity and caprice, but you, you do neither. You only live on dreaming of the nice things you would like to have happen to you but which never happen; and you wonder vaguely why the young lives about you which you occasionally chide for a fancied impropriety never listen to you and seem to flee at your approach. When you die you will be buried and forgotten, and that is all. The morticians will enclose you in a worm-proof casket, thus sealing even unto eternity the clay of your uselessness. And for all the good or evil, creation or destruction, that your living might have accomplished, you might just as well never have lived at all. I cannot see the purpose in such a life. I can see in it only vulgar, shocking waste."

"I thought you said you didn't evaluate lives," snapped Mrs. Cassan.

"I'm not evaluating; I'm only wondering. Now you dream of an oil well to be found on twenty acres of land you own in New Mexico. There is no oil there. You dream of some tall, dark, handsome man to come wooing you. There is no man coming, dark, tall, or otherwise. And yet you will dream on in spite of all I tell you; dream on through your little round of hours, sewing and rocking and gossiping and dreaming; and the world spins and spins and spins. Children are born, grow up, accomplish, sicken, and die; you sit and rock and sew and gossip and live on. And you have a voice in the government, and enough people voting the same way you vote could change the face of the world. There is something terrible in that thought. But your individual opinion on any subject in the world is absolutely worthless. No, I cannot fathom the reason for your existence."

"I didn't pay you to fathom me. Just tell me my future and let it go at that."

"I have been telling you your future! Why don't you listen? Do you want to know how many more times you will eat lettuce or boiled eggs? Shall I enumerate the instances you will yell good-morning to your neighbor across the fence? Must I tell you how many more times you will buy stockings, attend church, go to moving picture shows? Shall I make a list showing how many more gallons of water in the future you will boil making tea, how many more combinations of cards will fall to you at auction bridge, how often the telephone will ring in your remaining years? Do you want to know how many more times you will scold the paper-carrier for not leaving your copy in the spot that irks you least? Must I tell you how many more times you will become annoyed at the weather because it rains or fails to rain according to your wishes? Shall I compute the pounds of pennies you will save shopping at bargain centers? Do you want to know all that? For that is your future, doing the same small futile things you have done for the last fifty-eight years. You face a repetition of your past, a recapitulation of the digits in the adding machine of your days. Save only one bright numeral, perhaps: there was love of a sort in your past; there is none in your future."

"Well, I must say, you are the strangest fortuneteller I ever visited."

"It is my misfortune only to be able to tell the truth."

"Were you ever in love?"

"Of course. But why do you ask?"

"There is a strange fascination about your brutal frankness. I could imagine a girl, or an experienced woman, rather, throwing herself at your feet."

"There was a girl, but she never threw herself at my feet. I threw myself at hers."

"What did she do?"

"She laughed."

"Did she hurt you?"

"Yes. But nothing has hurt me very much since."

"I knew it! I knew a man of your terrible intenseness had been hurt by some woman sometime. Women can do that to a man, can't they?"

"I suppose so."

"You poor, poor man! You are not so very much older than I am, are you? I, too, have been hurt. Why couldn't we be friends, or more than friends, perhaps, and together patch up the torn shreds of our lives? I think I could understand you and comfort you and care for you."

"Madam, I am nearly two thousand years old, and all that time I have been a bachelor. It is too late to start over again."

"Oh, you are being so delightfully foolish! I love whimsical talk! We would get on splendidly, you and I; I am sure of it!"

"I'm not. I told you there were no more men in your life. Don't try to make me eat my own words, please. The consultation is ended. Good afternoon."

She started to say more, but there was no longer anyone to talk to. Apollonius had vanished with that suddenness commanded by only the most practiced magicians. Mrs. Cassan went out into the blaze of sunshine. There she encountered Luther and Kate. It was then precisely ten minutes before Kate's petrification.

"My dear," said Mrs. Cassan to Kate, "that fortuneteller is the most magnetic man I ever met in my whole life. I am going to see him again this evening."

"What did he say about the oil?" asked Luther.

"Oh, he was frightfully encouraging," said Mrs. Cassan.

In the Forest of the Night

PAUL FINCH

"They didn't really care much about animal rights back then,"
Nick Scotney said. "When would it be?... mid-1970s, I
suppose. There was nothing like the regulations governing ownership
of dangerous animals that there are now. Any circus you went to,
there'd be lions, elephants, chimpanzees. God knows what conditions
they were kept in. Can't have been good." That was one of Scotney's
stock-phrases; a euphemism he used often and to great effect.

Can you imagine being sectioned in that loony bin where half the
staff got prosecuted for using iced water and lecky cables to keep
discipline?

"Can't have been good."

What kind of life did that old dear have, you know ... the one they
took out of that ramshackle house, the one whose boils were full of
baby spiders?

"Jeeesus ... can't have been good."

We were all at the rear door of the grey, prefabricated building
which these days housed the little that remained of the *Shirdley Herald*.
Scotney had been on that title longer than the rest of us. Longer than
anyone, in fact. As well as him and me, there was Mandy Jones from
Classifieds and a young lass called Claire who worked in Admin. We
chuffed on our cigs as we watched the rain thrash the car park and the
angled metal roofs of the other buildings occupying our bleak out-of-
town industrial estate.

"What actually happened?" I asked. "This was a famous incident, wasn't it?"

Scotney, who edited our Features section, was a big, burly guy in his fifties. He had craggy brows, limpid blue eyes behind thick spectacles, and a mop of iron-grey curls existing in a state of constant unrest. He gave it some thought. "I suppose it was a famous incident at the time. Got me my first ever front-page. I was only a cub-reporter back then, of course."

That must have seemed a lifetime ago to him. Back when he'd started, newspapers had been the real deal. There'd been no internet to scoop you every time a story broke; no free-sheets to encroach on your advertising revenue. Even a local weekly like the *Herald* had a regular circulation of eighty thousand, and occupied extensive floor-space in a purpose-built town centre facility with its own press-hall and distribution depot. The snappers had had to develop their pictures in dark rooms, rather than email them digitally to the News Desk. The printers had produced perfect pages in hot metal, rather than the reporters having to key their stories direct into predesigned online templates.

The good old days. Or so I'm told.

"To be honest," Scotney added, "it was a shitty time. No-one really gave a crap about anything. I mean that circus . . . the one that caused all the problems; it was like a bunch of hillbillies had rolled into town. The caravans were sheds on wheels. The people running it were real scallies. You could tell that just by talking to them. And like I say, no-one cared. They could have been a bunch of tinkers for all the local authority were interested. They still let them pitch up and put on a so-called show for a few days."

"So what actually happened, Nick?" I asked. You often had to ask him twice. His thoughts tended to wander these days.

He blew a plume of smoke as he recollected the details.

"It all started with the police helicopter. It was pretty unusual back then for the chopper to be out and about. Cost 'em a bloody fortune just to get it in the air. And there was probably only a couple of lads on the whole of Merseyside who were qualified to fly it. So when you heard the chopper, you knew it meant trouble. Especially if it was the middle of the night. Anyway, here's what happened . . . "

῾∞῾

At seventeen, Nick was a sound sleeper. It took the combined drone of rotor blades far overhead and the trilling of the telephone down in the hall to tear him into wakefulness. He lay groggy in his narrow, pitch-dark room, listening to his mam blundering downstairs in her slippers, no doubt fumbling with the buttons on that awful crimplene dressing gown she wore. He hadn't been in the job long, but he was already developing that uncanny journalistic ability to detect a shit-storm even before it appeared over the horizon. He plucked at the toggled string next to his pillow. His beside lamp sprang to life. When he glanced at his watch and saw that it wasn't yet two in the morning, that confirmed it — only *he* was unlucky enough to receive a call at this hour.

"Nick!" his mam said, rapping on the bedroom door. "Mr. Dixon's on the phone. Get down and take it sharpish. First the busies, and now this racket — no-one can sleep."

Len Dixon, or 'Dicko', as he was known behind his back, was the *Herald's* news editor, and a grouchy bewigged old Scouser, who'd moved to Shirdley after getting caught fiddling his exes on the *Echo*.

"Sorry kid," he drawled. Nick could picture him slumped next to the phone in his flat, wreathed in cig smoke, a paper beaker half-filled with Grouse clamped in his nicotine-stained fingers — much the way he sat on the News Desk during the day. "You'll have to cop for this one. No-one else is available."

"Go on," Nick said, blinking the sleep from his eyes, pen at the ready.

"You can hear the chopper going mental up there, yeah?"

"Yeah, I hear it."

"Well listen . . . we've had a raft of calls."

"Paper's gone to bed, hasn't it?" Nick replied. The *Herald* came out Friday afternoons — and this was the wee small hours of Friday morning. Back at the factory, the night-subs should be putting the last touches to it right about now.

"Everything's on hold because this one's too good to miss," Dicko said. "That circus up at Shirdley Old Hall . . . ?"

"Yeah?"

"There's a story the leopard's escaped."

Nick straightened up. "Is it kosher?"

"Dunno. That's why I'm sending you. Just get up there, find out what's happening. And you'd best be quick, because if this one stands up, the busies'll be roping the entire area off."

"Okay . . . yeah." Nick was now wide awake. This was a little more exciting than he'd anticipated. An escaped leopard. Could this be his first front page lead? And then a sobering thought intruded. "Hang on, Dick . . . Len. I haven't got any wheels." Nick didn't drive, and even if he had been able to, neither he nor his father owned a car.

"Thought of that, kid, thought of that. Frank Roper's on his way to pick you up."

"Okay. Cool."

"Be there any minute, so you'd best get your shit together."

Nick pulled on a shirt, tie and jacket, crammed his notebooks and pens into a satchel and scampered to the front door, just as a pair of headlights glistered through its frosted glass panel. The initial prospect of being sent on a late-night job had not appealed to him while tucked up warm in his pit, but now he was seeing the advantages. To begin with, it was only September and was likely to be mild. Secondly, even if he didn't get a good story, if he was up most of the night he'd probably be able to take tomorrow off. They'd never refuse him that if he volunteered for time-in-lieu instead of overtime, especially as Friday was normally a housekeeping day.

Frank Roper didn't share this upbeat assessment.

He was the *Herald's* photographic manager. He would have initially followed Dicko's example and tried to find one of his underlings to cop for this late-night job, but in his case he'd evidently failed.

"What a fucking bag of shit this is," Roper said as Nick jumped into the chugging old Moscovitch. Roper was a sour, pug-faced man, with flabby jowls and licks of thinning hair greased down across his permanently sweaty forehead. He even wore the obligatory brown mac with scruffy shirt and tie underneath.

"Could be a decent story," Nick replied, as they rocketed away from the kerb.

"Yeah, course."

Shirdley Old Hall was the closest thing in the area to a stately home. Built in the mid-19th century, it had been in private hands until the 1950s, whereupon the blue-blooded owners, having run out of money, had sold it to the local authority for the knock-down price of £16,000. But according to Dicko, even at that figure Shirdley Corporation had "bought a lemon". The fabric of the big old house, which was not especially pretty to look at in the first place—it was a large, flat-roofed structure, built from grey solemn stone, with few architectural features of interest apart from a gargoyle or two—had been deteriorating badly for years. Not only that, when the Corporation had taken possession, it was empty; there were no antiques or attractive furnishings left, the décor was peeling and grubby. They'd made some improvements since then, cleaning up the downstairs area at least, so that it could be used for community functions ("Corporation bun-fights," in the words of Dicko), and turning what had once been a kitchen salon into a café to accommodate the locals who visited the grounds in summer. In fact, those grounds had proved to be Shirdley Old Hall's most valuable asset. As well as the ugly old building, the Corporation had purchased nine square miles of parkland. The initial part of this, those acres immediately encircling the Hall, had been well manicured at the time, and were still in excellent condition now— they incorporated lawns, flower beds, shady walks, fish ponds, greenhouses and topiary. In contrast, the outer collar of the estate was largely untamed, and over the last quarter-century had turned to wildwood. But, at least a mile deep and known locally as "the Timber", even this section of the estate — thick and impenetrable in summer, bleak and frozen in winter — was a novelty much enjoyed by the occupants of Shirdley, an industrial borough on the northwest outskirts of Liverpool.

There were two ways to reach Shirdley Old Hall by car.

The first was via the so-called "Victorian Gate" in Shirdley town centre. This was not actually Victorian, but had been gifted to the township by Queen Caroline in 1819. It was fifteen feet tall, made from cast-iron, and as such had corroded badly. It stood between two almshouses, which had once provided free lodgings for war-veteran pensioners but were now derelict. The whole thing was a bit of an eyesore, and these days, except on special occasions, it was kept locked. The narrow road behind it, which meandered through the deepest part of the Timber before approaching Shirdley Old Hall from its south side, was thus weedy and decrepit.

Much more commonly used was the second road — the one entering the estate from the north. On this side there was a car park and a well-maintained access-way, which connected with the town's outer ring road. The disadvantage of using this approach was that it was a much longer journey to it from central Shirdley, where Nick lived.

"Voyage and a half just to collect *you*," Frank Roper complained. Living outside Shirdley, in Maghull, if Roper had driven straight from his home to Shirdley Old Hall, he wouldn't have had to go anywhere near the town centre, though at the end of the day it was still only four or five miles extra.

"Don't think anyone else was available," Nick explained.

"Can't you drive?"

"Don't have a motor."

"Use one of the pool cars."

"Would have had to walk all the way to the office to pick one up."

"That would never do," Roper grunted, clearly feeling it a bigger imposition that he had been required to drive four miles out of his way than it would Nick having to walk the same distance.

They steered onto the estate by its north gate and followed the unlit access road, which was separated from the Timber by low stone walls on either side. The car headlights only hinted at the thick, leafy groves clustered beyond them.

"If this really is an escaped leopard, it'll have gone to ground easily up here," Nick commented.

"There'll be *no* escaped leopard," Roper scoffed. "When you've been in this job as long as I have, you'll learn to treat tip-offs like that as the piss-takes they undoubtedly are. I'll tell you what, I'll be surprised if there's anything happening at all."

But when they drove down the last part of the access road onto the Hall's forecourt, and around the big, gloomy edifice to its extensive rear lawns, where the circus had set up, they found a bustle of activity.

The first thing Nick noticed was a panda car; a pair of constables in flat hats—a tall one with red hair and a beard, and a short, younger one—stood next to it, discussing something with a rotund gent wearing a coat over his pyjamas. Various other characters, presumably circus folk, were shifting dazedly around in the background. Nick eyed them curiously, not quite sure what he'd been expecting— strongmen in leotards, bearded ladies, guys on stilts? Instead, he saw ordinary looking men and women—again, mostly wearing coats over nightwear. Small children, also in nighties and pyjamas, scampered among them, delighting in this unexpected midnight adventure.

The actual circus was located on the lawn to the east of the estate's south road. Its Big Top was a gaudy red and gold, but even from this distance it looked dingy and patched. Wagons, caravans and canvas-covered trucks were huddled around it; all were in beaten-up, second-hand condition. The grass where they'd parked was scattered with sawdust and animal dung, and crisscrossed with muddy tyre-tracks. The whole camp was lit garishly by strings of variously coloured bulbs suspended between temporary wooden posts. Somewhere in the background, a generator was rumbling noisily; it drowned out the distant *whirring* of the helicopter.

"Can I help you gentlemen?" the red-bearded policeman said, approaching.

"Er, yeah." Nick flashed his press card. "We're from the *Herald*. We were just wondering what's going on?"

"You see!" the rotund man said excitably; his accent an odd mish-mash of Italy and Lancashire. "I tell you . . . these damn newspaper people! They come here to spread more lies about us!"

It didn't surprise Nick that he and Roper weren't welcome. This particular circus had a rep for not being an especially salubrious one; since it had first arrived over a week ago, there'd been several letters in the newspaper columns, calling it mean and tatty.

The Italian/Lancastrian had a mop of black hair and chubby, beefy features, which until recently had been marked with stage make-up. Nick recognised the shadows of cruciform eye-liner, rouged cheeks, white smudges around the mouth. Clearly, as well as the head honcho, this guy was also one of the clowns. Perhaps absurdly, Nick had expected the boss here to have met them in riding boots, white jodh-purs, a red tail-coat and a topper, maybe with a coiled whip in his hand and a pencil-thin tash over his lip. Nick again eyed the other circus folk. Without their gaudy costumes and make-up, they looked a mundane bunch; in fact in some cases less than mundane — he saw scarred faces, hair slicked with grease, the glint of Gypsy earrings. No matter how beautiful the women appeared when they swung on the trapeze in their fishnet tights and revealing outfits, now they were puffy-eyed plain Janes, cigs hanging from their lipstick-slashed mouths, their hair in rollers and pins. Like the men, they too were looking on with what appeared to be serious concern, trying to earwig the conversation but not participating in it themselves — perhaps in these old-fashioned travelling societies that kind of thing just didn't happen. The boss sorted things out, and everyone else abided by his decision. Other opinions weren't required.

"What's your exact interest?" the constable asked, interrupting Nick's thoughts.

"Oh . . . er, we were told one of the animals has escaped. A leopard."

The circus boss threw his arms out in exaggerated gestures. "You hear the lies they tell? You hear these lies?" But for all his protestations, his expression was taut and sweaty. He looked like a man under real stress.

"You'll have to clear this area," the constable said. "This is private property."

"This is Shirdley Old Hall," Nick replied, glancing for support from Roper, but detecting no sign of him. "Isn't it in public ownership?"

The constable shook his head. "Not while the circus is renting it."

Nick now located Roper, the hefty rain-coated form prowling around the outskirts of the chaos, flashbulb flaring as he took random shots.

"Do you at least mind telling us why *you're* here?" Nick asked. "Obviously something's going on."

The constable chewed on his lip, before replying. "Break-in. Very routine."

"Someone's broken into the circus?" Nick tried not to sound as dubious of that as he felt.

"Look sonny, you know the form. I'm not going to tell you anything about a crime while we're in the process of investigating it. Any information will be given to you in the morning at Police Calls. Same as usual, 10am, Shirdley Central. Now take your vehicle and let us get on with our job."

The constable made to move away as if the matter was closed, but Nick knew that a more experienced hack would never be fobbed off so easily. "If there's an escaped leopard, surely that's something the public should know about?"

"How you hear these things?" the circus boss shouted. "How you hear them?"

Did it mean anything that he wasn't denying it any more? Nick wondered.

The bearded constable swung back. "I'm not debating it with you! If you don't piss off now, I'm booking you both for obstructing the police."

He turned away again, just as Roper came sauntering back, shoving his camera into his bag. "That's me done," he said.

"They're hiding something," Nick replied quietly. "I know they are."

Roper feigned fascination. "So what're you going to do? Creep around 'til you find a cage with its bars bent or its hatch hanging open? Look for a trail of paw-prints leading across the grass? All the time hoping no-one sees you? Good luck with that."

"Come on, Frank . . . we could be onto something here."

"Give over. You heard what he said. They're not going to cough. We've done our job by coming and asking." He dug in his coat pocket for his car keys.

Nick glanced back towards the circus boss, still talking animatedly with the two policemen; *very* animatedly. Nick's junior status meant that no-one on the paper, least of all a time served clock-watcher like Roper, would take his hunches seriously. Maybe they were right not to. If a leopard really had escaped here, wouldn't there be people around with torches and nets? Maybe weapons? Nick didn't know. How did you respond to an escaped dangerous animal? Surely the police would at least be armed? Perhaps they were waiting for armed units to arrive?

"Frank . . . we should just hang on and see what happens."

"Deadlines don't wait, Nick."

"There's supposed to be an escaped leopard."

"Is there bloody bollocks!" Roper shook his head at the gullibility of youth. "Look . . . why do you think Dicko sent *you*? Because it's a bag of shit, and he knows it. Don't you think he'd have come himself if he'd thought it was going to be a big story? Anyway, the paper's got to go to bed, so you have to call *something* in."

Nick sighed, knowing this at least was true. He stowed his notebook in his coat pocket, and glanced once more towards the circus boss and his cohorts, all now standing in a circle debating, while the bearded cop contacted his station by radio. The younger one was back inside the panda car; a member of the circus staff was in there with him; it looked like the young cop was taking a statement. In all honesty, there was nothing very urgent going on here. Anyway, if they weren't having it, they weren't having it.

Nick turned and headed on foot around to the west side of the Hall, where a public payphone skulked next to the closed-up ice cream kiosk. Roper's Moscovitch rumbled up alongside him while he dialled the News Desk. Nobody answered. Nick swore under his breath. The night-subs should be waiting for him to call it in, but they'd be moving back and forth between Editorial and the Stone, distracted by other piddling little jobs. He dialled again, and again, but still there was no response. Ten minutes had soon passed.

"Look mate, I've got to hit the road," Roper said, opening the phone-booth door. "Can't wait all night. I'm finished here and I've got to get all the way back to Maghull."

Nick nodded glumly. On the face of it, it seemed unfair — and perhaps a less obnoxious snapper would have thought that too — but in reality, now that no photos were needed, Roper had done his job. It was down to Nick to get the story in. Besides, it wouldn't take him long to walk home if he followed the south road towards the Victorian Gate. He only lived in the next street from there. Ironically, as soon as the Moscovitch's tail-lights had disappeared around the wing of the building, his phone-call was answered. He delivered the story, namely that there was *no* story — which the night-team was delighted by, because they were also ready to knock off and wanted as little extra work as possible — and hung up.

It was only as he trudged back along the south road, bypassing the circus again, that Nick felt his first stirring of discomfort. The road ran directly ahead of him for about three hundred yards, straight as a ribbon towards the dark outer bulwark of the Timber. From there on, the route would be dark and solitary. He'd be totally alone, surrounded by trees and undergrowth — for at least a mile.

What if the story about the leopard was true?

He glanced again at the circus. Folk were still milling between the vehicles. There was no sign of the two busies from this position, but the panda car was visible, so they hadn't gone yet. Didn't this seem an awful lot of fuss for a simple break-in? And a break-in where? Into one of those scruffy caravans? Into a tent, for Christ's sake! What were they after pinching? Popcorn? A bunch of pom-poms? It occurred to Nick that maybe one of the coppers would now come around the side of a wagon, spot him and call him back—he half-hoped they would—but they didn't, and soon the tents and caravans were falling behind him. There was a large penned area at this end of the encampment; it was difficult to see properly, but two humped, motionless outlines suggested elephants. If only it had been one of those that had escaped, he thought—at least you'd hear it coming.

As he approached the Timber, he tried to reassure himself that the distance from here to the Victorian Gate was actually nothing. In normal times he'd walk it in fifteen minutes. Normal times? What was he talking about? *This* was a normal time. There was nothing doing here. The cops had told him that.

He gazed determinedly along the road, which passed out of sight beneath an arch of leaf-heavy boughs. It probably only looked so dark through there because the circus lights were shining at his rear. After all, the moon was up. Its pale face occupied a distant quadrant of sky, rags of grey cloud cluttered around it, but it was casting enough radiance surely? He glanced left to right. The well-kept lawns were velvet-smooth in the silvery glimmer. Here and there lay rose-beds: he could make out each thorny stem, each crinkle-paper bloom. Everything would be fine. Once he got among the trees, the moon would shine in there as well. He'd find his way easily enough.

But finding his way was not the problem.

He glanced over his shoulder, wondering at how quickly the racket of the generator had receded. The Big Top and its associated vehicles already seemed amazingly distant. Beyond those, Shirdley Old Hall was little more than a dark, square-shouldered outline; a doll's house framed on a black backcloth.

"It's bound to be dark," he told himself in a chiding tone. "No point pulling my own pisser about that. It's going to be dark alright, but it's going to be quick too."

He hitched the strap of his satchel and increased his pace.

A figure to his left caught his eye.

He spun around.

It wasn't a leopard. It was a tiger, rearing back on its hind legs, clasping a waste-bin between its paws. If bathed in full daylight, he'd see its primary colours: the bands of bright yellow alternating with the slick black stripes, the snow-white of its face, the yawning red of its big, smiley mouth. The rounded plastic ears would have been reminiscent of Tigger had they not been bashed off by vandals. In fact, close inspection would reveal much damage caused by thrown bricks, and obscene scrawlings in marker pen. Such a shame to disfigure the last friendly face you'd see before the Victorian Gate in one mile's time.

He entered the trees.

As he'd hoped, it was not quite so dark once he was inside. The moon did indeed throw a dim shimmer through the high branches, dappling the road ahead and the surrounding glades, which though broken by thick clumps of rhododendron and tall, narrow trunks, were also spacious and airy, creating open vistas on all sides. The presence of trees was itself reassuring. If he saw the leopard he could climb one to safety. But then a voice reminded him that leopards also climbed. In fact, weren't leopards famous for launching attacks from out of trees? He glanced overhead, seeing only a caul of interwoven branches, twisting and turning and thick with tussocks of vegetation.

"There is no leopard," he reminded himself, having to physically shake to loosen the idea from his mind.

Even if he didn't trust those Gypsies back at the circus, where was the police helicopter? It would still be hovering overhead if there was a real crisis, wouldn't it, its searchlight spearing down through the canopy? He listened out. He no longer heard the rotor blades in the near distance. The only sound, in fact, was his own clicking footfalls on the rugged, broken surface. He glanced over his shoulder again, wondering what he'd do if he spied a sinuous, four-footed form already padding in his wake, but seeing only half an arch of circus light, sliding from view entirely as he rounded a bend in the road.

Now it was *all* moonlight—the whole thing, and this was less comforting: silver grey phantoms spattering through the clutching, cluttered overgrowth, embossing certain dingles, plunging others into deep shadow, creating fantastical, menacing shapes in the twilight realms between.

The best thing was not to look, Nick advised himself. No sense in trying to visualise things that weren't there, allowing the moon to play more and more tricks on him. Was that a tree root, for example, arcing up through the humus of the woodland floor, or something tensed and waiting to spring?

Just stare directly ahead. That was all it took. Just stare ahead and keep walking. With each turn of the silver-stippled road, he'd be another step closer to emerging at the far end. He still had a considerable distance to go—there was no point denying that—but he was making good time. In fact, the road was already angling downhill, which was excellent news. The Timber occupied the town's main river valley. It was only a shallow valley; the River Alt wasn't very big, and there were no escarpments enclosing it, no steep slopes—apart from on the far side, Nick supposed, where the uphill route would seem much tougher than the downhill one. But once he was on that upward path, having crossed the two bridges on the valley floor, he was practically home and dry.

He tried to distract himself by thinking about the new respect this adventure would earn him in the office. He'd been at the *Herald* only four months; he was still seen as a kid, someone to slap around and send for the tea. He didn't appreciate that very much, and would now have an escapade with which to refute it—but he didn't mind admitting that he'd give anything to be back there now, being ordered from one office to the next, dashing madly back and forth to that dirge of ringing phones and fingers bashing keys, the air rank with the outpourings of a dozen Lucky Strikes.

Movement. A loud crackling of branches and foliage.

Nick almost dropped to a crouch, glancing wildly up — seeing nothing, but hearing the lazy beat of wings as something flapped away through the September night.

A bird. Obviously a bird. But why not? There were owls in these woods; if one of them would only *hoot* now — give voice to itself in the warm darkness — it might make him jump, but at least it would provide companionship of a sort. Not that he was really lacking in that. There were all sorts of nocturnal creatures in this environment. These woods were teeming. The leopard could take its pick. Why would it come after him?

"There *is* no leopard," he told himself through tight-locked teeth, striding forcefully on. That boss-clown, or whatever he'd been, had insisted on it. That fat, shifty-looking hobo of a boss-clown, who'd been greased with a sweat of inexplicable fear.

Nick tried to hawk and spit, but could summon no saliva. Ahead of him, the vague shape of the road curved continually, though all he saw around each bend were verges dark with jumbled rhododendrons, moonlight rippling their leafy guts in ever-shifting patterns of silver stripes, silver blotches, silver spots. *Spots.*

It was maybe no surprise that he suddenly, desperately, needed to pee. He hadn't felt it creeping up on him the way he normally did. One minute his bladder was empty, the next apparently full. Obviously it was the high tension of this moment. Well, it hardly mattered. It wasn't like he was going to stop and flop it out here, was it? You were never more vulnerable than when you had your todger in your hand.

But how quickly his entire world had retracted into the lonesome space immediately surrounding him — the clicking of his leather soles, the rasp of his laboured breathing as he walked faster and faster, the ache of the satchel strap pulling on his shoulder. So many sensations, and all so intensely personal. It was astonishing to contemplate that this was the first time he had ever been out alone so late. Nick was too young to have worked nights before. Even when he hit the town on Friday and Saturday evenings, he was usually home by midnight. Of course being in the town when it was late, spying nothing but locked doors and dark windows, but knowing there were people on the other sides of them, even if they were asleep, was entirely different from being encircled by the black stanchions of trees, and dank, fathomless recesses filled only with dimness and silent, stationary shadows. Come to think of it, how strangely silent it actually was. Where were all the night-sounds? He was still a good distance from Old Lane, the main road running through Shirdley, the one onto which the Victorian Gate opened, but shouldn't he be able to hear the occasional purr of motors travelling along it?

He was almost at the first of the two bridges, he realised — not entirely with relief. Nearly halfway home, but between the two bridges would lie the really unnerving part of the journey: across the valley floor, where the undergrowth was so lush and thick it would literally hem the road from either side, where it was so dark he'd be lucky to see his hand in front of his face; the "Black Passage", as he'd christened it in his mind. That was the obvious spot for an ambush, if an ambush there would be. He tried to laugh at the thought. He was talking about a dumb animal, for Jesus' sake! Not a scheming human being. But then he remembered a childhood trip to Chester Zoo, and how one of the keepers had described the leopard as "the best *ambush predator* there is".

Ahead of him, the entrance to the first bridge heaved into the moon-light. It was an ancient cast-iron structure, which crossed over an old gully where a railway branch-line had once run, though that was long since defunct. There was no railing on its right-hand side because some brainless idiots had pushed a stolen car through it one night a few years ago. In fact the blackened, twisted wreck of said car was still down there — many was the time on hot summer afternoons, when younger versions of Nick and his pals had investigated it, crawling through the rusty, contorted metal, wafting at midges, fearing nothing more than one of the park rangers shouting down at them, calling them hooligans and telling them to bugger off. Course, he wouldn't see it if he glanced over the unfenced edge now — it was pitch dark down there, an abyssal canyon slicing through the heart of the Timber. He hurried on across, a little happier to be exposed again in the open air. Being on a bridge wasn't a problem in itself. Once you were on a bridge, you were safe—if the leopard came you would see him, either from the front as he stepped out to waylay you, or you'd hear his heavy paws pounding up behind. In either circumstance, you could run the other way.

Yeah, course you could.

The Black Passage loomed.

Nick had planned to smoke his way through this part of the journey, occupying his mind with deep, luxurious inhalations, but now realised that, leaving the house so quickly, he'd failed to scoop up his packet of Marlboroughs. In any case, it occurred to him that a winking red dot and the fragrance of burning tobacco might make him even more noticeable in the cramped, dark heart of this tangled forest. For surely he was finally at its heart. The road had levelled out. Gone were the open tenements of woodland. Gone was the filtered silver-blue radiance lying in zebra stripes across the road ahead. Instead, it was all blackness and a dense, muggy odour. Oily vegetation rose into a gloom as thick as jungle fog. The air itself was damp, sickly. This *would* be the time for something to attack. He drove on hard, wondering if he should start running, but asking himself, if he did, whether that would make him an even more obvious target, whether it would trigger an immediate assault from something which so far had been content merely to stalk.

He spotted something. A patterned form needling through low clumps of leafage on his left. His eyes strained in the murk, but no— he'd been wrong. There was nothing there. No undergrowth stirred. Not a blade of grass trembled.

"Idiot," he said under his breath, but quickened his pace so much that he was almost running.

How far to the river bridge? It couldn't be more than a few dozen yards. Another couple of turns in the road, and then, beyond the Alt, he was home and dry. Well, home and dry once he'd traversed that last stretch of road, the part rising towards Old Lane and civilisation, but rising for six hundred yards or more between high soil embankments broken by roots and leaf rubble and further clumps of shadowy rhododendron brush from which anything might leap.

At least he'd be close to the Victorian Gate, within shouting distance of Old Lane. Not like here . . . *wait, what the fuck . . . ?*

This time he didn't see something on his left, he *heard* it.

And he *really* heard it.

No fevered imagination on this occasion. He halted, cold drops of sweat spangling his forehead as he gazed hard to his left. Again no movement. No sound. The hush of the woodland. But this time it was too great a hush. Woods should breathe and murmur. But everything here had fallen still, anticipating a dramatic event.

Nick ran.

Fast, legs pumping, satchel joggling against his spine. The pain didn't matter. All that mattered was getting out of this place. *Good Christ, could he manage that?* He still had so far to go. And the harder he went, the louder the wind rasped in his chest and the blood beat in his ears, creating a cacophony of self-induced noise to chase himself with. If something was, as he suspected, ripping through the undergrowth on a parallel course, he'd never know for sure because he wouldn't hear it.

A curtain of brighter moonlight revealed the open spaces where the second bridge crossed the River Alt.

Nick lurched towards it. No longer running, but walking fast, feeling better just to see it, but still terribly aware of the invisible motion to his left. Though why shouldn't he hear such things? This was the Timber, famously home to badgers, foxes and even wild deer. Perhaps it was nothing more than a friendly dog looking for companionship—though that was probably a stretch. All the friendly dogs in this town would be basking in the warmth of family hearths, or curled on carpets by the kitchen range.

He hurried out onto the bridge. Below it, the land shelved precipitously down onto hundreds of square yards of marsh and bog and twisting, moon-glinting rivulets. Unlike the bridge over the railway, this one was broad enough to admit traffic if such a thing had ever run through these woods, stretching eighty yards from one faded marble balustrade to the other. But at least the air was cleaner here. Boughs of trees arched far overhead. There was a cathedral-like atmosphere, more silver-blue shafts piercing its vast, natural nave. And yet, as he crossed over, Nick still fancied that something was in close pursuit. He didn't look around, but unslung his satchel. He needed something in his hand — anything — that he could use as a weapon. His bladder was so full it was like a dagger through his abdomen. The act of running only made things worse. But he wasn't stopping to take a leak now. No, sir.

And then, mercy of mercies, he saw someone ahead.

Close to where the right-hand balustrade ended, next to where it was bookended by that tall chunk of weathered statuary.

"Hello!" he panted, veering towards the watchful figure. He was working on the basis it was one of the rangers, or even a patrolling police officer — they sometimes came through here on foot. Perhaps tonight of all nights they had been sent down in numbers, and this was the first he had encountered. "Hello, I think I've . . . "

He was mistaken.

It was merely that same lump of statuary that he'd known was here all along. Even in the strange shifting dimness of the forest cathedral, he'd have distinguished it for what it was — an art-deco sculpture, a Grecian nymph or some such thing, eroded now to a soulless effigy — but it was covered at present with pale plastic sheeting, blown on the wind or wound around it by mischievous youngsters. It had briefly possessed a more human outline: defined shoulders, a nodding head.

Nick snatched the plastic away. It fell to his feet in a crackling heap. There was no comfort to be had beneath. The moonlit face was barely human: cracked, grey, covered with grime and lichen.

He glanced back across the silver-lit bridge.

Nothing had trailed him onto it. But what did that signify? It could have crossed the marsh much earlier, and even now be sliding through the undergrowth on higher ground, waiting to cut him off as he approached the Victorian Gate.

"Don't wait 'til then," he said. He shouted in a voice so high and querulous that he didn't even recognise it. *"Don't wait . . . do it now! Now's your chance!"*

The eerie voice rang back to him. There was still no other sound.

He turned and hurried on. Some six hundred yards to go. The steepest part of the journey, but already Nick fancied that if he strained his eyes, he could see the sodium yellow glow of street-lamps through the thickly layered trees.

"No leopard," he muttered to himself, the road steepening but his proximity to safety giving him ever greater energy. The tall gate was still out of view, but the road was banking sharply round towards it, and yellow light *was* seeping through the black undergrowth rising on either side. "No leopard, nothing to fear."

It wasn't even likely the beast would be hungry. *Why* would it be hungry? It lived in a circus, for Christ's sake. It would be well fed. It might even be tame, probably more like a pet, a big, soft, silky-coated tom cat, which rubbed against its trainer's leg whenever he came into the cage.

The cage.

It lived in a cage.

And how filthy might that cage be? Especially in a fleapit circus like the one Nick had just left? How badly would the brute have been treated over the years? Whipped, chained, starved? What kind of *pet* would emerge from that experience?

"It doesn't matter," he said, once again at the top of his voice — still a quavering, unrecognisable yodel, "because *here we fucking are!*"

The Victorian Gate: a tall, black trellis, yellow street-light blazing through it. Ninety yards ahead, that was all. Ninety yards and closing.

He found that if he jackknifed forward, he could ascend the hill more quickly, plus it meant that he didn't look up the left-hand embankment to see what was thrashing amid the foliage at its crest.

Was an object still moving parallel to him, or was it now descending, zigzagging through the roots and rubble?

Seventy yards to go. His heart was pounding, sweat swam into his eyes. His satchel felt lighter—it was unfastened so he may have dropped a notebook or two. It didn't matter. He wasn't going back looking for them.

Fifty yards. The Victorian Gate was right in front of him, towering overhead. He could see Old Lane on the far side, and on the far side of that the boundary wall to the Nursing Home. His rasping breath sounded alien it was so harsh. But surely nothing would come for him now? Not unless that was the sound of its paws *pitter-pattering* up behind. He lengthened his stride, almost cried out. Dense rhododendrons again lay left and right—anything could pounce.

Thirty yards to the Gate; the narrow gap between itself and the right-hand almshouse was the gap he'd use to reach safety. The almshouses: squat, square cottages; boarded windows, broken open doorways. An ugly sight at the best of times, but he was so glad to see them now. He was so glad to *feel* the one on the right, its aged brickwork scraping the back of his coat as he hurled himself into the gap and sidled quickly through into the warm embrace of the street-lighting beyond . . .

Blissful seconds passed as Nick stood by the edge of the pavement. His breath slowing. His heart rate easing.

Hot saliva pooled in his mouth. He hawked it out as he angled forward, hands on hips, his dripping mop of hair hanging over his eyes.

God bless that lovely yellow light shining on all sides of him! What a colour, yellow: illuminating a world of normality, of brick walls and tarmac and road-signs, of a grid by his feet, crammed with toffee papers and lolly sticks. He tried to guffaw, but couldn't—his throat was too sore from gasping. No matter. The laughter could come in a moment, when he'd recovered himself properly. What a prick he must've looked, bullocking out into the open like that, frantic, sweat flying.

And no doubt with nothing to be frightened of. Nothing whatever.

Even if he was prepared to go back across the pavement and press his face against the bars of the Victorian Gate, peering into the chasm beyond, he wouldn't know for sure. It could be gazing right back at him, and he wouldn't see it. But in truth—in his heart of hearts, Nick had known there was nothing down there. He would never have taken such a chance if he'd thought there was. That journalistic sixth sense of his would simply have forbidden it.

But Christ, did he ever want to piss!

Now he *did* laugh as he lurched up against the almshouse wall—aaah, the pure pleasure of routine bodily functions. But he'd only half unzipped when he heard the approaching rumble of a car. Glancing over his shoulder, he grinned to see that it was a police vehicle. Maybe the same one from up at the Hall. Fat lot of good it was now. It was still some distance away and prowling slowly. They'd spot him no doubt and get out, especially if they caught him pissing in public, and even more likely if they saw him loitering, waiting for them to move on.

"Fucking busies," he muttered, still sniggering, stepping around into the almshouse entry. Last thing he needed now was hassle from that lot. There was a recessed doorway here, smashed down years ago, so he could have gone all the way inside if he'd needed to. But he didn't. There was shelter enough in the porch. He unzipped properly and finally let it go. Thank Christ for that . . .

What a tale he'd have to tell, but he'd leave this bit out. That he'd been dying for a piss all the way through. That would make it seem less like an adventure and more like a comedy. And he wanted to dine out on this one for many years to come.

Just out of interest, why had that police car been driving so slowly?

He zipped up again, distracted by the thought—and caught his skin in the fly. Normally he'd have howled and jumped around, but he barely noticed it. He was suddenly too busy staring into the dank interior—at the two burnings orbs, which regarded him back with scarcely a blink.

෨෬

Scotney blew out another long stream of curling smoke, before stubbing his cig on the wall. He sighed as the rain continued to pour. "Hard to believe it was all those years ago, now." He shook his head. "Poor Nick Curtis. I was the first reporter on the scene. Early shift, you see. The body was still inside. God knows what the last few minutes of that kid's life must've been like. Can't have been good."

All the Clowns in Clowntown

Andrew J. McKiernan

Binko stood his ground, white-gloved fingers twitching into nervous fists. The warmth from the overhead street-lamp drew sweat from his brow, sheening his greasepaint until it shone like fine-glazed porcelain. He stared into the night; the road ahead disappearing into darkness. He listened, waiting for the wind to shift. Only the dry-rattle of tumbleweed rolling across the barrens came to his ears.

But, for a moment, Binko thought he *had* heard something. *Just my mind playin' tricks, or someone playin' a radio too loud*, he thought, shaking his head.

Standing there on the edge of town, middle of the night, with nothing to keep him company but a tattered porno was downright creepy. It wasn't even supposed to be his job. That strange, old hobo Alfie should have been there. Instead, Alfie had found himself a children's party and a mall appearance in some deadbeat city.

"It's an overnighter," Alfie had said. "You'll keep watch for me just one night won't you Binko, old-pal, old-chum?"

So there he stood, heart pounding like some scared-shitless kid, hearing sounds that just weren't there.

He stood a little longer, breathing deep, waiting for the fight-or-flee panic to disperse. Eventually his heartbeat slowed. He relaxed his shoulders and unclenched his fists. Who was he going to punch, anyway? Maybe he'd punch Alfie for making him stand out there all night.

Binko slunk back to the battered wooden crate beside the lamppost and settled his well-padded butt. He poured a cup of tepid coffee from his thermos and took up the porno from where he'd left off—Miss October—just as the wind shifted again.

—the softest of melodies, carried upon a breeze: distant, sweet, and full of joy—

Binko's blood ran cold.

A palsy of terror seized him, limbs shaking, coffee spilling down his oversized pants. He grabbed the lamppost to steady himself and stared down the long road into town.

The music was unmistakable: faint, intoxicating, nauseating.

It's too damn happy, Binko thought. *Sickening. Like eating too much cotton candy.*

He took a tentative step away from the light, stomach churning with fear and anticipation.

Outside the streetlight's bright cone, the landscape resolved into grainy clarity. Stars gleamed on the black-velvet dome of night. The road stretched off across the flat plain of the desert, narrowing to a point on the horizon. And, just beyond that, a glow—soft, shimmering and multi-coloured.

The wind strengthened, bringing with it the smell of corn dogs and roasted nuts. Enticing. Repulsive. Binko felt the terrifying urge to juggle. To dance and turn cartwheels. Bile rose in his throat, and he retched on its bitterness.

He turned and ran, feet flapping against the road. Back through the industrial area. Past the balloon factory and the juggling school. He huffed and puffed down Main Street, ignoring the bright display windows of all-night pie shops and joke stores, running until he felt his heart would burst.

Alfie had never told him what to do if something happened; had never told him who to report to. But Binko knew he had to warn them. He had to warn them all.

The circus was coming to town.

❧

"They'll be here by dawn," Uncle Doody said.

Binko stared out the window. It was still dark. Even the stars were invisible this close to the centre of town.

"Don't go frettin', lad." Uncle Doody shut the blinds with a snap. "We've got plenty'a time to let everyone know. Sit down and have a spell, you've just run a mile. You'll drop down dead if you go much further without a breather."

Uncle Doody was a veteran. An old-school Vaudevillian whiteface who'd earned his own television show. A show that'd run twice a week for over fifteen years, syndicated to deadbeat channels all over the country. A show that finally crashed beneath an onslaught of rival programming and a general childhood ambivalence towards all that was whimsical and nice. In response, Uncle Doody had become cynical, acerbic, and often just plain vulgar. He rarely found work anymore and could only be trusted to play Roasts and Stag Parties. Events with children present were definitely out.

Yet, Uncle Doody was the closest thing to a Boss Clown Clown-town had.

Binko sat himself in an overstuffed chair, impatient and anxious to be doing something. Uncle Doody took out a pencil and paper and began scribbling.

"What's that?" Binko asked. "You drawing up our plan of defence?"

"No point." The old clown continued scribbling. "They come in, run their parades down Main Street, take a few of us, and then they're gone. Used to turn up every year, back when I was a kiddie. But the circus ain't too popular with folks no more. Haven't seen a circus for . . . hmm, maybe twenty-five years? Certainly before you were born. Good thing, too. This town's thrived without their meddling. Without them takin' our best and finest."

"So, just like that, people don't like circuses anymore?"

"Oh, they do. They do. Love 'em more than anything. But it was the animals, see. Bothered 'em seeing all those animals tied up, and locked up, and whipped into performin'. It was a moral choice. Give up somethin' they love so others won't suffer for it. Makes 'em feel guilty later on if they don't."

"Not guilty about us, though?"

"Oh, come on, Binko! You're a sensible whiteface, not some auguste who can't even tie his own shoelaces. They don't even *know* about us. They think we're just normal people livin' Clark Kent lives. Doin' a job. Goin' home every night to take off our suits and wash off our make-up. *Wash off* our make-up? That'd be like washing away who we are, Binko. That's why we're here in Clowntown. We're too different. We're just entertainment to them. A commodity to others."

Uncle Doody finished scribbling, rolled up the paper, and handed it to Binko. "Take this. Give it to Zippy over at the Emporium. He'll make sure word gets around. Then you go over to the cops. Won't do much good, but tell 'em anyway. They'll try and do something. As usual, it'll be a farce. Won't matter. By the time mornin' breaks everyone will know that there's trouble comin'."

✧◦✧

Eight blue-uniformed clowns were crammed into their old jalopy, half-hanging out of windows and doors, whistles blowing, truncheons waving. The car careened from curb to curb, siren wailing, narrowly missing a parked Volkswagen before disappearing into the distance.

Binko's shoulders slumped in despair as the Clowntown Cops drove off down Main Street.

No point, he thought. *Uncle Doody was right.*

The walk back to Binko's share-house normally took ten minutes, but he made it home in five. The streets were too quiet, the shadows too dark, for a casual stroll. He hadn't gone far when a phone started ringing in an apartment somewhere. Almost as soon as it was answered another started. The ringing of phones stalked him all the way home.

Zippy's gettin' the word around.

৯৶৶

No matter how many scented candles Kooky lit, they just couldn't get rid of the faint whiff of elephants. The smell had drifted in behind Binko, and at first they'd all thought it was him.

"What you been rollin' in?" Whacky Wally screwed up his face in disgust.

Annabelle was the first to recognise the smell. For a while they'd all tried to ignore it, but it had grown stronger, joined by other circus scents and sounds drifting in with the dawn. Air-conditioning only made the matter worse. Annabelle retreated to a far corner of the apartment, her large, polka-dotted handkerchief tied around her face like an old-western bandit.

The phone rang for the tenth, or twentieth, time. No one answered it. They didn't need to be told again.

"Get away from the window." Wally checked the locks on the door again.

Binko ignored him, and peered through the gap between the curtains. The sun was yet to rise and the light was feeble, leaching the street of colour. He could see all the way down Main Street. He sensed movement at the furthest reach of his vision, and a flicker of headlights.

"What is it?" Kooky whispered at his ear. "What can you see?"

"It's the cops. They're coming back." Binko couldn't believe his eyes. "They must have turned the circus around at the city limits."

The old jalopy rolled to a stop at the intersection of Main and Marceau. The doors did not spring open. Its occupants did not come piling out onto the street. There were no sirens or whistles. Six Clown Cops riding miniature motorcycles—knees pushed up around their ears—glided into formation around the jalopy.

"They're a bloody escort!" Binko's momentary hope unravelled before him. "The Cops've joined up already. Stinkin' weak bastards! They're leadin' the parade into town!"

Annabelle groaned. Wally collapsed onto the couch, shaking his head.

"Le'me see, le'me see." Kooky tugged at Binko's sleeve.

Binko brushed him away. Something was happening behind the lead vehicles. A banner raised. A band moving into position. A baton uplifted. Binko realised he should tell his friends to block their ears. His mind struggled to turn thought into words, his lips trembling in anticipation of their arrival. But they wouldn't come.

The baton dropped.

Cruelly, the band started with Sousa's *The Thunderer*. A fanfare of drums, trumpets and euphoniums erupted from the far end of the street. Like a tightening spring, the notes rose through the scale, spreading tension and anticipation. A beat of silence held everything tight. Expectant. Only to uncoil in an army of glockenspiels playing demonic counterpoint to the deep, two-step rhythm of timpani and cymbal.

Kooky screamed. Annabelle groaned. Wally held cushions to his ears.

Binko's muscles locked tight. He could only stare as the procession crawled slowly down Main Street.

☙❧

There were moments when Binko knew they wouldn't make it. Was sure they would not endure the barrage of sight and sound, the mélange of aromas that tantalised their senses. Some gave in sooner than others.

Through the curtains, Binko could see other painted faces peering from windows across the street. Before the band had passed, a few of those windows had opened, clowns leaning out to stare and cheer.

"No, no, no," Kooky's voice cracked like a pubescent choirboy. "Don't let them know we're here! Don't open your windows."

"They know we're here, Kooky." Wally tried to remain calm. "That's why they came. Let's just worry about us, eh?"

Behind the band, a troupe of acrobats tumbled. They rolled along the road, balancing balls and spinning plates on slender sticks. Elaborate gold-leafed circus wagons drawn by ten-horse teams rolled by. Some wagons were barred along their length, permitting only fleeting glimpses of lions, tigers, and bears. A monkey riding a dog dashed in and out of the procession.

Across the street, a door opened. Tickles and Giggles—auguste twins, never apart—stepped out. Good neighbours. Silly neighbours. Jaws slack, eyes wide with wonder, they shambled down the porch steps.

A roustabout in the crowd spotted them and peeled away from the parade. He walked up to them calmly, casually. Tickles and Giggles stared at the brightly coloured balls he held in his hands. Red smiles spread across their faces.

Giggles accepted the balls the roustabout offered him. He tossed one into the air. Then a second and a third. Around and around, bright colours blurring. Up and down, over and across. Their passage was mesmerising.

The roustabout touched Giggles gently on the shoulder, directing him towards the procession. Giggles juggled and laughed, never taking his sight from the balls. Tickles followed, always close behind her twin.

"They must have at least twenty of us already." Wally surveyed the scene over Binko's shoulder. "How many do they want?"

Binko retreated from the window and began pacing the room. Wally opened the curtains.

"Hey, what are you doing?" Kooky screamed, scrambling for the window. "You want them to just look in and see us? You want them to send some strongman over to knock down our door?" He grabbed the curtain and slid it across to cover the horrifying tableau that passed before them. Wally pushed him away and Kooky staggered, stumbled, the curtain held tight in his hand. There was the sound of cloth ripping, of stitches popping and metal clips snapping. The curtain tore free of its rail and Kooky fell back onto his padded arse. Drapery drifted down to cover him like a Halloween ghost. "Aww, crap! Look what you made me do, Wally!"

Wally rounded on him, snatching back the curtain, his happy-face a rictus of menace. "Look here you dumb auguste shit! They. Know. We're. *Here*! They know we're hiding. We just have to stay strong until they're gone."

"We're not all as strong as you, Wally," Binko said.

Wally considered this, took a deep breath, lowered and nodded his head. "Yeah, you're right, Binko. Sorry, Kooky. I'll find something to hold the curtain up. Are you okay, buddy?"

Kooky didn't answer. His eyes were fixed on the window, a grin creeping slowly at the corners of his mouth. Binko and Wally turned, wondering what could be holding his attention.

A carnie stood on the other side of the glass. He held up a unicycle, all bright spokes and polished chrome, for them to see. His toothless grin sent a shiver down Binko's spine.

Kooky stood and dashed for the door. His hands were fast—slipping locks and flipping latches. Wally reached him just as he turned the handle and pulled open the door.

The door swung back, catching Wally on the bridge of his nose. He screamed, reeling backwards into Binko, the two of them tumbling, bumbling across the room and onto the couch in a tangled heap.

Binko struggled for breath as Wally writhed above him in pain. He pulled his tangled limbs free and sat up, gasping for air. Wally held his hands to his nose, bright red flowing between his fingers and down onto his smock. The door was wide open. Kooky was gone.

"You fool, Kooky. You silly fool," Binko mumbled and closed the door while Wally applied tissues to his bloody nose. Annabelle sat in the corner, trembling silently, knees hugged tight to her body. She had pulled her handkerchief up to cover her face from brow to chin.

Binko picked up the curtain and threw it haphazardly over the rail, covering as much of the window as he could manage. Outside, a calliope passed by playing *The Greatest Show on Earth*.

"Won't be long now. There can't be much more," Wally said

through his ripe-tomato nose, trying to sound authoritative. Binko knew he was only guessing, hoping.

The phone rang for the first time since the parade had begun. Binko and Wally stared down at it. The sudden intrusion of its ring was so unexpected that it seemed an object both surreal and incongruous. A last attempt at social pleasantries that was somehow even stranger than the chaos in the street.

Wally shook his head and looked at Binko. "Who'd be calling at a time like *this*?"

"It's Uncle Doody, has to be."

Binko reached for the receiver.

৵৵

Uncle Doody had sent Chester the Jester out to scout the situation, and his report wasn't good. The circus wasn't just passing through and moving on as it normally would. The head of the parade had reached the end of town and stopped.

"It looks like they're settin' up, Binko," Uncle Doody said. "Never seen the likes of it. They've picked up more than enough clowns for a dozen troupes already. I don't know what else they want."

Uncle Doody sounded old and tired, his voice a weary whisper competing against the sounds of the parade. Binko could hear a bell-wagon ringing out a tune in the background.

"We might be in this for the long haul, Binko. I want you to stay strong, lad. Keep those rowdy house-mates of yours thinkin' about other things. If you can make it through the parade, you'll all be okay. Chester says the procession's about a twenty minute run from band to bum."

Twenty minutes! Binko thought. *It feels like a week already.*

"Sure thing, Uncle Doody." His voice shook and his lip quivered. *Kooky's gone, and the Giggle Twins have gone, and Wally broke his nose, and everyone I love is going crazy or on their way to that hell-damned circus,* he wanted to shout back down the phone-line. He wanted to tell Doody

215

he couldn't be strong any more, that none of them could be strong in the face of something like this.

"You there, Binko?"

He took a deep breath, swallowed back his fear and said, "Kooky couldn't hold out, but Wally and Annabelle are doin' good. We'll be okay, Uncle Doody. You worry about yourself. We'll be fine."

"Good lad. Good lad, Binko" Uncle Doody said, and the line went dead.

❧❦

For some, the last part of the parade was the worst. The bands, the organs, the bell-wagons, and a calliope had all passed. Their tinkling, pounding melodies drifted down the street. The sound of wagon wheels and horse hooves on asphalt remained only as a dull-throb behind Binko's eyes. For a time, there was silence.

"Maybe it's over," Wally whispered.

"Maybe." Binko didn't believe it, though, and moved to the window to look. He parted the curtain slowly, expecting to see a face up against the glass. No one was at the window, but the procession continued.

Sideshow freaks marched in silence: the fat man and bearded lady; a strongman leading a two-headed goat; fire-eaters spraying the air with flame; midgets and a rubber man. There were others, less identifiable, just as grotesque. Carnies and roustabouts and riggers walked amongst them. They turned their heads to smile at Binko as they passed.

Wally put a steadying arm around Binko's shoulders. He reached down to gently pry his house-mate's fingers from the window-sill. Wally could feel the shaking tension in Binko's body as it fought against unwanted desires; could see the smile threatening to take control of Binko's face. He closed the curtain as best he could and sat Binko down on the couch. "You okay, buddy? Need me to slap you round a bit?"

Binko shook his head to clear it a little, but it also served as an answer. "Nah. Thanks, Wally. I'll be okay. I just need a minute." He breathed deep and tried to relax the aching muscles in his arms and legs. He'd almost been caught for a moment there. *Midgets! He loved midgets.* But he'd been strong, like Uncle Doody wanted, and he'd won. It had been tough, though. Not a battle he'd be able to endure for long.

From outside, the sandpaper shuffle of elephant feet set a dull tremor through the house. Annabelle stirred. She groaned and whimpered. China and glassware rattled in cupboards and furniture shook. The curtain shifted on its makeshift rail and fell.

The elephants strode two-by-two, adorned in bright jewels, past the window frame. Sequin-gowned women rode their backs, hands waving, feathered headpieces bobbing. The lead elephant lifted its wrinkled trunk and trumpeted. The rest of the herd joined in, a beastly orchestra, their sound a little too much like laughter to Binko's ears.

"If only we had some peanuts," Annabelle mumbled from the corner of the room. "If we gave them some peanuts they might go away. Have we got any peanuts? Elephants like peanuts."

Binko grabbed the fallen curtain and ran for the window. He closed his eyes to avoid the view and fumbled with the curtain. The cloth was heavy in his hands: the rail too high on the window. "Wally, gimme me a hand over here, will ya?"

Wally dragged a chair across the room and held it steady while Binko stepped up to the rail.

Annabelle climbed unsteadily to her feet and searched her pockets. Her eyes scanned the room, resting for a moment on a bowl of old candies on the table. She shook her head. "No, peanuts would be better. I'll just go down the road and get them some peanuts."

"Oh, no you don't." Wally hurried to the door, blocking the way. Binko finished replacing the curtain and came up behind Annabelle. He put his hands gently on her shoulders. Compliant, she allowed him to lead her back to her corner of the room. Her handkerchief had

217

fallen from her face. Tears ran lines through her make-up, the bright colours of her face smearing to grey.

"Have you got any peanuts, Binko?" she asked between sobs.

Binko only shook his head. He had no words left to comfort her. He held her as she cried herself to sleep.

⤙⤚

The parade passed on, leaving the street silent and empty; the air saturated with fairground scents. Binko felt no feeling of relief, no survivor's elation, only a deep lethargy that filled his bones like concrete.

Wally lay curled up under an old army blanket on the couch. He breathed with his mouth open and a thin line of spit hung at its corner. Annabelle slept on, mumbling and twitching in her corner.

Binko grabbed some spare pillows from the linen cupboard and spread them across the floor. He'd feel more comfortable here in the lounge room with his friends, despite Wally's snoring. Enduring the noise and drool stains was a small price to pay for the strength they had found in sticking together.

He hoped Alfie was having a good time at his children's party. Bastard.

Binko lay staring at the ceiling as sounds drifted in from the far end of town—the rhythmic beat of hammers driving stakes into the ground; a lion's roar; laughter and carousel music. Eventually he slept, but the sounds found their way into his dreams, and his sleep was not restful.

⤙⤚

Binko awoke to a room filled with shadows. He felt as if he'd barely slept, stretching to work a kink from his back.

The lounge was empty. Annabelle's corner was vacant.

"They've just gone back to their rooms," Binko said, his voice an

218

anchor to hold back the panic. "Familiar, comfortable beds. Sensible. Should'a done the same m'self."

He didn't believe it for a second. The note on the coffee table confirmed his disbelief.

> BINKO,
> GONE TO FIND ANNABELLE. SOME GOON CAME ROUND OFFERING ELEPHANT RIDES. WASN'T AWAKE ENOUGH TO REALISE WASN'T A DREAM. WOKE UP JUST AS SHE LEFT. BACK SOON. STAY SAFE.
>
> WALLY

Binko recognised Wally's blocky script, but he'd never seen the sheet of bright-pink paper before. Something was printed on the reverse and he wondered where it had come from. He turned it over:

A Special Invitation To
ALL THE CLOWNS IN CLOWNTOWN

For One Night Only:
McKENZIE'S UNIVERSAL CIRCUS
& MUSEUM OF THE BIZARRE

Come One, Come All
Join In The Fun!
YOU'LL NEVER WANT TO LEAVE

The leering caricature of a ringmaster grinned at him from the page. His top hat was twisted at a jaunty angle, moustache as neat as a cat's whisker. The eyes were menacing, hypnotic swirls.

A knock at the door startled Binko from the staring, spiralling eyes. He dropped the flyer and spun to face the door. Wally hadn't locked it when he left and the chains dangled, impotent.

The knock came again, harder, more insistent.

"Hey, Binko! Wally! Anyone in there? Le'me in. It's Chester." The voice was a whiny squeak roughened by cigarettes. "Hey, I've got Arlo with me. Uncle Doody's gone. His place is empty. Let us in, will ya?"

Binko staggered forward and opened the door. Two clowns stood on the porch. Both were dressed in motley, but there the resemblance ended.

Chester was only four feet tall. He wore a suit of red and green, boots curled up at the toe, and waved a wooden sceptre at Binko. His jolly, coffee-coloured face stared out from beneath a three-pointed cockscomb cap, silver bells on the cap's points jingling.

Arlo stood behind him. Taller. Much taller. His motley was more vibrant, multi-coloured: a random rainbow of diamonds stretched from neck to toe. His face and head were covered in a black half-mask and cap, revealing little of the features beneath. A long, narrow cane completed the ensemble, held tight in both hands against his breast.

"Shut the door. Shut the door." Chester pushed his way past Binko and Arlo followed. "They'll target this place if they know we're here. They want everyone. They wanna take us all!"

"Yeah, I know. I saw the flyer." Binko shut the door, setting the locks and chains as Chester and Arlo headed for the kitchen.

"Hey! What'd ya say about Uncle Doody?" Binko asked.

"He's gone," Chester called from the kitchen.

"Where?"

Chester returned. "Don't know," he said through a half-chewed chicken leg. "Musta got 'im. His place was empty when we went to report back. No damage. Nothin' mussed up. The door was wide open, though."

"One of them flyers in the hallway, too," Arlo added. He'd made himself a sandwich and opened a Coke.

"But Uncle Doody wouldn't have been sucked in by this lot," Binko said. "He was stronger than that. He wasn't even a circus clown! Never was. How'd they get *him*?"

Chester finished his chicken and pointed the bone at Binko. "What'd ya think T.V. *is*, Binko? It's a twenty-four hour circus for the masses! Course they got 'im."

"Doesn't seem to bother *you* too much though, does it?" Binko asked.

"What'd ya mean?"

"You and Arlo. You just waltz in and help yourselves to a feed! Uncle Doody's gone! Kooky and Wally and Annabelle are gone. Why are you *here*? Why aren't *you* at the circus or cowering in some apartment?"

"Nah." Chester walked over to the window. "If a Renaissance Fair came barrellin' into town you'd have to lock us in straight-jackets. But the circus? Don't bother *us* much. Arlo and I, we only play for royalty and the like. Sophisticates. Not the sorta commoners who attend a circus."

Arlo grunted his agreement.

Chester looked out the window and then gathered up his sceptre. "We can't stay here though. You either, Binko. You'd better come with us."

"But I can't go out there!"

"Yeah, sure you can. We'll stuff your ears and nose with cotton wool. You got cotton wool, don't you? You won't hear or smell nothin'. Just remember, close your eyes if you see anythin' makes you feel funny."

Binko stared at Chester. "Is that supposed to be some sick joke?" He knew he couldn't step outside. Once he was out there, it would be the end of him. The end of town was only a short walk away. His feet would carry him there and he'd have no choice. He *knew* it.

"What? What joke?" Chester asked.

"'*If you see anything that makes you* feel *funny.*' That's what you said. Is that some sort of joke? Medieval humour? I don't need a *circus* to be funny. I'm *always* funny. Look, I can be funny right here!"

Binko searched the room for a prop, anything he could use to hang a gag on. He couldn't go outside. No way! He'd end up in the Big Top for sure.

There came a knocking at the door —*shave and a haircut, two bits*— and they all froze.

"*Shhh*," Chester warned and crept towards the door. He held his sceptre like a bludgeon. Arlo stood, cane at the ready. Locks clicked, chains dropped. Slowly, they opened the door.

As one, they sighed. The aroma that wafted in! Warm, homely, fresh baked. It was heavenly. A basket of pretzels lay abandoned on the doorstep.

"There's a card." Chester passed the basket to Binko.

Binko reached for a pretzel and stuffed it in his mouth before reading the card.

> **Binko,**
> **Won't you come and join us?**
> **We're having so much fun.**
> **It's not the same without you**
> **And your squirting-flower gun.**
> **Your pals,**
>
> **Wally, Annabelle & Kooky.**

Binko spat the pretzel from his mouth. Suddenly, it was tainted and brittle; eggshell and bone in his mouth. He threw the basket across the room. He didn't even *have* a squirting flower gun. His friends knew that! What had they done to his friends?

"They know we're here. Get your things, and let's go," Chester said. "They must be roundin' up the stragglers, Binko. They'll be looking for you. We gotta move now, while we still got some light."

∾∾

Binko followed Chester and Arlo down Main Street. Every wall, door, and telegraph pole had been stickered with bills posted for the show. Flyers and elephant droppings littered the street. Balloons hung limp from the telegraph pole gallows that had snared them. The cotton in Binko's ears and nose itched. He breathed in and out through his mouth, trying not to sneeze, the sounds of the circus muffled and distant.

Chester led them on a rambling route—right at Fratellini, along Keaton, down Chaplin. Twice they spotted carnies and freaks patrolling the streets. They ducked into darkened alleys and hid behind dumpsters, or under parked cars, until the threat had passed. Once they heard screams and a gunshot.

"Zippy had a gun," Chester said. "Maybe that was him? Maybe he took some of 'em out?"

Binko couldn't imagine Zippy with anything more dangerous than a water pistol.

"Where the hell are we going?" he asked.

"Just up here. Not far." Chester led them down a narrow and dingy alley. "I wanted to come at 'em from the side. The front door'll be too well guarded. They'd see us before we even got close."

"We're not going *inside*!"

"Shouldn't have to if what I've got in mind works. Not into the Big Top anyway. You'll see. C'mon, over you go." Chester indicated a wire fence at the end of the alley. Through its diamond-upon-diamond weave, Binko could see the circus.

Less than a hundred yards away, the Big Top rose into the sky. The king-pole reared through the canvas at the centre, taller than a three-storey building. Bright red and yellow canvas flowed out and down in an enormous cone held taut by webs of rope and wire. Bright-coloured wagons and smaller tents clustered around like children at the feet of a parent. Towering over everything else, a Ferris wheel revolved in the background, firefly-lights aglow, soft music sweetening the air. A postcard-perfect scene.

Even through the cotton wads, Binko could hear the Ferris wheel calling sensuously from across the lot. He could hear laughter, and cheering, and the calls of concessionaires from the midway. Somewhere, a big cat roared.

"Look, over there." Chester pointed to where the rear of the lot butted against the old rail line. A train stood on long abandoned tracks.

It was a 2-8-0 steam-locomotive, easily a hundred years old. The engine was jet-black, with gold trimming around the boiler and driving wheels. A conga-line of coaches, wagons, and flatcars were coupled behind the engine. Most were freight cars—rough, wooden-slatted things as dark and uninviting as coffins—cars for transporting livestock.

"I can't do this," Binko said through clenched teeth. A coldness clutched at his guts, and yet the sounds of the circus still whispered of dancing bears and brightly painted teeter boards. "I can't do it, Chester."

"Yeah, sure you can." Chester patted Binko on the back. "Just keep your head low. Ignore the ballyhoo. You don't listen to the ads in a TV break, do you? All that spruikin's just the same. Adverts for things *you* don't need."

Binko's grip tightened on the fence; cold wire dug painfully into his fingers. "I know I don't *need* them," he said. "I don't even *want* them, but . . . " He looked from the Big Top to the train and back again. "They're going to load everyone up? Aren't they?" he asked.

"Yep, I reckon they are, and the show's gonna be startin' *real* soon, Binko."

All his friends would be in that tent. Annabelle and Kooky and Uncle Doody. Wally and Zippy. The clowns he saw in the streets and behind the counters of stores. The clowns he'd grown up with. Everyone who'd made Clowntown his home. They would all be gone. "What do you want me to do?" he said.

Chester motioned him to crouch down, plucked a wad of waxy cotton from Binko's ear, and whispered his part in the plan.

They waited for the Big Top to open, and then another hour for all the clowns to be ushered in, before making their move.

Arlo tossed Chester over the fence, and then gave Binko a boost. Binko landed heavily on the rough and dusty ground.

Chester laughed and helped him to his feet. "Lucky you weren't born an acrobat." He dashed across the no-man's land between alley and wagons, and Binko followed. They crawled under an empty trailer and crouched beneath greasy axles. Binko looked back to the wire fence and Arlo waved. A fanfare erupted from the Big Top; a band playing the *Liberty Bell March*.

"Hold on, Binko." Chester threw a comforting arm around him. "You can do this. Just hang in there."

They could see down the midway from where they were. It was deserted—a ghost town of empty coconut-shies and shooting galleries seen through the spokes of a wagon wheel. Crumpled candy wrappers rolled through the dust, as lonely as tumbleweeds.

Chester pointed to the Big Top. "I'm gonna sidewall my way in. You know what to do, Binko. Wait for the signal, then make your move. If anyone sees you, mace 'em! Good luck, lad. I'll see ya when this is all over." He crawled out from under the wagon and was off like a rabbit, disappearing under a tent-flap.

Binko stayed, alone in the dust and shadows. He looked back for Arlo, but he was gone too. He hummed a tune in an attempt to block the noise from the tent, and waited for the signal.

❧❦

"*Roll up! Roll up! Roll up!*"

The voice of the ringmaster filled the lot. It echoed inside the Big Top and bled from speakers strung up and down the midway. The sound was harsh and vulgar. It was Binko's signal to move.

"*Welcome, one and all, to McKenzie's Universal Circus and Museum of the Bizarre! The greatest show you will ever see in this, or any other world!*"

From his hiding place under the wagon, Binko groaned. How could they all have been so stupid? So gullible? Sucked in by such showy pageantry? Listening from the outside, it all seemed so wrong.

225

"Sights that will dazzle. Sights that will amaze. Sights that you will find nowhere else, ladies and gentlemen. Nowhere! They are all here to entice you. To entrance you and amaze you!"

Binko found nothing enticing about that voice ... or about the freight cars waiting on the rail line out back.

"I guarantee, ladies and gentleman, by the end of this show you will never *want to leave."*

A great cheer arose and the band struck up again. Laughter and applause thundered through the lot.

Binko scrambled from beneath the wagon, his red and white suit covered in dirt, axle grease slicking his hair. He took the wire-cutters Chester had left for him and edged towards the Big Top.

"Don't worry about the thick ones," Chester had told him. "They're for the king and queen poles, and we don't wanna to bring *them* down 'til all the clowns are clear. Go for the finer wires that hold the quarter and side poles. We wanna weaken the sucker, not bring it down 'round our ears."

Binko reached the walls of the Big Top — heavy canvas sheets, laced together with eyelets and ropes, punctuated along their length by poles held taut in a cat's cradle of guy ropes and wires. All he had to do was stay low, follow the wall, snip every second or third wire along the way, and be finished and ready to trip the generator by the finale. Easy.

The wire-cutters were a little stiff, and the first wire took a while to cut. Eventually it snapped with a twang. The music and cheering inside the tent had not let up since the fanfare — there wasn't a chance of him being heard by anyone over all that racket.

One by one he cut the cables that helped support the main structure. The damage wouldn't be noticed. Wouldn't bring down the Big Top unless a big storm blew up — and that was unlikely. The sky was clear; deep and dark with night.

He reached the entrance marquee and skipped past the closed curtain, smiling and giggling at how well he was completing his part of the plan. How, only a few feet away behind a thin membrane of canvas, they suspected nothing of his sabotage.

Half way, half way. Not many to go now. He'd be finished and at the rear of the tent in no time.

He wondered where Chester and Arlo were.

He wondered if Kooky, Wally, Uncle Doody and Annabelle would be all right. They were just on the other side of the canvas. Brainwashed? Helpless?

He stretched out his hand to touch the wall. It vibrated with the sound of mirth; the cheerful blast of the calliope; the thump-thump-thump of a kettledrum. It vibrated with life. His hand took up the resonance, transferred it to his bones and up his arms, filling his skull.

He leant forward to peer through a gap in the lacing.

Through the canvas wall, past the wooden braces supporting the stands, between the pantalooned legs of the crowd, Binko could see that the circus was in full swing. Every act looked to be performing at once. They competed for space in and above the arena. Acrobats, trapeze artists and tight-rope walkers spun through the air. Sequined showgirls, dancing horses, fire-eaters, and sword-swallowers all circled the ring in a tightly choreographed kaleidoscope of colour.

Singly, and in groups, the clowns in the audience were rising. Slowly, ecstatically, they left their seats and made their way towards the centre ring—brightly-painted zombies marching happily to their doom.

As the clowns stepped into the ring, a roustabout handed them each a prop. He passed out unicycles and stilts, air-horns, rubber-chickens, and battery-powered bow ties. The clowns eagerly claimed the props and began their acts. They danced, and cavorted, and tripped over each other's feet. There were pratfalls, and slapstick, and plenty of pies thrown. Religious fervour infused their eyes—rapturous and distant.

Binko wanted to shout at them, tell them to wake up!

Each clown's time in the spotlight, though, was brief. Barely had they pulled a gag before the ringmaster tapped them on the shoulder from behind. He whispered in their ear, and the clown stopped to take a triumphant bow towards the diminishing audience. A cheer erupted for each clown as they turned and left through the ring door.

Binko realised that the cheers were recorded. There weren't enough clowns left in the stands to create such a ruckus. But it was applause! An ovation, the likes of which most clowns would never hear, and its source didn't matter. A part of Binko understood this, and for a moment, his composure slipped. If he could just get his hands on the right prop, he'd perform the greatest gag of the night. Get the biggest cheer. Maybe impress the ringmaster so much he would be made Boss Clown? Now *that* would be something.

He shook his head, disgusted at his own weakness, and pulled away from the gap in the canvas. He had a job to finish. All the clowns in Clowntown depended on him, and he wouldn't let them down.

"Oy! Bozo! Who said you could run away from the circus?"

The voice was close, abrasive. Binko dropped the wire cutters and spun around, hand fumbling in his pocket for the mace.

A scowling carnie stood close, his face a dry and cracked landscape of acne scars and stubble. The stench of corn dogs and chewin' baccy hung on his breath.

"Come on, then." The carnie grabbed him by the shoulder. "Still time for your moment in the spotlight." He began to drag Binko back towards the entrance marquee.

Binko pulled the can from his pocket, aimed straight at the carnie's weathered face, and pressed the trigger.

Long strands of silly string streamed into the air, curling over the carnie in a slimy, pink mess that draped his shoulders and covered his face.

Damn! Wrong can! Binko pitched it as hard he could. It flew from his hand and bounced off the carnie's forehead with a satisfying crunch.

"Argh! Bastard clown!" The carnie peeled silly string from his face and hair. He lunged for Binko. The two of them collapsed in a heap, wrestling, rolling through the dust.

"Hey rube! Hey rube!" the carnie screamed between punches. Binko tried to force his hand over the carnie's mouth to stifle the cry for help. The carnie bit down hard and Binko screamed.

Rough-voiced shouts and hulking shadows closed in from behind the rows of wagons. A great weight landed on Binko from behind, driving him to the ground, pushing the air from his lungs in a rush of pain. Fists landed on his kidneys, his gut. Booted feet found his ribs with cruel accuracy.

Something hard came down on the back of Binko's head: suddenly his vision narrowed, darkness descended, voices receded. The world was reduced to a point of light that seared his brain. Calloused hands lifted him from the ground, and mercifully, the light went out.

☞◦᠅

. . . ay kup, ay kup inko, ake up . . .

The refrain played around Binko's mind, a carousel of gibberish that left him dizzy and nauseous.

. . . ake up, ake up . . .

Pain pulsed behind Binko's eyes and a tight knot of muscle ached at the back of his neck.

"Binko, wake up." The voice was soft but insistent, a susurration of syllables close to his ear.

Binko opened his eyes and turned his head. Chester grinned at him like a madman from the shadows. "We gotta get you out'a here, Binko."

They were inside the Big Top, in the performer's vestibule between arena and backyard. Canvas stretched above them into darkness. Binko lay in a bed of straw, hidden from view behind two elephants. Rough ropes bit into his wrists and ankles, holding him tight. He could hear talking and movement on the far side of the room. See the faint light of electric bulbs.

A bright flash filled the tent, blinding until he blinked away the glare.

"They're photographin' everyone, Binko," Chester explained. "Makin' 'em all sign work agreements. Branding 'em too, before they pack 'em on the train."

"Our faces? They're photographing our faces?"

"Yep."

"But, our faces are who we are. They're like fingerprints. Like our souls!"

Chester nodded, working quickly at Binko's bonds, untying his feet and hands. When he was done he helped Binko to stand and led him through the shadows, past elephants, and llamas, and a lion pacing its cage.

A steady flow of clowns were leaving the arena. Carnies and roustabouts kept them moving, prodding them into line with bull-hooks and riding crops. The clowns looked around, confused and unsure of themselves, too dazed to protest. One by one they were led to the processing station and photographed, the dazzle of the flash shocking them deeper into stunned compliance. Without much prompting, they signed the single sheet of paper placed in front of them—a scribbled "X" was enough to secure their permanent employ-ment. Identity recorded, contract signed, the clowns were led to a pot of coals and marked with a glowing brand that filled the air with the stink of burnt flesh. Rough hands stifled screams, smearing make-up into grotesque masks of fear and pain. Some clowns struggled in the tight grip of the carnies. Others passed out. All were dragged out the back door of the Big Top, off to the waiting train.

"C'mon, Binko. You okay? They're almost done. Arlo needs us to finish this." Chester tried to pull Binko away, but he wouldn't move. He was staring at the line of clowns—at Kooky and Annabelle who stood only moments from processing.

Kooky still held the unicycle at his side. His eyes gleamed with pleasure. A silly grin stretched across his face. Annabelle was cata-tonic—a shuffling mess of tangled hair and pom-poms, prodded along by laughing roustabouts.

"Come on, darlin'," a roustabout lashed out with a punctuating whack. "Keep it movin'. We still gotta photograph that pretty face of yours."

Binko moved towards them, but Chester pulled him back by the hem of his shirt.

"What'ya gonna do, Binko? Rush in there and take 'em all on? Save the maiden in distress? They'll eat you for breakfast! They almost did already. Annabelle'll be all right. They'll *all* be all right if we just keep to the plan. Be strong, Binko."

The music and cheering in the Big Top stopped abruptly, as if someone had lifted a needle from a record. Sounds previously hidden revealed themselves to Binko's ears: a generator chugging away outside the tent, throaty snarls from big cats in their cages, the hiss of the branding iron on clown-flesh.

Keep to the plan? How can I stick to a plan in the face of something like this? Plans are logical, organised. This is madness, chaos, hell. How can you draw strength from that?

No more clowns joined the line from the Big Top. The last of them were through, and the Ringmaster followed.

He was a large man, nothing at all like the caricature on the poster. Dressed in a black suit, adorned at cuff and collar with braids of gold, top hat on his head, he strode into the vestibule and looked around.

"Good show! Good show!" He patted roustabouts and carnies on the back as he passed along the line. "Get this lot processed, boys, and we'll pull up stakes. We're leavin' this ghost town to rot. We got us enough clowns now to tour forever. *McKenzie's Perpetual Circus and Clown Menagerie* is on its way!"

He swaggered out the back door, the circus crew cheering and clapping at their master's bluster.

"Ain't got no time left now, Binko," Chester said. "They'll have 'em all loaded up in a jiffy. I've gotta stay and grab that camera when the lights go out. If they've got our faces, they've got us forever. We need you to knock the power out, Binko. You've gotta go *now*."

A menagerie . . . all of us working the circus forever.

Binko knew this wasn't hell, not really. It was just the ticket booth leading the way. Hell would be waiting for them at the other end of the railway line. He nodded and crept towards the tent wall. Before ducking under the canvas he took a last look back. Annabelle was in the processing chair. The camera clicked, flooding the vestibule with light. Annabelle didn't blink. She didn't even move as the brand was raised and brought down on her arm.

Binko turned and fled.

❧❦

The generator sat in the shadows—a giant octopus spreading its tentacles across the lot, feeding power to the Big Top, and the Midway, to the spotlights which lit the backyard. Beyond it, Binko could see a line of flares that marked the trail along which the clowns were being herded.

He waited until the last clown in line had passed and ran for the generator, careful to avoid the guy wires beneath his feet.

A roustabout appeared from behind a trailer, unzipping his pants, intent on his task. Binko dropped, sliding the last few feet to the generator, hoping it would hide him from view. He stopped beneath the generator, the diesel engine running hot above, dust in his eyes and mouth. The roustabout stopped, boots close enough for Binko to touch. A rank stream splattered the dirt inches from his face, rivulets forming a steaming puddle of piss and mud. He held his nose and waited while the roustabout finished, zipped up, and moved on.

Binko crawled from beneath the generator, scalding his neck on the exhaust pipe and stepping in the piss on the way.

He opened a panel in the side of the generator and stared in at the chugging engine. It was a confusion of machinery—a nest of pipes, and wires, and metal things that meant nothing to him. He had no idea how to sabotage a generator!

He'd just have to cut as many wires and hoses as he could. One of them was bound to cause damage of some sort.

He reached into his pockets for the wire-cutters. *Aww shit!* He'd dropped them back where the carnies had caught him. *Aww shit! What am I gonna do now?*

"All out and over. All out. All over."

The voice came from the direction of the train, a great bellow that had to be the ringmaster. It was Binko's final signal. The last of the clowns had been loaded onto the train.

He looked around for a discarded tool, a piece of metal, a broken bottle, anything with which he could stop the generator. He found nothing.

The ringmaster was making his way back down the trail, a top-hatted silhouette against the night. A phalanx of carnies, roustabouts, razorbacks, and sideshow freaks followed behind.

"All out and over. All out. All over," he shouted again. "Time to get this show movin', boys. Pull up stakes and load her up. I want us out of here by dawn."

The circus crew spread out, some moving towards the Midway to pack up the rides and stalls. Riggers headed for the Big Top to pull down the stands and lower the roof. They moved through the lot, busy as ants. They hadn't seen Binko, but they would as they worked their way closer. He had to act fast.

He reached his hand into the engine bay and fumbled around, fingers stretched to grasp as many hoses and cables as he could. His knuckles brushed the engine block, white-heat searing gloves and flesh, and he held back a scream. He gripped like a vice and pulled as hard as he could.

Wires snapped. Hoses cracked and tore from their fasteners. Binko went sprawling backwards into the dust, still clutching a handful of engine guts. The generator coughed, spluttered. Lights all around the circus dimmed and flickered. Darkness fell in the instant the generator ground to a halt.

Binko ran, using the dying light of the flare-trail to guide him. He slipped past the Ringmaster. Confused shouts rose from the circus crew as he sped by. He could smell diesel on his clothes, feel it soaking his gloves.

Somewhere, on the other side of the Big Top, an explosion ripped through the air.

Binko stopped, risking a backwards glance. Flames leapt from the Midway, orange light twisting with the shadows. From inside the Big Top, a lion's roar was prelude to screams of pain and terror as Chester let the big cats loose.

Binko turned and ran for the train.

☞⚜☜

Confused and frightened faces stared out from between the rough-planed planks of the freight cars.

"The circus! The circus!" they cried. "Someone is burning down the circus."

Sky-rockets lit the sky, bursting into chrysanthemums of rainbow light. The clowns stopped their crying to stare in delight, jaws slack with *ooohs* and *aaahs*.

"Come on," someone called as Binko passed. "Climb aboard! We're running away to join the circus."

They don't even want to be saved anymore. Is this what we really are? Binko couldn't believe it. Not after everything he'd been through.

He looked for familiar faces, the faces of his friends—but recognised no one. Their make-up was too smudged, smeared, running like dark tears down pale cheeks. Smiles melted into frowns.

He couldn't leave them in there. Animals on their way—*to slaughter, to slaughter*—to market.

Binko stepped up to one of the freight cars. The sliding door had no lock, just a lever. A rusty metal lever that might take some strength to shift, but he could do it. He knew he could.

"Don't, Binko. They'll only run back." Chester stood on the trail with Arlo. The circus camera was strung around his neck, dangling to his knees. Behind them, the fire on the Midway bathed everything in a warm glow. Circus crew ran around putting out fires, working on the generator, trying to control the animals prowling the lot.

"They'll all be okay, Binko," Chester said. "You did good. They mightn't seem too grateful right now, but they will once the glamour's worn off. They'll be thankful for what you've done."

He turned to Arlo. "Go and see if you can convince the driver to move us on. We're gonna need to get gone real quick."

Arlo ran back towards the engine. His walking cane had been unsheathed, transformed into a razor thin rapier which glinted like blood in the light from the fire.

"I hope Arlo's persuasive." Chester led Binko back to the caboose, loosening brake-wheels on the freight cars with his sceptre. "They'll have those fires out in no time. Might take 'em a while to calm the animals down, but I sure hope they fix that generator before we leave. Arlo spent a bit of time with that Ferris wheel whilst we were dealin' with other matters. I'd hate to see all his hard work go to waste."

੭~ᕠ

Red as sin, the caboose was a garish full-stop to the long line of clown-filled freight cars. Firelight played off its painted surface and reflected in darkened windows. On the roof, a squat cupola peered back along the length of the train. Steps and a long, curved handrail lent easy access to a narrow platform at the back. The carriage appeared empty.

"They used to call them clown wagons, you know?" Chester jumped up onto the platform and turned the final brake-wheel. "Kinda fitting, don't you think?"

Binko looked back to the circus. The flames were still rising, but it looked like the spread had been stopped. He hadn't heard an explosion or animal call in a while, either.

A whistle sounded from back towards the train's engine. It was loud. Much too loud.

"Come on, Binko! Arlo's got this beast moving. Get up here, will ya?"

The whistle sounded again and Binko watched as some of the circus crew turned. They might not have been able to see him standing there in flickering shadows, but they knew what the whistle meant. He heard the train lurch into motion behind him; felt it as a twitch in the earth that tickled the soles of his feet. The carnies were pointing, yelling, running down the path towards the train.

No, no, no! Binko thought. *We've come too far to end this here.* He turned. The train was still moving slowly, crawling along the tracks, and he did not have to run fast to catch up. He reached out a gloved hand, grabbed the curved handrail and jumped. His feet caught the edge of the steps, scrabbling for purchase, and slipped. He dangled from the handrail, shoes dragging furrows in the dirt. Chester reached out with a tiny hand and Binko swiped for it, missed. The train lurched again as a fresh load of power was transferred from the engine, spreading along the line of railcars. Chester, already over-balanced, toppled forward.

Binko seized the handrail with both hands and pushed up from the ground. He flicked his legs out hard and straight, opened in a slight "V". His back arched, momentum from his legs carrying him up into the air, still holding tight to the rail. He was no tumbling-clown, but he knew a few moves.

Chester landed in the crook of Binko's legs. He held tight as he was carried up and over, caught in the arc Binko's body inscribed in the night.

Binko, now almost upside down, let go of the handrail, hoping he'd timed everything right. He grunted and threw his upper body forward, up, back towards the train. The weight of his legs, and the extra bulk of Chester nestled in his crotch, completed the trajectory Binko had set for himself. Chester dropped from between Binko's legs and landed gracefully on the caboose platform. Binko followed a second later, legs and arms aching, astonished at what he had just done.

The train was picking up speed, but it still wasn't going fast enough. A rabble gang of carnies and roustabouts burst from the path as the caboose passed. They reached out with grimy hands and bull-hooks, snaring the handrail, trying for the brake-wheel. One climbed onto the platform and made a grab for Binko. Chester swung his sceptre hard and low. The sceptre knee-capped the roustabout with a sickening crunch, sending him toppling back off the train. A rough-faced carnie caught onto the back of the carriage, reaching over and turning the brake-wheel.

A high-pitched squeal came from the rails beneath them, a sound that tore at the mind like cats fighting or a baby's scream. Sparks flew up from the wheels, strobing the ground with light. The caboose groaned as the coupling between it and the next carriage strained to hold. Binko pounded at the carnie's tattooed arms. He bit at the knuckles which turned the wheel. If he didn't open up the brake-wheel the coupling would snap. The train would tear itself away from the caboose.

Chester had his hands full. His sceptre twirled and sang through the air, swinging left and right into the faces and groins of their attackers. One by one they tumbled from the train, falling heavily into dust and saltbush.

The carnie at the brake-wheel laughed at Binko's attempts to displace him. "If we can't have the lot, we're sure gonna make a special attraction out of you, Bozo!"

Binko stared at the carnie's face, remembering the last person to call him Bozo—the carnie outside the Big Top, the one he'd tried to . . .

He put a hand into his pocket and smiled. Raising his arm, he pointed an aerosol can straight at the carnie's face.

"Ahh, I've seen that trick before," the carnie smiled.

Binko fired. The carnie screamed as capsicum spray flooded his eyes and clawed at sinuses. He released his grip on the brake-wheel, clutching at his face, falling back off the carriage and disappearing into the distance.

Binko grabbed the brake-wheel and spun it as hard as he could. The brake released and the torturous squeal stopped. Sparks sputtered away to nothing and the train surged forward, freed of its anchor.

Chester dispatched his final assailant and laughed with maniacal glee. "We did it, Binko! We did it!"

Binko sank down, exhausted, onto the step at the edge of the platform. His feet dangled, swaying with the increasing rhythm of the train.

He watched as the circus sprang back into to life. With the generator finally fixed, rainbow strings of light flowed along the tents, the wagons, the rides. Music poured from speakers. Spotlights carved white cones in the smoke. It was a magical sight.

"Watch this, watch this," Chester said from over his shoulder.

In the circus lot, the Ferris wheel began to turn, a constellation of lights in motion. It groaned around its central axle and something gave way with a screech of grinding metal. The wheel broke from its housing, rolling across the lot, crushing wagons and trailers as it went. It barrelled into the Big Top—two hundred and twenty tonnes of steel, stretching cables and fabric. The canvas tore, cables snapped. The king pole fell, and the entire structure collapsed—a giant bellows fanning the flames of the midway. The Big Top caught alight too: oiled canvas curling, blackening, flaring into the night.

Binko had no idea how many people were still inside. He tried not to think about it. The whole scene was becoming distant: a miniature display shrinking to a candle flame on the horizon.

He thought of the clowns packed into the train. Of the joy and terror imprinted on their faces. The homes and freedom they'd left behind. The fools they'd made of themselves! All for a day at the circus.

"They'll be okay, won't they?" he asked, knowing they'd be feeling scared, betrayed.

"They'll get over it, eventually" Chester said. "We're a resilient bunch, Binko. Been taking pies and pratfalls for hundreds of years. That's gotta harden us up somewhat. They'll need your help, though."

"What about Clowntown? How are we going to get back to Clowntown?"

"Clowntown's not a *place*, Binko," Chester grinned. "It's a state of mind! A way of being who we *are*."

Chester took his sceptre and dubbed it gently onto Binko's shoulders. "You've got a million miles of track ahead of you, Binko. Find a place and teach them how to be free clowns again. Remind them who they really are. It will take time, but you've proved your strength. You're Boss Clown now."

Binko thought of the track, stretching forward and back like a measure of their lives; of Alfie the hobo, who'd return home to a ghost town; and of McKenzie's Circus, who weren't the sort of people to let matters rest. Mostly, he thought of the clowns, still packed tight in the freight cars. Even above the sound of the train, he could hear their muffled shouts and protests, their cries for the circus. They stomped and banged on the walls, begging to go back to juggle and dance.

He ignored the noise to focus on the job he'd been given. The job of leading the clowns home. Of leading them back to themselves. It would take time.

The sun rose up behind them, slowly revealing the landscape on which they travelled. The plain was wide and empty, passing by without change. Tears blurred Binko's vision as he searched for a place for them to stop.

Nine Letters About Spit

ROBERT SHEARMAN

Dear Sir,

In response to your letter, dated 15th August, I will state that we do indeed sell dogs. I can state that most unequivocally. We are a pet shop, sir. Selling dogs is what we do.

I am confident that we can furnish your needs, and look forward to your paying a visit to our establishment at your convenience.

I should add, moreover, that we do not merely supply dogs. We have cats, parrots, budgerigars, mice, hamsters, all colours of goldfish, and have recently acquired four baby turtles. All of these, naturally, will be made available for your additional perusal.

Yours sincerely, etc.

❧❧

Dear Sir,

In response to your letter, dated 19th August, I would beg, sir, for some additional information. You say that you require dogs tailored to your specific needs. But you do not say what these needs might be. If you would indulge us with some indication, sir, then maybe we would be able to recommend accordingly.

241

If you want a dog as loyal companion, I would suggest a Labrador or a German Shepherd or an Alsatian would be ideal. We have a very friendly Alsatian at the moment, we call him Fyodor, but of course you can change the name as you see fit. If a guard dog, I would advise some sort of mastiff. Is the dog intended to be a gift? If for a child, we have a great array of puppies, of all breeds, all of sweet temperaments. If for a lady, our new range of Chihuahuas always proves very popular, or maybe a poodle; both dogs are considered perfect accessories for the fashionable gentlewoman about town.

Your letter suggests moreover that you are looking to purchase *dogs* — in the plural — as opposed to *a dog* — in the singular. And I seek only to reassure you, sir, that we boast a full complement of dogs, and can satisfy your needs should you want two, or half a dozen, even twenty of the creatures. (Your letter suggests moreover that you are looking to purchase *many* dogs — in a large plural — as opposed to a *few* dogs — in the small plural. We seek only to reassure you, sir, when we say we can provide twenty, that I was using a round number, in fact we can provide twenty-three, we have twenty-three dogs at the moment.)

I should add too, of course, that in addition to the dogs we also sell cats, parrots, budgerigars, hamsters, fish, and four baby turtles. I say with full confidence that there is no finer pet shop in St Petersburg, and we look forward to satisfying your special needs. Whatever they may turn out to be.

I have the honour, sir, to be your servant, etc.

P.S. — There are, of course, some very fine pet shops on Nevsky Prospekt, and I dare say in all conscience I cannot compete with those. Ours is a family pet shop, sir, run by myself and my daughter Nina, and (until recently) my late wife Natalya. Theirs though are pet shops run as *industries*, with animals passing through their hands day and night, in one door and out the other, and may be by appointment to the Tsar, and display it in the window, sir, and the money spent on those dogs may be more than the worth of my entire shop. But I sincerely put it to you that there is no finer *family* pet shop than ours, run with simple love, in the whole of St Petersburg. And I have the honour once again, sir, to be your servant, etc.

ತ⊸∽

Dear Sir,

Thank you for your letter, dated 23rd August. I can confirm that we will be 'at home' for you, as it were, at your especial convenience, on Saturday next. Moreover, we will have the shop closed for your private viewing, so that you can inspect the animals at your own leisure without interruption. Moreover, I will assure you that I shall be present, a faithful servant in the background, etc., sir, to answer any questions you may have. Moreover, I shall guarantee that the dogs will all be scrubbed and clean and brushed within an inch of their lives and acting upon their very best behaviour.

You still have not revealed what your especial needs for the dogs may be, but it is no matter, each and every one will be standing to attention to demonstrate whatever particular attributes may take your fancy.

Moreover, I feel I should apologise. It has come to my attention, sir, that you are a famous personage, a man of science, and I humbly seek your pardon in my earlier missives to your most honourable self for not being in full acknowledgement of that there fact. I am a plain man, sir, and I confess I had never heard of you. But now that I am in the know, I ask whether you might consider, should this not be an imper-tinence, and should you naturally find my dogs and my establishment to your particular satisfaction, allowing me to advertise the fact that you are my customer? The shops on Nevsky Prospekt say 'by appointment to the Tsar'. It would be a signal honour, say, if you would permit a similar sign, hanging in my window, saying we were 'by appointment to Ivan Pavlov, open brackets, famous scientist, close brackets. I would, of course, offer you a discount for the dogs. I might even throw in a dog for free.

I remain, sir, in keen anticipation of your arrival, etc.

さみ

Dear Sir,

Please, sir, accept my apologies for what has occurred. I am mortified.

Let me state, first, that when you said you would visit my shop on the Saturday, I bluntly took you at your word, and had not appreciated (as I now perforce must do) that you would have meant 'Saturday, or some close to Saturday', or, 'not Saturday at all, but in the environs of Saturday'. Had I realised, sir, that by Saturday you had really meant Thursday, I would have closed the shop in readiness (as I promised), I would have had the dogs groomed for display (as I promised) — and, moreover, I would have ensured that I was on the premises to greet you.

I was abroad from the shop, sir, on Thursday, because I was accepting a consignment of hamsters. I say this to you, sir, so you will realise that my absence was not borne out of laziness or inconstancy, I was engaged nonetheless in business. Of course, hamsters do not sell as well as dogs: that is the tragedy of the thing. I would have foresworn each and every hamster in Russia had I realised they would come between you and me, and between you and my dogs.

And then you would not have been left alone with Nina.

What can I say, to put this right? Nina is my daughter. Forgive a father's indulgence. She is still a young girl, and she is headstrong and she is impetuous. I assure you that when she had you ejected from the shop it would have been done (mistakenly as she clearly was) for reasons that she thought were best.

She is a sentimentalist, Mister Pavlov, sir. She is a woman, and women are made of sentiment, and it is a dear and tender thing, but it is not a useful quality in a pet shop owner. She will name the animals, she will pet them as if they are ours. She calls the Alsatian Fyodor, she calls the poodle little Olga-kins. I tell her it is ridiculous. That these are products to be sold, and the customer will have the right to do whatever he likes with these products, to rename them as he sees fit. But ever since her mother died last year — and it was a shock, sir, so sudden and so sad, and I doubt that myself or Nina will ever truly get over it, and finding her body like that, so still and somehow so small — ever since, she has fixated upon the animals, she has poured her love into them. And she has so much love to give, sir. Sometimes, if we sell a pet, she will sit in her room for a day and cry. And I shall say to her, but my darling, we *need* to sell them, that is what they are *for*, how else can we eat? And she will tell me that she knows that, but she may doubt the character of a particular customer, she thinks a particular customer will not treat our animals well; she begs me to go and find this particular customer, to rescue the pet we just sold him, to buy the animal back. Of course, I do not do this.

I tell you all this, sir, not to frustrate you or to exhaust your patience, but to give you a context for what happened, you as a man of science and all.

She was not prepared for the precise and intimate inspection you wanted to give our dogs. And I must admit, I do not follow her descriptions of what you did either, and fear she may have misunderstood. You told her you were interested in 'psychic secretions'. And you went to each and every dog, and put your fingers in its mouth, and tugged hard. You said you were looking to see whether or not you could stimulate the dog's salivary gland, that the specific needs you had for the dogs you left unspecified in our correspondence was that they must drool copiously. It was the fact that you so distressed Fyodor that did it, sir; the Alsatian is a favourite of Nina's. Nina said that when you thrust your hand into Fyodor's mouth you did it with too much force, sir, that you hurt Fyodor. That is why she shouted at you, sir. That is why she called you such names (she has confessed some of the names she called you), that is why she chased you from the shop. It is unfortunate too, sir, that you came during regular business hours, and that one of our burlier customers, I'm sure only wanting to help, had you frogmarched from the premises and plonked you down so hard in the gutter.

I know I should punish Nina, sir. But understand a father's love. She was protecting the dogs as if they were her own children, and I can only feel the same impulse. Since the death of Natalya (my wife, sir) we have been all on our own here. And I can't explain it. But whenever I *see* Nina, whenever I hear her voice, my heart gives a skip, it swells, it misses a beat. It is entirely involuntary. It is a reflex action over which I have no control. I know I should be angry with her, but she triggers something within me, I feel such a rush of love that it overwhelms me quite. And I'll think of her mother—even though she looks nothing like her, if anything Nina has taken after me, same hair, same jaw, none of Natalya's more refined features—but she makes me think of her mother, and I'm in love, I almost sway with the force of it, and I hang on to that little happiness, I don't want to let it go.

I hope, sir, you can forgive the misunderstanding. And may return to my shop at your convenience. I shall be here, sir, next time, whenever that may be, the hamsters may go hang themselves, and I shall attend to your needs, and Nina, she will be away somewhere, I can send her out. And you can have all the dogs to look through, and the cats, and the parakeets, and the fish, and the baby turtle. (We only have the one turtle; one was sold, two died, it was a shame.)

I remain, sir, your most faithful and apologetic, etc.

ॐॐ

Dear Sir,

It has been two weeks now, and yet I have not received acknowledgement of my letter to you, dated 30th August, in which I made a full and frank apology in respect of what occurred in my pet shop, vis a vis you, my dogs, and my daughter, on 29th August. The least I might have expected was a response; I was hoping, moreover, for an apology back, not least because my daughter claims you brutalised our dogs, and my daughter does not lie.

I will choose to believe, sir, that the letter you sent has been mislaid in the post. Or that you entirely forgot to reply, so lost in your strange salivating experiments, and that this fresh communication from me will prompt you to do so. We remain, as ever, sir, available for the sale of dogs, no matter what your requirements, and we will most happily accept your custom.

Yours sincerely, etc.

☞◦☜

Dear Sir,

A whole month has now passed, and I can only conclude that the slight you have shown my daughter by not making an apology is intentional. I understand too that you have purchased a number of dogs at Ivanov's Pet Emporium on Nevsky Prospekt. If that is the case, then more fool you. Ivanov's dogs are too posh and refined to salivate, it would be beneath their aristocratic dignity. Whereas the dogs I sell are good, hardy, earthy Russian dogs without pretension, and would drool for your pleasure night and day. Even our Chihuahuas have some peasant grit in them.

I wish to inform you moreover, on my daughter's prompting, that we still intend to hang in our window a sign saying we are 'by appointment to Ivan Pavlov, open brackets, famous scientist, close brackets'. We had the sign made up when we fully expected you would be buying our dogs, and indeed you led us on, you gave us every reason to believe it was so. And you *have* shopped here, sir, no matter the circumstances of your departure. Besides, the sign cost money. (If you object to the sign, then we will take it down, but we would ask you at least to pay for the board and the inks that fashioned it.)

I write, moreover, to tell you I am troubled. Since your visit Nina has taken an inordinate interest in the salivatory instincts of our dogs. It is most unlike her. She attempts to keep it hidden from me, but a father knows. And sometimes I will spy her, prodding away at their mouths, poking inside; one time I even caught her yanking upon poor Fyodor's tongue. She carries a little saucer, and holds it under the mouths to collect the drool; and then she *studies* it, she sniffs at it, compares it to other drool samples she has already taken, I've even seen her dip her finger into it to taste it. The dogs take it in good spirits; they love Nina, and really, who could not? But they are confused by this development, and so am I.

Yours, etc.

స్త్రా

Dear Sir,

We have had our differences, but I write to you now as a fellow scientist. Or, at least, as the father of a fellow scientist.

The fact of the matter is this: there are a lot of animals here, and feeding them is a matter that requires great enterprise and methodical planning. Animals are brutes, and look forward only to their next meal. We have a lot of animals to feed, and when they see another of a rival species being given preferential treatment, they get excited and angry. We need to feed the parrots before the budgerigars, because the parrots are bad-tempered and squawk furiously otherwise. We feed the hamsters before the goldfish, because the hamsters go crazy in their cages, throwing their little bodies against the cage bars and rattling them so. We feed everything before the turtle, because the turtle can't make a fuss.

To summon the dogs, Nina rings a bell. Then the dogs know to come in, to line up, to eat.

One day she rang the bell for them, and then there was a crisis: the parrot got out of his cage! Nina had already fed it, but must not have closed its cage properly—and now it was out, and careening around the room—and it was full of food, and it was exultant, and it celebrated by raining down droppings on all the animals still hungry below. It took the work of several minutes to get it back behind bars, and at least as long again to clean up all the mess.

When Nina turned back to the dogs, she saw that they'd been salivating. There were entire puddles of spit underneath their panting heads. She concluded that the salivating was triggered either by the ringing of the bell, or by the rain of bird excrement upon their heads. She experimented. Fresh excrement seemed to have no effect, but when she once more rang the bell, the dog drooling recommenced. She decided not to feed them at all; she merely rang the bell instead every half hour—and each time she did, in anticipation of the food she was withholding from them, they'd salivate freely.

Nina believes that this is a remarkable thing. That the dogs now associate hearing a bell with tasting food. They almost seem to bliss out on it; she rings the bell enough times, and they roll over lazy and happy, as if they've eaten their fill, as if we've tricked them into believing there's meat in their bellies.

We should probably feed them soon, though, or they'll starve. I thought there might be a practical application to this discovery, that we could save money by not giving them food at all, and merely by ringing a bell cheaply and at no cost we could satisfy their dietary needs. Nina is certain this isn't the case, so feed them we must. (And the amount of dog spit on the floor is causing the shop to smell.)

Nina reports that she has tried the same experiment on the turtle, but the turtle shows no interest in drooling whatsoever.

Yours, in mutual respect, etc.

❦

Dear Sir,

You will have heard, I am sure, of our great success! We are the talk
of St Petersburg. Even Ivanov on Nevsky Prospekt must be gnashing
his teeth with jealousy. I write to you not in smug pride, to show you
that we were right, and you were wrong. But, as Nina says, in humble
understanding now of what you were trying to achieve, and recogni-
tion of your part in our fortune.

This is the conclusion we have drawn from our experiments. People
don't much like pet shops. But they give their hearts to animals that
can do funny tricks.

And they'll flock to our shop. No, not shop, our little theatre.
There are banners outside, have you seen them? 'Nina Allanovich and
Her Salivatory Dogs.' They pay their tickets, in they come. Children
get in half price, it's fun for all the family. We have them sit in a circle,
like a circus ring. We sell them warm snacks, we serve vodka and
blini.

And then the lights go down, and oh! the magic starts.

Nina steps out on to the stage.

We've bought Nina a dress; it was a ball gown, second hand, once
worn by some dead duchess or another, and it cost quite a few roubles,
but you'd never know it wasn't designed for Nina herself, it fits
perfectly. Dressed in blue, with the most gorgeous little bows at the
back, and she looks so *elegant*. And she looks like a *woman* now, the
way it emphasises her bust. She takes her first bow, and I can't help it,
my heart still skips at the sight of her. And the men in the audience
applaud, each time, they wolf whistle, they cheer. It's as if they can't
help it. It's like a reflex action. Ring the right bell, they'd all be
drooling for my daughter too.

Nina rings her bells. The dogs perk up, stiffen. Their mouths begin
to drip with water. Grown men are stunned by the salivatory prowess
of our dogs. Women gasp at the sight, they recoil even, but they're

excited too, they hold on to their husbands so tightly, they enjoy the excuse. And children point and laugh. And we've been clever, we've learned tricks to this trade. We give the dogs food colourings to dye their saliva, it comes out in all different bright colours. Fyodor's saliva is always green, it stands out so well against his light fur. And at the climax of the act, Nina plays the national anthem — and, on cue, as she rings the bells near the appropriate dogs, they'll drool out the colours of the flag, of Mother Russia, red, white and blue, and we all stand and salute.

(We admit that some of the supporting acts don't go down so well. No one cares about the lettuce eating turtle, and you can't get the cats to do anything useful. But they're only there as the warm-up.)

The Tsar has heard of us. We have been summoned to Moscow. There we will give him a private performance. It will be the proudest day of our lives.

Nina seems less sentimental with the dogs than before. She doesn't pet them like she used to. She tells us she daren't, that it'll confuse their responses. I ask her whether she still loves them, and she says she does. I ask her whether she still loves me, and she laughs, and gives me a hug, and she's still wearing that that blue dress, and I think of her mother, I think of how elegant Natalya had been when she was young — and we had no money for dresses in those days, but it didn't matter, elegance isn't only about what's on the surface — and I'm in love, I'm in love, I can't help it, and I wouldn't want to.

We understand now what you wanted with our dogs. That you had ambitions for a circus act of your own. And we forgive you, dressing up a simple entertainment as something like Science, something sounding so grand and important — why couldn't you just be honest with us? We don't need facts, we need something fun, something to distract us from the hardship, to give all our hearts a little reason to skip. But there's no need for resentment now, and you did give us the idea after all.

So we want to say, no hard feelings, Mister Pavlov. And we will be happy to show us our dogs, and offer you two free tickets to any one of our performances (Fridays and Saturdays excepted) as a demonstration of our good faith. We look forward to seeing you at your convenience.

Yours sincerely, etc.

৵৶

Pavlov,

She has gone. She has left me. She has gone.
Oh God.
We were so proud as we entered Moscow. We thought we would be the toast of the city. We thought we would set the world on fire. Nina looked in shop windows, planned all the jewellery she would buy when she was rich. She planned even to get the dogs gold-encrusted collars, that might be picked up by the stage lights. For myself, I promise it, I didn't want anything—I just wanted my beloved Nina to be happy. I thought too that if she were really happy, then she would be kind to me again.

But Moscow has no need of drooling dogs. The Tsar has all the animals he could dream of. He has bears to dance for him. He has elephants swinging their trunks, gorillas that stomp their feet to music and sing.

Nina went on to stage confidently enough. But suddenly, surrounded by all the wealth in that room, her dress seemed like such a mean thing. She seemed like someone pretending to be a duchess. No, worse, someone pretending to be pretty. No, worse still, someone pretending to be a shop owner, a little bourgeois, someone climbing the ladder, when we are peasant stock through and through, we are the children of peasants and always will be no matter how much we dress it up differently, no matter how brightly our dogs might drool.

The dogs were conditioned by now to salivate not only at the sound of the bells, but the sound of audience appreciation, the applause and the cheers. But there weren't any. And they got confused. Fyodor stared out, jaws clamped shut, not a drop of spit to be seen, the mouth so resolutely *dry*, and it didn't matter how much Nina paraded in front of him, or how loudly she deafened him with that bell.

I could see her get desperate. I wanted to shout out, to tell her to leave the stage. To get out now before it was too late. But instead, she tried all the harder. "Come on!" she shouted at Fyodor. And Fyodor gazed up at her, eyes wide with love, it wanted to please her, but it didn't know what she wanted. "Come on, damn you!" And she kicked him. Again and again, hard.

One man got up — I like to think it was the Tsar, maybe it was the Tsar himself — he shouted, "What is this act, Nina Allanovich and Her Dying Dog?"

And I can see her now, blinking with humiliation in the stage lights, standing there over that still body of the dog she had once loved — and she looked like a little girl again, like my little girl, and I wanted to wrap her up in my arms then and there, and tell her it was all right, that everything would always be all right.

And at the Tsar's words the audience started to laugh. But it was the wrong kind of laughter, it was mocking and cruel, and the dogs didn't know what to do with it. They didn't drool. They were sick. They vomited over the stage, in turn, as if one egging on the next, all the colours of the rainbow.

"Get her off!" shouted someone. Disgusted and, well, *bored*. Maybe *that* was the Tsar. I don't know.

And I tell you now. That there will come a day of reckoning. When the ordinary Russian people will no longer put up with such humiliation. When the Tsar won't be able to take something good and noble and decent, and destroy it in one fell swoop. When a man and his daughter will be able to lead a band of salivating dogs across the country in dignity and freedom. Not today, maybe. But the day is coming soon.

We left Moscow. We began the trip back.

Last night I woke to a letter from Nina.

Dear Sir, she'd written. The act isn't working. You're holding us back. I've run away to join a circus. I have fallen in love with a contortionist, and we're going to America, where there's opportunity, and anyone can be what they want. Don't try to find me. Yours sincerely, etc.

She's gone, and she's taken the surviving dogs with her. I don't know what she'll do to them. But I worry. She's in love with a contortionist, after all.

I'm glad she's in love. I'm glad, if it means her heart skips whenever she's with him, the way mine always did for her. The way mine always will, whenever I even think of her. I'm glad. If.

I shall be home soon. But I do not know what I will find there. The parrots will have starved in their cages. The cats will have turned feral. The turtle, at least, should be alive, but I doubt he'll be too happy to see me.

I feel, sir, I have done you a disservice. That I have blamed you for things which were never your fault. And I would like to say that I hope we can somehow be friends. But I think I should warn you. In all conscience. I think, if I ever saw you again, for what you've started, I'd kick you very hard where it hurts. I wouldn't be able to help myself. It'd be pure reflex.

Yours sincerely. Etc.

To Run Away, to Join the Circus

ALISON LITTLEWOOD

When Matthew was eight, he ran away to join the circus. He didn't want to join the circus, but that's how his mum said people ran away; and so he did it, as soon as Brogan's Big Top was in town. He crept under the rope that separated the parts you were supposed to see and the parts you weren't, and he looked back and thought: *That's that, then.*

He walked in amongst the tents and the shabby caravans and the trailers. He didn't like it, couldn't see into any of the windows, couldn't tell if anyone was watching him. Then he came to the cats.

They were big cats, three lions in cages like prisons on wheels. Matthew approached one. It was bigger than he'd thought a lion would be. It smelled bad and its fur was mangy and its long, curved claws were blunted where they'd been cut across.

"Hoy," came a shout. "Get away from there." Matthew turned. He thought it would be someone dressed in glitter, or a clown maybe, but it was just a lad wearing jeans and a grey t-shirt. His posture was loose, lazy even, and it was easy to see he belonged here where Matthew didn't. "Do you want them to eat ye? Do ye? They'll eat ye."

He had a Scottish accent. Matthew wanted to ask if he, too, had run away to join the circus, but instead he ran, away from the strange smells and the shabby homes and the whole *place*, the feel of it, where he didn't belong and never could.

Back towards the home he knew.

❧❧

When Matthew's mum was being strange, *touched* as their neighbour put it, Matthew would walk up the hill to the barrow. He knew it was somewhere he could be alone, because there was nothing there; yet according to his mum that wasn't true. Matthew knew it *was* true, though, because he'd seen it. There was the hilltop with its view over the town, a single standing stone, and the barrow itself—the burial mound—which sounded exciting but in truth was just a low bank of earth long-since overgrown with grass.

There were doors in that mound once, his mum said once. *It's not safe. They could open, and then where would you be?*

But there were no doors. Matthew had looked for them. He had walked around and peered into the grass and poked it with his toe. There were definitely no doors, no matter how hard he wished he could find them.

❧❧

Sometimes, Matthew's mum didn't know him. She called him by name but looked into his face as if he was a stranger; as if trying to work out who it was behind his eyes. Matthew didn't like it, but there was always the barrow, and lurking somewhere in the back of his mind, there was the circus.

❧❧

When Matthew was eleven, the circus came back. He saw the white tents sprouting from the ground, and that evening, he left the cottage and hurried towards it.

It was a different circus, but looked the same anyway. The big top was in front, the ropes and tents and caravans behind. A clown was handing out tickets to a woman and her children, and when he saw Matthew, he winked and gave him one too.

256

Matthew grinned. He didn't know if the clown had miscounted or given him the ticket on purpose, but he went inside anyway. There was music, loud and brash, and it was dark. Then there was a ringmaster, and his voice was loud, too. There were magicians, a juggler, acrobats and elephants, and a girl who did tricks on a white horse. There were lions, clowns, then lions *and* clowns, who ran away from them, shrieking.

Then all fell quiet. A single spotlight shone up high and Matthew realised there was a girl standing up there, on a platform. She was all dressed in sequins, her red hair like flame, and she had a small, delicate face. Matthew only had time to think: *pretty*—and she sprung from her perch and she *flew*.

She let go of her trapeze and everyone gasped. She somersaulted once, twice, caught a new trapeze that had swung out to meet her at just the right moment. She was small and lithe and spun in the air. Then others emerged from the dark and joined her, spinning and flying all around, everywhere at once in a great shining web. They glided through the air and caught each other's hands and held them. They glittered. They were like butterflies: *no*, Matthew thought, like *hummingbirds*. And then they started to vanish, just like that, disappearing into the dark one by one until only the girl was left. She looped around the tent. Matthew couldn't see how she was holding on; he looked down but there was no safety net, never had been. He realised she must be gripping something with her teeth, saw them shining clear and white in the dark.

Then she, too, was gone.

The crowd erupted into shouts and wild clapping. Matthew clapped too, so hard his hands hurt.

He saw the girl again when he was leaving. There was a path of lit torches and the performers stood by them, handing out leaflets, telling everyone to tell their friends. Matthew took one before he realised it was her; then looked up and saw her green eyes fixed on him. They tilted upwards, like a cat's.

"You'll come back," she said.

257

"No." Matthew blurted it before he could stop himself, and he sighed. "No, I won't." He walked towards home, and he didn't look back no matter how much he wanted to.

☙❧

Each window of the cottage was burning brightly when Matthew got home, and his heart sank. He had hoped to sneak in quietly; now he stood there, suspended between going on and walking away. After a moment, he went on.

The door handle was warm under his hand. He turned it and went inside.

His mother stood in the middle of the room. Her hair was awry, lit by the fire behind her, a crackle of brightness. The flames raged, an inferno. She must have piled every spare log onto it. Now she brandished the poker in her hand. Her eyes were gleaming, filled with something a little like triumph. Matthew noticed, somewhere in the back of his mind, that her cardigan was fastened with all the wrong buttons.

"Now, we'll see," she said.

"Mum?"

"Don't call me that." Spittle flew from her mouth and frothed on the carpet. "Never call me that. You aren't my child. I know you're not."

"*Mum*!" In spite of himself, the evening he'd had, Matthew felt tears pricking his eyes. A spark cracked and rose from the fire; he briefly remembered the girl he'd seen, flying about the big top. Then she was gone and this was all that remained.

"It's *me*, Mum. It's Matthew. I'm home."

She looked puzzled.

"We should go to bed, Mum."

She strode forward, grasped his arm tight. Then she was pulling him across the room, half carrying him with her, towards the fire.

"Mum—" Matthew pulled away but she had him again, this time by the hair at the back of his head. The next instant, she had pushed him down towards the fire. Flames darted from it, licking greed-ily. For one moment Matthew remembered bonfire night, how the village kids dared each other to go closer to the fire, the red heat of it on his skin; but then it was worse, much worse, and he cried out in pain.

"I want him back." His mother's voice was a hiss.

Matthew struggled, clawed at her hand. A sob burst from his throat. His eyes were dry as bone and he felt his lips crack.

"Send him home," she shrieked. "I want this thing *gone*. Send Matthew back to me!"

Then he was free and stumbling across the room, the smoke dense in his lungs, the air blessedly cool on his face. He pawed at it, thinking his skin must be crisped and crackled, but it was not. He turned to see his mother sink into an armchair, her arm over her face. She looked up; her tears caught the light, two molten rivers. "I just want Matthew," she said. "Please. I want my son."

Matthew backed away from her. Then he turned and groped his way towards the door.

ॐ✤

At first, Matthew didn't know where he was going. Then he saw the large white tent looming and realised he'd retraced his steps, was once again at the circus. It was quiet and it was closed.

You'll come back, she'd said.

Now he *was* back, but it was too late. Matthew kept walking, heading around the big top to the caravans. A rope separated them from the outside world and Matthew stepped over it, looked back, and thought: *That's that, then*.

He walked between the hulking shapes, barely noticing where he went. Then he rounded the corner and saw her.

The green-eyed girl was heading into a caravan. Her back was turned, but Matthew knew who she was anyway. She tripped up the steps so lightly he couldn't hear her feet and then she turned, raised her eyes, and saw Matthew. Her face was lost in shadow, but he saw her grin by the gleam of her teeth.

Matthew took a step forward, another; he felt as if he couldn't do anything else. Then a hand fell on his shoulder.

"You lost, boy?"

The voice was deep and gruff and so Matthew was surprised when he turned and saw a thin man, a wiry man, an unimpressive man. For a moment he wondered what on earth this person was doing in a circus; then saw a smudge of white make-up clinging to the man's cheek, and he thought he knew.

"I said, you lost?"

Matthew nodded, pursing up his lips and shaking his head.

"I see." The man glanced towards the caravan. The door had closed; the girl had gone. "Well, you don't want to go with *them*. Their sort, they'd take a lad like you and spirit you away and *eat* you." He said this last with emphasis, finished with a wide grin. His teeth were yellow. He leaned in closer and his nose wrinkled. "Hm, you'd be safe enough if they got a sniff of you. You smell half cooked." He grinned. "They likes 'em raw."

Matthew only stared.

"All right, boy. You look hungry and you look lost. I'll find you something to eat." He caught hold of Matthew's sleeve, but there was a sharp *snick* and the caravan door opened again.

She was there. Matthew couldn't see her eyes, but he knew what they would look like. He pulled his arm free and the man grimaced in disgust. He muttered "suit yourself," and was gone.

The girl beckoned.

❧

The trapeze artists didn't eat Matthew. They were all there, in ordinary clothes, but he could tell it was them, could sense their capacity for lightness and grace, their *airiness*. They laughed and joked, flashing their teeth. Matthew expected them to ask when he was going home, but they did not, and after a while he realised he felt a little odd. At first Matthew couldn't work out what it was; then he realised that, for a little while, it had felt as if he belonged.

৵◌৵

The next day, Matthew watched the trapeze artists practice. He had slept in a spare bunk, washed in the sink, sluicing the burnt smell from his hair and skin. Now he smiled as his new friends spun and flipped through the air. One of them let go, somersaulting over and over, and somehow Matthew didn't flinch, didn't feel afraid as she plummeted and landed in front of him. It was the girl with green eyes.

"Now you try," she said, grinning.

Matthew shook his head, but she took his hand and led him to a ladder made of fine rope. He hesitated, then followed her up, knowing he could just cling there when he reached the top, could watch her and climb down again. But when he got there he turned and saw the trapezes and the way they were interconnected, one leading to the next as clearly as a solid pathway.

She let out a trilling laugh and launched herself into the air.

Matthew shivered with the thrill of it. He saw another trapeze close at hand, and before he knew what he was doing he had caught hold of it and jumped.

The air was his. It rushed past his ears, cleansing, cold on his skin. He gasped. He had done it: he was flying.

৵◌৵

"You're a natural," said Grigor, afterwards. He was the head of the troupe. "Born to it. I knew it as soon as I looked at you."

Matthew didn't know what to say. He beamed. He looked around the ring, and his grin didn't fade even when he saw the thin man from the previous evening standing in the wings, staring at him without expression.

৵৵

Later, the thin man came to him. "A message from the boss," he said. "He wants to know if you're staying. We're moving on."

Matthew caught his breath. He had always known the circus must move on, but had pushed the thought away. Now he thought of his mother and his hand went to his cheek.

"Well? What's it to be?"

Matthew shook his head; he couldn't speak. He found his eyes filling with tears. The man frowned, put his hand on Matthew's arm. He said something Matthew didn't catch, but it was different this time; his tone was kind. Matthew opened his mouth and the words spilled out; he found himself telling the man everything, about the way his mother had turned on him.

When he'd finished, the man paused. "It's a test," he said.

"A what?"

"The fire—it's how you test for a changeling. She thought that you were not you, correct?" he sighed. "There is one of the old places, near here: a barrow. People thought fairy folk lived there, once. They would emerge from the hillside and steal human children away, leave their own in their place. They'd take the humans as slaves and give the parents the trouble of raising their changeling. They made them look just the same, so mostly the mothers never knew the difference."

Matthew stared.

"So you frighten the changeling with fire. It flees and the human child is returned. They told of it in the old days. Not so much any longer." He paused. "The old doors are closed now."

"What?" Matthew looked at him sharply. "What did you say?"

The man shook his head, as if shaking away dreams. "Just stories." He gestured around, indicating everything, the big top. "So, boy. Are you staying or not?"

৵৵

"There is only one thing you need to know," Grigor said to Matthew. "The folk stick together. We are a family; we are there for each other. The folk do not betray each other."

Matthew swallowed; he couldn't help it. Grigor's eyes were intense. Not so bright a green as Elise's, his were more . . . *turquoise*, he thought—but intense. He nodded, and Grigor smiled, patting him on the back. He gave Matthew a costume to wear. It was covered in sequins. It felt like skin against his body, moved with him and clung to him. He stood taller when he was wearing it, as if he was someone else.

Matthew tried a couple of switchovers, shifting from one trapeze to the next. He had thought he would be more afraid, but somehow he was not. Now he observed the others, taking note of the order in which they flew, the rhythm of their interplay. Then he just watched without thinking of anything at all. It was like before; they were a web—no, a *cloud*, a gossamer cloud, hanging there above the ring. *Of* the air, not suspended within it.

He half-closed his eyes and they were only points of light. They shone all colours, darting and shimmering high above him.

৵৽৽৻

Matthew wasn't ready to take part in the show, but he took money at the door and ushered people in and sold refreshments. When the circus let out, he went to light the torches and hand out leaflets to the crowds trampling across the grass. "Tell your friends," he called, and he glanced across the field to see Elise doing exactly the same thing.

As he watched, she looked around and started walking away from the crowds, towards the caravans. Matthew frowned. There was something about her expression he hadn't liked; it had been furtive, almost sly. He gazed after her a moment longer, then stuffed his leaflets into his pocket and followed.

He walked softly until he caught sight of her; then he stopped. Elise had ducked behind a caravan, was peering out in quick glimpses.

Matthew caught his breath. It must have been a trick of the light, but he thought he had never seen her look so *alive*, her hair so bright, her eyes glowing. Then he saw what she was looking at.

A child had wandered away from the crowds. It was a golden-haired boy, no more than five or six; his thumb was stuffed into his mouth and tears glistened on his face.

Elise stepped forward and she called to him. The boy looked up and his tears turned to smiles.

Matthew watched as she went to him, whispered in his ear, stroked his hair. He couldn't seem to move. Then Elise took the child's hand and led him away, not towards the exit but inward, where the caravans nestled thickest, and the spell was broken. Matthew shook himself and hurried after her. Now he couldn't seem to see her at all. He stopped wandering aimlessly and instead headed for her caravan, went up the steps and knocked. There was no answer. It was dark inside. The place seemed deserted.

Matthew shook his head. What was he doing? The child was fine. Of course Elise would take care of it; he only had to look at her to know that. She had looked so kind, so beautiful.

Then he remembered what had been said to him the night he arrived in the circus; his mouth twitched, and he laughed.

You don't want to go with them. Their sort, they'd take a lad like you and spirit you away and eat you.

He frowned. It was odd, wasn't it, that the man had spoken against the trapeze artists, even in jest.

The folk don't betray each other.

And they did not; the circus folk stuck together. Matthew had seen it. So why would the man have tried to keep Matthew from them?

∻

Matthew hurried to the clowns' tent, pushed his way inside. The man was there, his thin frame lost in giant pantaloons; there was a smile painted on his face, but Matthew could see he wasn't smiling.

"I need to know what you meant," Matthew demanded.

"What?"

"You said the old doors are closed, now. What did you mean?"

He was silent.

"When the changelings — the fairy folk — are frightened away by fire, where is it they go? If the old places are closed, where do they go?" Matthew paused. "Elise, Grigor, the rest of them. They're not circus folk, are they? They're the folk my mum talked about." Matthew was breathing hard. "Please. I just need to know what they are. They're so — *beautiful*. I loved that about them. Now I just don't *know*."

The thin man bent so that his eyes were level with Matthew's. It was a while before he spoke. "I know what you're thinking," he said quietly. "But you should remember: the folk do not betray each other."

Matthew looked away. "I'm *not*. I don't mean to. It's just — I need to know, that's all. If it's real. If *they* are."

"The *folk* do not betray each other, boy."

Matthew stared at him. He started to shake his head, but he caught the odd emphasis in the man's words, and now he realised what he meant. Matthew let out a sharp laugh. "No," he said, "*no*, that's stupid. I'm not one of them. My mum, she — but I didn't fail the test. I only ran away. My mum was mad. It's not that I was one of *them*; I wasn't even scared, not really. Fire doesn't scare me. I was just scared of what she might do next, that's all."

"Is there a difference, lad?"

Matthew backed away. Then he turned and ran, out of the tent, away, back into the dark.

∂∾∽

The torches were still blazing by the entrance to the big top, and Matthew grabbed one of them, wrenching it from the ground. He looked neither left nor right as he carried it towards the caravans; the people he passed were no more than shadows, and no one tried to stop him, no one called out his name. He was one of them.

265

Elise's caravan stood quiet and dark, the curtains drawn. Matthew slowed as he approached, padded up the steps and knocked on the door. He was ready, and when he heard the metal scraping of the bolt, he pushed.

There was a gasp from inside and Elise staggered back, the torch-light making her face shine as she moved away from it.

Now that he was inside, Matthew didn't know what to do. He stood there, the flame a bright barrier between them.

"What are you doing, Matthew?"

"Elise, I'm sorry. I need to know, that's all."

She didn't ask: *what*. She didn't ask a question at all. She merely said: "You'd better not."

"Why? Because the folk don't betray each other?" Matthew suddenly felt stronger. He thrust the torch forwards and Elise gasped, edging away until she reached the wall.

"No, Matthew. That's not the reason," Elise said, and then she bared her teeth. Matthew caught his breath. Her teeth weren't just gleaming; they were *sharp*. And he thought of the way she'd reached out to a small child, calling in that soft voice, smiling that smile.

"Where's the child you found, Elise? What did you do with him?"

"What do you mean?" This time, Elise's smile was innocent. "He's with his mother, where he's always been. She never even missed him."

"I don't believe you."

"It doesn't matter."

Matthew scowled. Then he stepped forward and shoved the flame towards Elise. She shrieked and darted away, quicker than he could see, and Matthew swung the flame around, too fast; sparks flew up, and he dropped it.

There was an unearthly shriek. The carpet caught at once and the fire spread before him, towards his feet, *under* them. Matthew tried to step forward but it was no use, it was spreading. He looked up and met Elise's eyes. They were no longer green; they were turquoise.

She screamed again and he stepped forward anyway, but the heat was too much. The smoke was filling his lungs, his mind. He was at home again, in the cottage, his mother shouting in his ears. Matthew covered his face, staggered back towards the door. His skin was scorched. He felt his lips crack. His mother's eyes were cold, pitiless. The flames were dancing around her. The fear rose into his throat, choking him, and he fled.

҂ᴏᴥ

Matthew hid behind a tent and watched as people fetched buckets of water, blankets, hoses. There were shouts all around, the distant wail of sirens. He swallowed, wiped his eyes. They stung. He didn't know if it was from the smoke that still rose from the caravan, black and thick, or if the tears were real.

He stayed until he could see the caravan in its ruin, a black, sodden skeleton, dark and empty; then he turned and walked to the edge of the ground. He stepped over the rope, and when he was standing on the other side, he didn't look back.

҂ᴏᴥ

As the next night drew in, Matthew started to recognise the places around him. He'd hitchhiked much of the way; now it was only a few miles, and the evening was quiet and calm, the air cooling, so he started to walk.

The cottage was nestled into the hillside as it had always been, its windows aglow. It looked soft and welcoming; it looked like home. Matthew walked up the path. His mother would be there, he told himself. She would be well, and she would know him, be glad to see him. But as Matthew let himself in at the gate, he thought: *What if she isn't well?*

He turned away from the door, instead going around the side of the house. He stood for a moment by the window. Then he took a deep breath and turned and looked inside.

His mother was there. She sat by the fire, and she looked happy. But Matthew saw that she was not alone. She had a visitor, some company; they were sitting in the chair facing away from him but he could see a little of their arm, their shoulder. As he watched, his mother laughed at something they said.

Matthew turned and leaned back against the cottage and looked up to see a bright moon shining overhead.

He looked in at the window once more. His mother was chatting and smiling. Then the fire sparked. She turned, gestured towards it. Her visitor rose, picked up the poker, and prodded at the flames. Then he turned and Matthew froze, a cry caught halfway in his throat.

He was looking at himself.

The visitor was Matthew, wearing his old clothes, smiling his old smile. He was the one who was sitting with his mother. And, until his eyes flicked towards the window, he'd looked happy too.

Matthew ducked down beneath the sill. He felt dizzy; the stars wheeled about the sky.

There was a sound behind him, then he heard the front door open. Matthew stayed perfectly still, his heart beating too fast.

"I could have sworn I saw something," he heard his own voice say. There were footsteps, then nothing, and the door closed again, a key grating in the lock.

Matthew hid his head in his hands. What was that *thing* inside there? But his mother had taken him and held him in the flame. She'd tested *him*, tested *Matthew*, and he'd failed; and this thing had come and taken his place.

She had looked so happy. So did *he*.

Matthew let out a sound that was something like a sob. Then he jumped to his feet to look through the window once more. He could have been wrong: *must* have been wrong. The boy had been a visitor, nothing more; he'd been tricked by the light from the fire. But the curtains were now drawn. There was only his own reflection in the dark, blank glass.

Matthew couldn't breathe. He could see his face, and he didn't recognise it: it was not the face he was used to seeing. He opened his mouth in a silent wail and the reflection opened its mouth and it wailed with him. Matthew saw, then, what lay within its mouth; he saw its teeth, their whiteness, their clear sharp points, and he threw back his head to the sky, letting out the sound that had been inside him, trapped and hidden, since he'd returned to this place; since he'd betrayed his friend, since he'd betrayed the folk.

It was not a human cry, and it was *out*, it was flying towards the stars, and when Matthew saw where it was leading him, he rose into the air and followed after it.

The Contributors

RAY BRADBURY (1920–2012)has written more than 500 short stories, novels, plays, screenplays, television scripts and poems. Lauded as one of America's most elegant and poetic writers, acclaimed by many to be the inventor of dark fantasy, he has won many major awards, including the World Fantasy Award for Life Achievement and being named a Nebula Grandmaster.

MURIEL GRAY graduated from Glasgow School of Art and then worked as an illustrator and then assistant head of design at the National Museum of antiquities in Edinburgh. Playing in a punk band led her to present Channel 4's seminal music programme *The Tube* with Jools Holland and Paula Yates. A successful presenting career in television and radio followed, with Muriel also founding a television production company that grew into one of the leading UK independents. Her writing career began with the best-selling horror novel *The Trickster*, followed by two more, *Furnace* and *The Ancient*, which Stephen King described as "scary and unputdownable". She has contributed many short stories to anthologies, and written for comics. A horror and fantasy fan from childhood, Muriel was always a secret but obsessional geek, who hid *The Pan Book of Horror* under her bed covers and read it with a torch. One of her greatest disappointments is that she has not yet been abducted by aliens.

JOHN CONNOLLY was born in Dublin, Ireland. He is the author of 16 books, including *The Book of Lost Things*, *Nocturnes*, the Samuel Johnson books for younger readers, and the Charlie Parker series of mystery novels, the latest of which is *The Wrath of Angels*. Like most writers, he is waiting to be found out.

TOD ROBBINS (1888–1949) was the author of two short story collections and several novels, including *In the Shadows* and *The Master of Murders*. *The Unholy Three* was adapted by Tod Browning as a silent film in 1925, and Browning went on to make a feature of "Spurs": the controversial *Freaks* (1932) for MGM. The movie has gone on to gain a cult following, and was ranked 15th in Bravo TV's list of *The 100 Scariest Movie Moments*.

RIO YOUERS is the British Fantasy Award–nominated author of *Old Man Scratch* and *Westlake Soul*. His short fiction has been published by, among others, Edge Science Fiction & Fantasy, IDW Publishing, and St. Martin's Press. Rio lives in southwestern Ontario with his wife, Emily, and their daughter, Lily Maye.

TOM REAMY (1935–1977) was, at the time of his death, one of the most popular young writers in the Science Fiction field and a key figure in 1960s and 1970s SF fandom. He became active in this area, both as a fan writer and artist, while still in his teens in the early 1950s. It was also during this period that Reamy began to produce his own fantasy and SF stories. His only novel, *Blind Voices*, was published posthumously in hardcover and mass-market paperback editions, and was compared critically with the works of Richard Matheson and Harlan Ellison.

THOMAS F. MONTELEONE has published more than 100 short stories, 4 collections, 7 anthologies and 25 novels including the bestseller, *New York Times* Notable Book of the Year, and Bram Stoker Award winning *The Blood of the Lamb*. He's also written scripts for stage, screen and TV. His fourth collection of short fiction, *Fearful Symmetries*, won the Bram Stoker Award. His omnibus collection of *Cemetery Dance* columns about writing, genre publishing, television, film and popular culture entitled *The Mothers And Fathers Italian Association* from Borderlands Press also won a Stoker for non-fiction. He is also co-editor of the award-winning anthology series of imaginative fiction, *Borderlands*. He is also the author of the bestselling *The Complete Idiot's Guide to Writing a Novel* (now in a 2nd edition). With his wife, Elizabeth, and daughter, Olivia, he lives in Maryland and, other than all the high taxes, likes it a lot.

JOE HILL is the award-winning author of two novels, *Heart-Shaped Box* and *Horns*, a collection of short stories, *20th Century Ghosts* (originally published by PS Publishing), and a comic book series, *Locke & Key*. You can get nearly daily doses of his thoughts over on Twitter, where he goes by the handle of joe_hill and his blog can be found at joehillfiction.com

WILL ELLIOTT came to international attention with the publication of his debut novel, *Pilo Family Circus*. The book won several awards, is the basis for a play by the Godlight Theater Company in New York, and was short-listed for the International Horror Guild award for best novel. He has written a memoir (*Strange Places*), a fantasy series called the Pendulum Trilogy, and his new novel *Nightfall*, a dark comic fantasy, has been published in Australia. He is 33 years old and lives in Brisbane, Australia.

Born in Wales in the UK, LOU MORGAN grew up in a house with an attic full of spiders and now lives on the south coast of England with her husband, son and obligatory cat.

PETER CROWTHER is the recipient of numerous awards for his writing, his editing and, as publisher, for the hugely successful PS Publishing (now including the Stanza Press poetry subsidiary and PS

Artbooks, a specialist imprint dedicated to the comics field). As well as being widely translated, his short stories have been adapted for TV on both sides of the Atlantic and collected in *The Longest Single Note, Lonesome Roads, Songs of Leaving, Cold Comforts, The Spaces Between the Lines, The Land at the End of the Working Day* and the upcoming *Jewels In The Dust*. He is the co-author (with James Lovegrove) of *Escardy Gap* and *The Hand That Feeds*, and author of the *Forever Twilight* SF/horror cycle and *By Wizard Oak*. He lives and works with his wife and business partner, Nicky, on the Yorkshire coast of England.

JAMES LOVEGROVE was born on Christmas Eve 1965 and is the author of nigh on 40 books. His novels include *The Hope, Days, Untied Kingdom, Provender Gleed*, the *New York Times* bestselling Pantheon series (*The Age Of Ra, The Age Of Zeus, The Age Of Odin, Age Of Aztec*), and *Redlaw*, the first volume in a trilogy about a policeman charged with protecting humans from vampires and vice versa.

CHARLES G. FINNEY (1905–1984) is best known for his first novel and most famous work, *The Circus of Dr. Lao*, which won one of the inaugural National Book Awards: the Most Original Book of 1935. Born in Missouri, he served in China with the United States Army, where he originally conceived of *Dr Lao*. He also later worked as editor of the *Arizona Daily Star* in Tucson, Arizona. Finney's work was a huge influence on writers like Ray Bradbury, Arthur Calder-Marshall, Tom Reamy and Jonathan Lethem

PAUL FINCH is a former cop and journalist, now turned full-time writer. He cut his literary teeth penning episodes of the British TV crime drama, *The Bill*, and has written extensively in the field of children's animation. However, he is probably best known for his work in horrors and thrillers. To date, he's had 12 books and nearly 300 stories and novellas published on both sides of the Atlantic. His first collection, *Aftershocks*, won the British Fantasy Award in 2002, while he won the award again in 2007 for his novella, *Kid*. Later in 2007, he won the International Horror Guild Award for his mid-length story, *The Old North Road*. Most recently, he has written four *Doctor Who* audio dramas for Big Finish—*Leviathan*, *Sentinels of the New Dawn*, *Hexagora* and *Threshold*. His horror novel, *Stronghold*, was published in 2010, his *Doctor Who* novel, *Hunter's Moon*, in 2011, and 2012 will see the publication of his Arthurian adventure novel, *Dark North*. Paul has also written scripts for several horror movies. The most recent of these, *The Devil's Rock*, was released to the cinemas last July. Five more of Paul's horror and thriller scripts are currently under option. Paul lives in Lancashire, UK, with his wife Cathy and his children, Eleanor and Harry. His website can be found at: http://paulfinch-writer.blogspot.com/

ANDREW J. MCKIERNAN is a writer and illustrator living and working on the Central Coast of New South Wales, Australia. First published in 2007, his stories and illustrations have since been short-listed for multiple Aurealis, Ditmar and Australian Shadows awards. His work can be found appearing here and there, like a slow growing fungus. Visit his site at http://www.andrewmckiernan.com

ROBERT SHEARMAN is probably best known for bringing back the Daleks to the twenty-first century revival of the BBC sci-fi series *Doctor Who*, in an episode that was nominated for a Hugo award. But he has largely worked in the theatre, his plays winning the Sunday Times Playwriting Award, the World Drama Trust Award, and the Guinness Award for Ingenuity, in association with the Royal National Theatre. He is a regular playwright for BBC Radio, and his two interactive series of *The Chain Gang* have both won Sony awards. He has written three collections of short stories, *Tiny Deaths*, *Love Songs for the Shy and Cynical*, and *Everyone's Just So So Special*, and collectively they have won the World Fantasy Award, the British Fantasy Award, the Shirley Jackson Award, and the Edge Hill Reader's Prize. A fourth collection of horror tales, *Remember Why You Fear Me*, is due from ChiZine in the autumn. He is currently writer in residence at Edinburgh Napier University. "Nine Letters About Spit" is part of his 100 short stories project, posted weekly at justsoso-special.com.

ALISON LITTLEWOOD is a writer of dark fantasy and horror fiction. Her first novel, *A Cold Season*, is published by Jo Fletcher Books, an imprint of *Quercus*. Alison's short stories have been picked for *The Best Horror of the Year #4* and *The Mammoth Book of Best New Horror #23*, as well as featuring in magazines including *Black Static*, *Crimewave*, *Not One Of Us* and *Dark Horizons*. She lives near Wakefield, West Yorkshire, with her partner Fergus.

The Editors

MARIE O'REGAN is a British Fantasy Award nominated writer of horror and dark fantasy, based in the Midlands, UK, where she lives with her husband—author Paul Kane—her children and the creature of the night known as Mina, the family cat. Her fiction has been published in the UK, US, Germany and Italy, and she has had reviews, interviews and articles published in many magazines both in the UK, US and Canada—her essay on *The Changeling* was published in the award-winning *Cinema Macabre*, from PS Publishing. Her first collection, *Mirror Mere*, was released in 2006 by Rainfall Books in the UK, and she served as Chairperson of the British Fantasy Society for four years (2004-2008), during which time she co-edited several publications, including *British Fantasy Society: A Celebration*, as well as a number of FantasyCon Convention souvenir programme books. She has also edited the BFS flagship magazine, *Dark Horizons*, and their newsletter *Prism*. In 2008 Marie co-Chaired what is widely regarded as one of the most successful FantasyCons and in 2011 she Co-Chaired the biggest one ever. She is the co-author of interview book *Voices in the Dark* (McFarland Publishing), co-editor of *Hellbound*

Hearts (Simon & Schuster) and *The Mammoth Book of Body Horror* (Constable & Robinson), plus the editor of *The Mammoth Book of Ghost Stories by Women*. To find out more, visit www.marieoregan.net

PAUL KANE is an award-winning writer and editor based in Derbyshire, UK. His short story collections are *Alone (In the Dark)*, *Touching the Flame*, *FunnyBones*, *Peripheral Visions*, *Shadow Writer* and *The Adventures of Dalton Quayle*, with his latest out from PS Publishing: *The Butterfly Man and Other Stories*. His novellas include *Signs of Life*, *The Lazarus Condition*, *RED* and *Pain Cages*. He is author of the novels *Of Darkness and Light*, *The Gemini Factor* and the bestselling *Arrowhead* trilogy (*Arrowhead*, *Broken Arrow* and *Arrowland*), a post-apocalyptic reworking of the Robin Hood mythology. His latest novel is *Lunar*. He is co-editor of the anthology *Hellbound Hearts*, *The Mammoth Book of Body Horror* and the forthcoming *Beyond Rue Morgue* from Titan. His non-fiction books are *The Hellraiser Films and Their Legacy* and *Voices in the Dark*. His work has been optioned for film and television, and his zombie story "Dead Time" was turned into an episode of the Lionsgate/NBC TV series *Fear Itself*, adapted by Steve Niles (*30 Days of Night*) and directed by Darren Lynn Bousman (*SAW II-IV*). He also scripted *The Opportunity*, which premiered at the Cannes Film Festival, and *The Weeping Woman* — filmed by award-winning director Mark Steensland and starring Tony-nominated actor Stephen Geoffreys (*Fright Night*). You can find out more at his website www.shadow-writer.co.uk which has featured Guest Writers such as Neil Gaiman, Charlaine Harris, Robert Kirkman, Dean Koontz and Guillermo del Toro.